the

paris

affair

the
paris
affair

pip drysdale

SIMON &
SCHUSTER

London · New York · Sydney · Toronto · New Delhi

THE PARIS AFFAIR
First published in Australia in 2021 by
Simon & Schuster (Australia) Pty Limited
Suite 19A, Level 1, Building C, 450 Miller Street, Cammeray, NSW 2062

10 9 8 7 6 5 4 3 2

Sydney New York London Toronto New Delhi
Visit our website at www.simonandschuster.com.au

A catalogue record for this
book is available from the
National Library of Australia

ISBN: 9781760854324

Cover design: Christabella Designs
Cover images: lambada/Getty Images; Ilya Akinsin/Shutterstock
Typeset by Midland Typesetters, Australia
Printed and bound in Australia by Griffin Press

The paper this book is printed on is certified against the
Forest Stewardship Council® Standards. Griffin Press holds
chain of custody certification SGSHK-COC-005088. FSC®
promotes environmentally responsible, socially beneficial
and economically viable management of the world's forests

For the lovers, the dreamers and the Murderinos

Chapitre un

I met Thomas three days ago in the laundromat. Romantic, I know. I was bored, I saw him checking me out, I liked the look of him, and so I asked him a question in my broken, shitty French. But he's not French. He's British. He has big, rough fingers, and right now those fingers are interlaced with mine.

We're lying in his bed, on the border of the 7th arrondissement and the air smells of candle wax and his cologne. My gaze is on an oil painting circa 1750: a man in a high, frilly neckline. He has no chin and a stern expression on his face. It's valuable. I know quite a lot about art, so I can tell these things from the subject, the craquelure and the grandiose gold frame. But even without all that, I could guess. Nobody keeps an ugly painting like that unless money is involved.

'My parents are in town this weekend,' I whisper, my eyes now on our clasped hands.

'Already?' he says. 'That's nice.'

By 'already' he's referring to the fact that I only moved to Paris five weeks ago.

I look over my shoulder at him, my blonde hair catching the light. He has blond hair too, but his is caramel and has a deep side part. It's the exact same colour as the tan on his forearms that hasn't faded from the summer yet. His eyes are that kind of brown that flecks orange in the right sort of light, his eyelashes are long and pale at the tips, and his body is lean and healthy looking.

'Yeah, they want to meet you,' I say with a small, coy smile. And then I watch for his reaction.

Is that a minute clench of the jaw I see? A bob of the Adam's apple? The usual signs of panic? He's wondering how I went from cool girl to stage-five clinger so quickly. Now he's thinking, *It's the sex. That's what did it to her. The sex was clearly* that *good*.

I let a moment pass. Let the anxiety settle in nicely.

'You don't have to,' I say, breaking eye contact and looking back at the man on the wall. Guy on the wall does not approve of the stunt I'm pulling at all. He can see straight through my little game. But guy on the wall was from another era. He wouldn't understand. 'I just know Mum would love to meet you,' I add. 'She thinks you're super handsome.'

His muscles tense up. I can almost feel his heartbeat accelerate. I swear to god the heat pulsing off him under the covers just went up a couple of degrees.

'What? How does she know what I look like?'

'I sent her a photo. Why?'

2

Now Thomas is thinking, *Shit, it's only been three days and her mother already has a photograph of me? Wow. I'm the man. The MAN. But I need to escape. ESCAPE.*

This is the exact reaction I'm hoping for.

Because he needs to think us ending things is a good thing. That it's his idea. Things get messy when a man's ego gets hurt.

'I'd like to.' His voice comes out a pitch or two higher now. 'But I have plans this weekend.'

Thomas is fibbing. He *doesn't* have plans. I know this because we spoke about perhaps seeing each other on Saturday night or Sunday afternoon via text this morning and his exact words were: 'I'm all yours this weekend. Wide open.' That was when I knew I had to end things. That, and he liked three of my Instagram pictures in a row.

But I expect now that he's told the lie, now that those syllables are hanging in the air, that text is floating back to him. He's thinking, *Shit, shit, shit.*

Poor Thomas.

This is why dating is stressful.

This is why I avoid it.

Well, one of the reasons.

I pull away and sit up. The air is cool on my skin. Goosebumps form as I look around for my clothes. They're lying in a pile on the floor by the bed, right by the condom wrapper. I loop my arms through my bra straps and fasten it behind my back as I scan the titles on his bookshelf. They're mainly photography books – Henri Cartier-Bresson, Man Ray, Robert Doisneau – and a couple on positivity-slash-manifestation. I pull my white T-shirt over my head and can feel his eyes on me as I stand up, reach for my short black skirt and put it on.

'Are you leaving?' he asks. And there's an edge to his voice but I can't tell if it's panic or relief and I'm intentionally not looking at him so I can't read his expression.

'Yes,' I say as I do up my boots. *Ziiippp.* The sound echoes in the silence between us.

'Why?' he asks. Small.

I turn to face him and try to match the sour expression of the man in the ugly, expensive painting. 'This isn't going to work,' I say.

My bag and jacket are lying on the brown leather sofa. I move over to it, pick them up and head for the door. And without even saying goodbye I open it, move out into the hallway and let it bang behind me.

I rush down the three flights of stairs – the same wooden staircase I came up just two hours ago – as quickly as I can. I pull open the security door and head out into the mauve dusk light, go right, past the red and white lights of a *tabac* and disappear around the corner.

And that, ladies and gentlemen, is how it's done. That's how you lose a guy in less than three minutes.

∼

There's a main road ahead of me and as I walk towards the hum of traffic, a rubber band flicks something deep within my chest. Because I'm not some psychopath (I know this for certain because I've done an online quiz). I don't fuck with people's feelings for fun. And I liked Thomas; really, I did.

Which is precisely why I needed to pull my bunny-boiler routine now, before things went any further. Because I could tell from the way he looked at me, from how he held my hand so tight after sex, that if I didn't do something soon he'd get attached. And he needs to find a normal girl who'll want normal things. Someone who listens to 'How to keep your man' podcasts and doesn't sabotage things the moment a guy wants more than a casual hook-up. Someone looking for a white dress, a set of his-and-hers towels, a dum-dum-da-dum-dum and a couple of offspring.

And that's not me.

Not anymore.

And not just because I tried love once and it didn't do what it said on the box, not just because I'm pretty sure the whole thing is bullshit. But because every time I open the newspaper a new continent is on fire, World War III is about to erupt, a big corporation is screwing over the vulnerable or some expert or another is talking about how sooner or later water will cost more than gold. It's depressing. So, what? I'm supposed to ignore all that, pretend that Orwell isn't the new Nostradamus, couple up, invest in white goods, pop out a baby and then leave it here in this shitstorm?

No thanks.

I prefer my life clean. Simple. My weekends free to write.

So this is best for both of us.

I look around as I weave between taxis, motorcycles and bicycles and cross the street. There's an H&M sign glowing in the distance, lots of cursive, neon restaurant signage, one of those bottle-green Parisian newsstands with postcards on racks, and a homeless man sleeping beneath a pile of cloth in a doorway across from it. I get to the other side and am about to walk the short distance home when 'Hot in Herre' starts playing from my handbag. That's Camilla's ringtone – she's my best friend. Who am I kidding? Camilla is my *only* friend but that's entirely by choice; I don't really like that many people. They're fake and try to make me fake too and it's tiring pretending I don't see it.

I reach for my phone and move out of the pedestrian traffic, past the rows of postcards into the newsstand to talk.

'Hey sexy,' I say, pushing a finger into my free ear so I can hear her beyond the hum of traffic and chatter of pedestrians. I can still smell Thomas's cologne on my fingertips and I have a flash of memory. His breath on my ear. Goosebumps.

'So, I have news,' she says in a sing-song happy voice.

'You got the job?' I ask, hopeful. She's still back in London, works in corporate communications at an investment bank, hates her boss, hates her job, and has been waiting for word on a new one just like it for weeks.

'No. But almost as good,' she replies. 'I think I saw my soulmate tonight.'

~

I first met Camilla twelve years ago when we shared a flat at university. We bonded over big dreams – I was going to change the world one hard-hitting news story at a time and she was going to revolutionise *Vogue* – and a shared hatred of passive-aggressive Post-it notes left on the fridge. But then life went how life went. Camilla finished her degree with first class honours but graduated into a market where the only job for a journalism student was corporate communications. And I quit after my first year to get a day job in an office (marketing) because my boyfriend at the time, Harrison, was a musician on the verge of big things. In my defence, we were a team, he was supposed to be my love story, and someone had to pay the rent until he got his big break.

That someone was me.

In hindsight I suppose I could have kept writing; hindsight will always fuck you up like that. But somehow at the time there wasn't enough oxygen for two artists in our relationship: our roles had been set. He was the creative one and I was the support staff. And at the beginning I didn't really mind. He was hot and he toured Europe a lot and I'd use my holiday days to go along. I'd spend my days wandering through galleries filled with Klimt, Picasso, Warhol and Duccio, learning from gallerists about how the old masters used pinhole techniques for perspective, how the cracks in a painting can tell you as much as a fingerprint and what led each artist to the moment the world said: 'ahhh'. It was always that last part that fascinated me most: who was Duchamp before *Fountain*? What did Picasso's earliest sketches look like? Would *The Kiss* still be Klimt's most famous painting, had a set of three 'pornographic' ceiling panels not been destroyed in a fire in World War II? So for me, it wasn't the likes of the *Mona Lisa*, but rather the early works, the lost works, the clumsy sketchbooks that held secrets undisclosed by the glossy brochures handed out by galleries, that had me fall in love with art.

Harrison, on the other hand, spent his days 'rehearsing' (code for fucking Melody, who will become more important to this story quite soon). I kept telling myself we were living the dream, and it looked that way to anyone back home in grey old Kent who was scrolling through my social media but if I'm honest, really honest, it was lonely. He had my heart and he wouldn't give it back; he wouldn't even let it beat beside me half the time. Every year that passed saw him becoming a bit more depressed that he wasn't famous yet, while my life force was bled dry trying to make him happy. By the third act my soul was as shrivelled and dry as a fossil.

It took eight long years for his big break to finally come. A record deal. With a major label. A song he'd written about me called 'When She Sleeps' would be the first single. It felt like finally – *finally* – all that pain, all that sacrifice, had been worth it. Finally things might get better. Then one evening, about a week later, I got home from work, poured myself a gin and tonic, plonked myself down on the mauve leather sofa I'd paid for and Harrison sat down next to me. He took my hands in his. His eyes began to water. And my heart began to pound: he'd always been anti-marriage, said he didn't believe in it, but this was it, he was going to propose. Everything was finally working out.

His exact words were: 'Harper, you know what John Lennon said about how life is what happens to you when you're busy making other plans? Well, that's what happened to me, baby. You were my plan. *She* just happened. Don't be angry.'

But I *was* angry.

And not just because he was leaving me for Melody, his keyboardist. I'd given up on my own dreams in favour of his, I'd lost eight years of my life – that's 70,128 hours, I checked – and here I was with no degree, no writing career, a credit card debt (independent tours are expensive, you know), a job in an office that I hated, and no idea who the hell I was anymore.

It took a long time for me to realise that was the day I was born.

~

'Where did you meet him?' I ask Camilla, scanning the headlines of the newspapers laid out in front of me: last night the Paris police shot dead a man in a park after a stabbing rampage, the mayor is coming under scrutiny for something I can't quite understand, and

Le Monde's headline translates as 'No Justice for Matilde Beaumont?' She's been in the papers a lot over the last couple of weeks, so her picture looks almost familiar now as it smiles back at me: young, blonde, pretty. She could have been cast as Laura Palmer in *Twin Peaks*. And as I scan her features I can't help but wonder how it happened. How does a normal girl like her end up on the front page of the newspaper?

'In the elevator at work,' Camilla says, breaking my chain of thought.

'Well, what's his name? Send me his Instagram profile,' I say, still staring at Matilde's picture. 'I'll vet him for you.'

'Oh I didn't actually talk to him,' she says. 'But he looks just like the sketch.'

Six months ago, Camilla paid some guy on Etsy to draw a picture of her 'soulmate'. She provided her full name, her date of birth and her address. She says he needed that information to tap into her aura and she has been convinced ever since that she can use that sketch to find her other half. I, on the other hand, have been convinced that it's some sort of elaborate identity theft scam. The jury is still out as to which of us is correct, but that right there tells you everything you need to know about us, our respective life philosophies and the vital balancing role we play in each other's lives.

My phone beeps with a text.

'Hang on, Mills.' I pull the phone away from my ear and squint down at the message.

Urgent! Need you to cover an exhibition tomorrow night at Le Voltage. 7 pm. Brand new series. Due Friday 10 am. Make sure you network! H.

That H stands for Hyacinth, my new boss. This new job is the reason I moved to Paris. I put the phone back to my ear. 'Can I call you back later? I've just got to deal with a work thing.'

'Okay, sure. Big love.'

And then we hang up and I stand there rereading Hyacinth's message. An exhibition tomorrow night. Due Friday.

Shit.

Because tomorrow is already Thursday.

That doesn't leave me much time to write something impressive. And it *needs* to be impressive. Uber-impressive. Because this will be only my third story for *The Paris Observer*. My first was a review of a gypsy-jazz band. I thought my piece was amazing but it only got a depressing twelve likes and two shares. And my second, a walking tour of Paris's street art, is still on Hyacinth's desk awaiting the 'constructive notes' she told me were coming. Mine's an entry-level position and they're easing me in slowly, but if I don't hit it out of the park soon, Hyacinth is going to start wondering why the hell she hired me. And I can't afford to screw this up. I've worked too hard to get here.

Because after Harrison left me, let's just say things got a lot worse before they got better. It didn't matter what I drank, who

I fucked or what colour I dyed my hair, every time my lungs moved they hit my newly returned and wounded heart. It wasn't so much losing Harrison that haunted me; it was losing myself. I'd let this happen to me. I'd ignored everything I'd seen happen to my mother and let him in anyway. And he'd done exactly what I was scared of: taken what he could get from me and left.

In short, I'd betrayed myself.

And then, one very ordinary day that wasn't marked by anything I can recall now, I was sitting at my desk, pretending to put together a pamphlet for work, when something truly miraculous happened.

I started to write instead.

I hadn't written anything other than marketing copy in eight long years. But as I typed out the first line – *Why I hate John Lennon* – a light flicked on inside of me. And I knew: this was it. This was how I could make things right. Yes, I had given up my own dreams in favour of his, but I was only twenty-eight and I could still become a writer. And so every night that's what I did: I wrote. I wrote rave reviews about the music Harrison hated. I wrote about the art I now knew so much about thanks to his tours. I wrote about fitness trends, movies, intermittent fasting, music, sex, mascara and had a recurring micro-column inspired by my love of true crime podcasts called: 'How not to get murdered'. I even wrote about tax time once. Basically, I'd write about anything and everything as long as it added to my portfolio and took me one step closer to my dreams. And I did it largely for free.

Then one day, after about two years of that, Camilla sent me an advert for a journalism job in Paris with the note: 'What's the worst that can happen?' It asked for one year of fulltime experience and a portfolio. I only had the latter, but I applied anyway. There was a call, a Skype interview, a Eurostar trip, an offer and now we're in October and here I am.

They pay me a (meagre) salary and I can put 'Journalist' on forms beside: 'Occupation'.

Yes, as of three weeks ago, Harper Brown (that's me) officially works for *The Paris Observer* online magazine. It's *so* official that my voicemail now says: 'Hi, you've called Harper Brown at *The Paris Observer*. Leave a message and I'll get right back to you.' I'm their newest art and culture writer. That makes two of us now: me and glum Wesley.

I mean, no, I'm not writing hard-hitting pieces that end human trafficking or expose white collar crimes, but it's a cool job in a cool area – Bastille – and I'm thrilled to have it. It's a stepping stone to my dreams. Which is why it really matters that everything I submit to Hyacinth is impressive. So that, one day, when an opportunity in news comes up she'll think of me. But how the hell am I supposed to put together something 'impressive' between Thursday night and Friday at 10 am?

Unless . . .

There's a small fridge full of Evian and soft drinks in front of me, and I check my reflection in the glass: dark roots that fade into crème blonde at the ends and eyes that are either green or hazel depending on the weather. But right now, those eyes are sex-smudged with mascara. *Shit.* I use my fingers to try to wipe them clean.

Because I was planning on going home right now, but we all know what John Lennon said about life and plans . . .

Chapitre deux

I'm on Rue Bonaparte, eight steps away from the gallery, Le Voltage. It has a black wooden façade, and stuck on the inside glass is a red and cream poster. It's styled in Seventies font and reads, 'Noah X Exhibition, jeudi, le 14 octobre.'

X.

Wow.

Could he get any more pretentious?

I bet he's one of these types who refuses to wear shoes or has half his body shaved for no decipherable reason. I move towards the window, squint through the glass and try to make out the canvases on the walls. Because I've had enough lonely conversations with frustrated gallerists to know how exhibitions run by now: work needs to be hung, lighting adjusted, ahead of time. Whatever I'm supposed to write about tomorrow night will already be on the walls. And if I can just catch a glimpse of it, a sneak preview, get a feel for Noah-bloody-X, I can start the article tomorrow morning. That will give me a strong head start.

But shit, shit, shit – they're all white. Please don't have gone all Malevich *White on White*, that'll be impossible to write about . . .

No, wait, they're not white. They're covered in something. Cloth.

I glance left to the door. There's a handwritten sign on it that reads '*Fermé*', but there's a light on inside so maybe, just maybe . . .

Fuck it. I need to try.

I reach for the handle and push. It opens with a creak. Hooray! I move inside, shutting it quietly behind me. The air smells like damp, dust and furniture polish and I stand still for a moment, listening for movement. But there's nothing. It's just me, and the canvases all covered by cloth.

Still, the door was unlocked, a light is on and there are two alarm sensors flickering red from the corners of the room, yet no alarm has been set: someone must be coming back. I don't have a lot of time. I tiptoe over to the canvas in front of me, reach for the edge of the white covering and gently pull it off.

Plain black frame. A sheet of glass. And beyond it: a canvas. The edges are old, distressed Marvel comics stained in deep shades of burgundy and purple. Interesting. They've been torn away to reveal a woman, sitting on a shimmery golden background – think thirteenth and fourteenth century Italy. She's naked – aside from a red kabbalah string tied around her wrist and a small gold nose ring. She's hugging her knees, ankles crossed as she stares straight out at

16

the viewer. She has porcelain skin, light blue eyes, fire-engine red hair and a grey-metal gun lying on the floor beside her.

I reach for my phone, snap a picture and quickly glance down at it.

Shit. All I got was my own reflection and the flare of a couple of streetlights in the glass.

I snap a few more from other angles and the last one is strong. No reflections.

I start to drape the cloth back over it but then—

'What the hell are you doing?' comes a male voice. American.

Shit.

I turn my head quickly. He's tall, young – maybe thirty-two? – has floppy brown hair and tanned skin and, wow, he has the bluest eyes I've ever seen. Skies-over-the-alps blue. His chest is broad, like he works out, and he's wearing a pair of black jeans with a white T-shirt and a navy blazer. He's the kind of guy I'd usually flirt with, but he's carrying a big set of jangly keys and he looks *way* too pissed off for flirting right now.

He must run the gallery. Shit.

'Sorry,' I say, as he strides towards me and I awkwardly pull the remainder of the white fabric over the canvas. I swallow hard, trying to figure out how to get out of this. I have to come back here tomorrow night to review the exhibition. I can't get myself banned . . .

'Didn't you see the sign on the door?' he snaps, nodding towards it. He's half a step away from me now; I can smell his cologne. His eyebrows – thick, well formed – are raised. 'We're closed. You can't just come in here.'

His eyes trace my body: neck, clavicles, breasts. They linger on my hips then snap back to my face. Our eyes meet: *zap.*

My throat closes up. But I need to say something. I can't just stand here. Staring.

Luckily, I fuck up a lot in life so I'm well practised at getting myself out of fixes like this. I reach for my failsafe: damsel in distress.

'Oh shit, is that what the sign says? I don't speak French,' I say, all doe-eyed darling. 'It's just I saw you were having an exhibition for Noah X tomorrow night,' I nod to the poster in the window, 'and he's my favourite French artist . . .'

Something flickers behind his eyes; does he believe me?

'And I just wanted to see . . . I'm sooo sorry.' It all comes out in one, long, rambling breath. And that's just perfect. Because I sound flustered. I look flustered. And here's a life lesson for you: no man can resist flustered.

I look up at him, blink twice, and wait for him to soften. Wait for his eyes to do that thing they do when a man is mentally undressing you.

But his blue eyes narrow. Uh-oh, this is not good.

'You know I could call the police, right? This is trespassing.'

Wait, what?

My throat grows tighter. 'But the door was unlocked.'

'Riiigghht,' he says. 'What did you say your name was?'

I do *not* want to tell him my name. What if he looks me up, figures out where I work and this somehow gets back to Hyacinth?

'Grace,' I lie. I reach out my hand to shake his.

'Well, Grace,' he continues, ignoring my outstretched hand, 'tell me, what precisely did you think those covers were for then? Keeping the dust off?' And then he stands there, arms crossed, just looking at me and waiting for a reply.

My ears ring.

'Look, I'm really sorry, you clearly want me to leave,' I say in my firmest, most grown-up voice. I head for the door, reach for the handle and pull it towards me. A gush of cool air hits my cheeks and I step outside into freedom then—

'Wait,' Mr Blue Eyes says.

And there's something in his voice that makes me stop mid-step and look back. A hook.

'What?' I ask, still edging my way outside. He's standing in the middle of the room now, arms by his side, and the air between us is thick and silent.

The muscle on the left side of his jaw is twitching but his eyes have softened.

Oh, right, I know what's going on here: he's freaking out.

He's thinking about Google and Yelp and the reviews I could leave if he doesn't smooth things over. *Rude manager! Kicked me out!* Maybe I will . . .

'Did you like it?' he asks. It's conciliatory. Like he's hoping I'll forget he just yelled at me. 'The painting.'

And there's a part of me that wants to say 'no' and just leave him there to stew, but I *do* still need to come back tomorrow to see the rest of the work. It would be so much better if we could make amends. Be friends. Even if he does think my name is Grace now . . .

I let out a deep breath and let the door close as I step back inside. 'Yes,' I say, 'but I love anything pop art. And I mean, she's naked with a gun; it's total vulnerability and absolute strength all in one. The Marvel comics are great too; it's a very modern representation of femininity. And I love that she's staring out at the viewer as though begging for their gaze. Begging for connection,' I say, eyes to him now. Small smile. 'Or is she challenging them?'

He grins, his forehead creases. Jesus, his eyes are practically neon up close. Something in my stomach flips. I break our gaze, glancing round the room.

'Do you think I'd be able to take a look at the others?' I ask, nodding at the other canvases all still shrouded in white. That would be perfect. Then I wouldn't even have to come back tomorrow. I could write my article in peace from my bed, wearing knickers and a T-shirt, with a bottle of red and Netflix going in the background . . .

'Hell no,' he says, moving over to the large wooden desk at the back of the room where he picks up a flyer. 'But . . .' he says, as he moves over to me. He's standing just a millimetre too close for a stranger and I can smell his cologne again. It smells familiar but I can't quite place it . . . like earth . . . no, leather. No: wet cement after the rain. 'You should come to the exhibition.' He hands me the flyer; his hands are big and rough.

'Great, thanks. I will,' I say, like I wasn't planning on it anyway. I take the flyer and move quickly towards the exit.

'I'll see you tomorrow then, Grace.' He opens the door for me. 'Try not to get arrested in the meantime.'

'I'll do my best,' I say as I move out into the crisp night air. 'And you see if you can figure out how to use those grey metal things. I think they're called keys.'

Then the door closes and he's on one side of the glass and I'm on the other and everyone's happy. Mr Blue Eyes averted a disaster: nobody will be writing nasty things about him or his gallery on Google or Tripadvisor. And me? Well, I'm heading home with exactly what I came for: a photograph of a new Noah X painting and a head start on my story.

Chapitre trois

My bedroom window looks out onto the rooftops of Paris. All grey metal and terracotta chimneys. So no matter what colour the sky – pink, mauve, tin, electric blue, treacle black – it always looks like an Instagram post. An Instagram post with a direct view into my neighbour's apartment. Every night she lies in bed, watching something on her laptop. Sometimes she touches herself. Sometimes her boyfriend comes over and they have sex. Either way, I try not to notice. Of course, she can probably see me wandering around naked too, but whatever. That's urban living for you.

Still, I shouldn't be so blasé. That poor girl in the newspaper, Matilde Beaumont, was probably blasé too, and now look: one night she disappeared without a trace and four months later her body was found in a forest to the south-west of Paris. If I was still writing my 'How not to get murdered' column, the takeaway from Matilde's story would be: always walk with your keys between your fingers and stay the fuck away from the woods.

But that window is my favourite part of the room. The rest of it is all old white-grey paint and enclosed spaces. I have no closet – just a hanging rail and piles of folded clothing in my suitcase beside it. Not that I'm complaining. According to glum Wesley, apartments in Paris usually take six months, four guarantors, a shady landlord, hefty insurance and a pound of flesh to secure, and so I wouldn't even have an apartment if one of Mum's school friends (Anne) hadn't taken pity on me. She's very rich, very blonde, lives somewhere in North America now, and she has a place here she rarely visits. It's in the 6th, bordering the 7th, right by Jardin du Luxembourg and Montparnasse. Yes, I live in Postcard Paris. My apartment building has one of those grand wooden doors with an enormous black knocker, a cobbled courtyard and a chandelier that magically turns on whenever you walk down the stairs. It feels a bit like being a Disney princess.

I pull out my earplugs and reach for my phone. The time reads 6.55 am. I'm up five minutes early and that feels like a minor victory. It's always nice not to be ripped from sleep by the church bells that ring every morning at 7 am.

I sit up, my limbs heavy, and look out the window: this morning the sky is streaked with pink cloud. I snap a picture and upload it to the Instagram account I set up when I moved here: @new.girlinparis. I add #goodmorning and #paris then take my phone through to the living-area-slash-kitchen and flick on the light.

To my left is a white sofa (just a matter of time before I spill something on that) with a series of pink, terracotta, olive green and yellow striped pillows and an old Louis Vuitton luggage case as a coffee table. In front of me sits a big bookshelf full of books

23

and CDs, a lamp and another Louis Vuitton case. Above that is the only window in this part of the apartment – it's on the ceiling and requires a stick and a special knack to open it. And to my right sits a table, two chairs and a big wooden cupboard I found my sheets and towels inside. Behind me is where the coffee lives. The kitchenette: two hot plates (one is broken and the other has two settings: off or volcanic), a microwave where I heat up the creamed spinach I pretty much live on (I'm definitely going to develop some sort of nutritional deficiency soon, but at least it won't be scurvy), a sink, a fridge, and just enough room to open one, but not two, of those appliance doors at once. Anne's bedroom and ensuite (which I'm under strict instructions not to enter and aside from once, just to look around, I've complied) is to the right of that, just past the main bathroom.

I flick on the kettle. There are three mini bottles of Scotch right beside it, but I will not drink this morning. I have no issue with drinking at 7 am, but I want to be clear-headed at 10 am because today is Thursday. We have our editorial meetings on Thursdays where we pitch ideas to Hyacinth. I want to do well. I look past the amber liquid and out through the kitchen window. It's open and rain-stained and there are three terracotta pots outside filled with the brittle corpses of herbs or flowers. The sound of the kettle hissing echoes off the walls and the church bells ring in the distance as I reach for my phone and do the thing I told myself I wasn't going to do anymore.

First, I pull up Google and then I type in: *Harrison Daze*. If you want to know what haunts someone, check their search history.

I glance down at the results, scanning through the list of links. One day I'm going to run this search and find Harrison has been nominated for a Grammy or something. That will be a dark fucking day. But not today. Today it's nothing I haven't seen before. Just articles praising him in ways that make me want to drown my phone in the sink.

I've been watching Harrison's life from afar, watching it flourish – moving to LA with Melody, large scale support tours, photographs with a Beatle – ever since he left me. Every time something else goes right for him, it feels like there is no cosmic justice. It fucks up my entire day. I have to imagine bad things befalling him just to calm down. Nothing life threatening – just, you know, vocal nodules.

And I know I should just stop looking, but I can't. It's like a bruise I can't stop pressing.

But, still, it's better to watch him through this electronic window than to pick the lock on his physical front door and break in again.

I only did that once, by the way, and only to get some of my stuff back.

People get all judgey when you admit to things like that, but if other people didn't do similar things I'm pretty sure that YouTube channel for Mr Locksmith wouldn't be so bloody popular and I'm pretty sure that Amazon wouldn't have 3976 five-star reviews on the professional locksmith set I bought for the occasion. There can't be that many locksmiths out there losing their tools. But that's the thing about a lot of people: they aren't brave enough to admit they might have darkness. That sometimes they might do questionable things. Instead they sit back, sip on delusion and judge those who *do* own their demons. But people like that scare the shit out of me. Because those are the people who one day are triggered, see their darkness, get a fright, go postal and end up as the surprise main character in a true crime podcast.

I'm still staring at the search results, listening to the kettle whistle and then click off, when a text message fills the screen.

Hi Harper, I'm not sure what happened yesterday but I think you're right, it's best we end things. Just let me know you're okay. T.

Oh goodie.

Just what I need before caffeine.

A message from Thomas.

A flash of his caramel arms, the smell of candle wax, the gaze of the man in that ugly painting by his bed.

I put my phone down on the countertop and make my coffee then take a sip of it as I glare at the screen, rereading his message.

I'm not sure what happened yesterday?

There's no simple way to explain that.

There's only the truth.

Around the time Harrison left me and I finally denounced the idea of true love forever, I started seeing things differently. I guess once you see through one socially sanctioned lie, everything is up for debate. Things like: work hard at a sensible job and everything

26

will turn out fine, fall in love and you'll be happy, don't drink at 7 am or you're an alcoholic. That sort of thing.

Because . . . why?

Why is drinking at 7 am any worse than 7 pm – isn't time itself a man-made construct? And nobody judges the guy throwing down a Xanax with his cornflakes, why is that so different?

Why does love get such a great rap when it can quite logically only end in one of three ways: disillusionment, death or divorce?

And if working hard at a sensible job is the answer, why are there so many people working multiple jobs and still unable to pay their bills at the end of the month? Still unable to buy their children new shoes? All while they down antidepressants in a bid to forget the unforgettable: their dreams.

Exactly. It seemed to me society was founded on a series of rather precarious rules and narratives and I didn't want to be disappointed again. Not like this.

So now I only live by one rule: do no harm.

And Thomas was a hair away from getting attached, it would have harmed him if I'd stayed, so I ended it.

And I didn't *want* to end it. It was a sacrifice. Because he was six foot two. Also, he was hot (in a groom cake-topper kind of a way), a financial journalist for Endroit (Paris's major media conglomerate) and really good in bed. On paper we were a good match and I would have liked him as a fuck buddy. But I've learned the hard way that guys might think they want a fuck buddy at the beginning, but once they've gotten used to you and seen that you don't get clingy, all that always seems to change. They start looking at you differently. Sooner or later they start holding your hand. And when it hasn't changed for you too, egos get hurt and the guy gets mean. They call you a slut. A bitch. A psychopath. And then, if you're like me, you get so hurt you go home and do an online test just to check they're not right.

Which is why it's important to get out before anyone gets attached. I've trialled a few exit strategies now – blatant honesty, blocking, ghosting, slowly disappearing – and the only one that works one hundred per cent of the time is making them feel like they've dodged a bullet.

Ta-da.

But I can't tell Thomas all that.

It'd hurt my thumbs to type it all out and he wouldn't understand anyway.

He'd just tell me I'm scared, lend me one of his books on positive thinking, and try to change my mind the way people always do when I say these things out loud. Like my saying them is what makes them true and if they can just shut me up it might go away.

But the truth is, despite growing up watching my mother have her heart broken on a biannual basis, I *still* wanted love to be real as much as the next person. And when I met Harrison I thought maybe it was.

It wasn't.

And there are only so many times life can show you the same truth before you accept it. So here's what life has shown me about love: it's nothing more than a beautiful biological hoax; the only way nature can get any sane person to stick around long enough to procreate. And that wouldn't even be a problem, I'd totally buy into the program if it wasn't so fucking temporary. If it didn't always end badly. But it does. All it does is fuck you up and slow you down.

And I don't have another 70,128 hours to waste.

I take another sip of coffee and consider my response. We only hooked up once, I acted crazy and yet he's still being a good human and checking I'm okay. So if I reply with anything semi-sane he might give me the benefit of the doubt and want to start things up again. But if I continue on the meet-the-parents track and reply with something uber-crazed he'll have it in writing. He could show people. And we work in the same industry.

So basically I'm fucked either way.

This, right here, is why sensitive people like me drink.

I reach for one of the little bottles of Scotch, twist open the top and pour it into my coffee then take a sip. Another. One more. There. A calm warmth flows through my veins as I glance out the window. There's a grey and white pigeon sitting on one of the pots now. It gurgles some sort of pigeon sound and I take another sip of boozy coffee.

'Bonjour, Mr Oiseau,' I say, tapping on the glass. *Oiseau* is French for bird, but don't get excited – my French is pretty sketchy.

I did 'A' level French but most of what I know, I figured out via Reverso. '*Tu ferais quoi?*' I just asked him what he'd do if he were me.

He gurgles something back and flies away. And there I have it, my answer, delivered via a pigeon and a very boozy coffee.

I should do nothing. Walk away. Just ignore the message.

Thomas will forget me soon enough. We may live in the same vicinity, but this is Paris. It's a big place. As long as I don't make a habit of doing my laundry on a Sunday evening at that specific laundromat, it's likely we'll never bump into each other again. Soon I'll just be a memory to him and my legs will be twisted in someone else's sheets. Someone like . . .

I open one of the five dating apps on my phone and scroll through my newest messages, glancing down through the profile pictures.

Someone like . . . Nicolas.

I click through to his profile. Good pictures. Good face. His profile says he's five foot eleven which in dating language means he's five foot eight when he's standing up straight, but at least he doesn't lead with his Uber rating. He'll do. And so, as I finish my coffee, I reply to his message with: *Hey x*

Chapitre quatre

The little clock in the top right corner of my computer screen taunts me. It's already 9.47 am. Wait, no, 9.48. That means I only have twelve minutes until our weekly editorial meeting where we talk about new ideas, compare how many likes and shares everyone got this week, and Hyacinth makes someone cry.

I've been safe so far: nobody wants to make the new girl cry. But this is my third editorial meeting, and I get the sense my grace period is drawing to a close.

I glance over at Wesley. He's sitting across from me frowning at his computer, the blue rectangles from his screen reflecting in his round glasses. He's already got sweat patches forming under the arms of his light blue shirt. I can't tell if they're in anticipation of our meeting or from his sprint into work.

Wesley and I emerged from the Bastille metro station at exactly the same time this morning. And so I did the only sane thing to do in that sort of situation: I rushed like hell so we wouldn't have to make inane chitchat for the twelve long minutes it takes to walk to the office from the station. And when I say I rushed, I mean I jogged part of it. That's how strong my commitment was.

When I arrived at the black, cast-iron gate nestled between two vast lighting shops that marks our office, I thought I was safe. But before I punched in the door code and made it inside, there he was behind me. Panting. Saying 'Hello' and following me in.

And so we rode the teeny-tiny elevator in awkward silence, until the doors slid open and he bolted out and I was left thinking: *Wesley doesn't like me very much.* But he was the only art and culture writer before I arrived. Maybe he sees me as a threat.

Now in the office, I reach for my cup of coffee, take a sip and glance around. Printers buzz. People whisper. The strip lighting on the ceiling flickers. I was surprised when I first walked in here: it doesn't look like a portal to an online English language magazine that syndicates its stories all over the world. It looks more like a makeshift employment agency, one bounced electricity payment away from closure. It's a sprawling, messy open-plan room for us plebs, a glass-walled office for Hyacinth, a meeting room, two bathrooms and a poky little kitchen.

I turn back to my computer, glance over my list of ideas one more time then press 'print'.

The printer that sits beside Wesley hums and then spits out my pages. He flashes me a look of hatred – how dare I be ready – his eyes the colour of chocolate croissants. God I'm hungry.

I give him a small, tight smile, reach for the pages, lay them down next to me and, with my final eight minutes, I go to Instagram, tap the little magnifying glass and type into the search function: *N-o-a-h-X*.

I might as well start my research.

There he is, right at the top: @NoahXartist.

I click on it and scan the images.

Boring.

Boring.

Boring.

Old work – all geometric shades of grey that don't translate well to social media. Ill-conceived comments: 'My toddler could have painted that'. An announcement about the exhibition tonight. Some more grey.

I glance left to his profile photo but it's just another shot of one of his paintings. But – ooohhhh wait – there's an Instagram story just waiting to be watched. Maybe he's in it.

I tap on it and a picture fills the screen.

But it's not of him. It's a series of five coffee cups with the hashtags #upallnight #Montmartre #coffee and #artistsoninstagram.

So basically he's #dull.

I exhale and Wesley shoots me a look.

I focus on my phone screen, typing #NoahX into the search function. There must be something interesting about him out there somewhere. Something questionable he was tagged in . . .

Up comes a page of square images. I scan them.

Two lines down, there's a shot of a young couple – she's dark, he's fair – posing beside a canvas. I click on it. It's from an exhibition in Berlin. I keep scrolling.

Photographs of articles written about Noah X. I make a note to look those up after our meeting. A shot of a very beautiful woman of about forty with a short strawberry blonde bob. She's wearing a tailored navy suit beside a piece so huge it dwarfs her. It's a magazine clipping. A gash of light catches on the glossy page.

I tap on the photo and read the headline: 'Agnès Bisset discovers yet another emerging art star: meet Noah X.' It was posted in September 2018.

Interesting.

I keep scrolling. Keep looking. And then there it is.

Something.

Or rather: some*one*.

The hot gallery owner from last night. He's standing there all white teeth and blue eyes. I smile as I remember him, the way he smelled. I tap on the image and read the caption. *Noah X at his exhibition in New York.* #2019 #OMG #love #contemporaryart #hessohot #NY #NYforever #NoahX.

Wait . . . what?

My blood speeds up as I read the words again: *Noah X at his exhibition in New York.*

I swallow hard. Make sure my synapses haven't misfired.

So that wasn't the gallery owner I met last night.

It was Noah X.

I can hear my voice saying, 'He's my favourite French artist.'

He's not even French, Harper, he's American.

And I know I could be embarrassed right now, mortified that I stood there oblivious to who he was, talking about him in the third person while he let me. But I'm not. All I can think is: *Touché.*

Because that's the exact sort of thing I might do.

Noah X just became a lot more interesting to me.

But now the air fills with the sound of a chair being pulled across the floor.

'Are you coming?' Wesley asks. I look up at him, he's standing now, holding a sheet of paper, a notepad, a pen and a coffee cup with a red cat on it.

'Of course,' I say, picking up my own coffee cup, notepad, pen and the printouts before following him along the grey carpet towards the meeting room.

'Harper,' Hyacinth says as I move inside. I try to read her expression – is that an I-loved-your-story or an I-hated-your-story blank stare?

Everything you need to know about Hyacinth can be gleaned from her name and title: Hyacinth Cromwell-Scott, Editor-in-chief of *The Paris Observer*. She's very British, very tall, has lived in Paris since the '80s, has worked on everything important and knows everybody worth knowing in Paris. I know all this because I did my due diligence (i.e. cyber-stalked her) before I came over on the Eurostar for my interview. What the internet didn't warn me of, however, was her poker face; it's impossible to know what she's thinking from her expression. Most of the time I find myself trying to figure out whether I'm on the verge of losing my job via decoding the grammar in her messages. It's harder in real life. There's no punctuation.

'Close the door.'

Shit. Not good.

I do as she says then turn back to the room. Along the wall facing me, windows with peeling paint look out onto the streets of Bastille: a row of green and turquoise Vélib' bicycles, a street-side café with black graffiti covering the stone-washed apartment above it and trees with leaves that are turning the colour of rust. I take a seat beside Wesley and glance around at the other faces.

Twelve people are sitting at a big round dark wood table. Even though everyone introduced themselves on day one, I'm still not sure of all their names. The only one I'm certain of is Stan, the blond guy sitting at the other end of the table from Hyacinth. Partially because he does the news and politics stories and that's the job I wish I had, and partially because when Hyacinth was walking me from desk to desk on day one, introducing me to everyone, he said, 'Wow, you look just like the dead girl we're not allowed to write about anymore'. Then he glared at Hyacinth.

That's the sort of thing that gets you remembered.

So there's him. Then there's Wesley, Hyacinth, five randoms I've seen around intermittently and suspect might be freelancers, and three girls facing me, their hair backlit by the window behind them. Three little angels. The middle one is Claudia. She's loud, brash, Italian, wears bright lipstick, and she's the one that cried last week. She was barely in the office when I first started, but flounced in every now and then to talk loudly about how fantastic Paris Fashion Week was. But when she wrote about it, Hyacinth did not 'love her work'. Mainly, however, Claudia writes about celebrity gossip, most of it secondhand and sifted from American or UK tabloids. Even though we might be broadly described as belonging to the French version of a tabloid – *la presse people* – France has stronger privacy laws than its international counterparts, and so Hyacinth gets very antsy when she thinks we might get sued.

This was quite the culture shock, coming from the UK where tabloids routinely declare all sorts of personal and shitty things about celebrities and get away with it. I'm not really sure about the two beside Claudia – I think maybe it's Nathalie and Helena – but we're all going out for team-building drinks tomorrow night, so I'll figure it out then.

Everyone is dead quiet but the hum of traffic floats in from outside. I reach for my cup of coffee and take a sip.

'So, my darlings,' Hyacinth begins, dragging out the word: daaaarlings. 'Who would like to take the floor first?'

'Me,' says Stan-who-has-my-dream-job.

'Great, Stan,' Hyacinth says. 'What have you got?'

'I think it's time to run my Femicide piece,' he says.

When he says 'Femicide' I immediately think of some graffiti I saw in Montparnasse soon after I arrived in Paris, in the space between unpacking and starting this job. I'd gone to see the grave of Simone de Beauvoir and Sartre; I'd taken a photograph of the lipstick marks on their tombstone and uploaded it to Instagram. But on my walk home, there was this stone wall with the black spraypainted words: '*une femme est tuée tous les deux jours en France*'. It stayed with me and I looked it up later that night. And it was true: a woman *is* killed every two days in France. I'm not sure how that compares to the rest of the world but it sounds like a lot.

'All the leads on Matilde Beaumont have dried up,' Stan continues. 'According to my sources they're about to close the case. People forget. And then it happens again.'

Stan takes special care to linger on the word 'sources' and there's a reason for this. The police in France don't trust the media as a rule, and keep us at a distance, not even using us to gather information from the public. So press reports are cobbled together from leaked information and snippets from whoever will talk to us. Thus, Stan thinks having a source at the police makes him special, and, well, it sort of does.

'Stan, I appreciate your passion,' Hyacinth snaps. I get the feeling they've had this conversation before. 'It's done. It's been covered to hell and back. And, yes, it's important, but it's also a downer. People don't visit *The Paris Observer* to hear about girls turning up dead. They want to hear about which restaurant to go to. What's on at the ballet. That sort of thing. And we need people to read our magazine or nobody will pay to advertise. I'm sorry but the answer is still no.'

I'm not stupid enough to argue with her, but this is blatantly untrue.

People love to read about murder. Death. It helps to remind them they're still alive. At least, I think that's why I like it.

'Right,' Hyacinth continues with a big smile that is strangely scary because her eyes stay botox-still. 'Who else?'

'I'll go,' says the girl to the right of Claudia.

She starts talking about a perfumery in Le Marais where you can mix your own scent. I remain aware of her vocal modulations and the way her hands are gesturing in front of her; her wedding ring catches the light. But I'm thinking about tonight, about the exhibition: as much as I'd love to chat to Mr Blue Eyes again, let him know the jig is up, I also can't risk it. I can't let him know who I am, where I work, or why I was there last night. Because I don't know him well enough to know what he'd do with that information. He might think it was funny. Or he might call Hyacinth, make a complaint and blow my whole life up. It's too much of a gamble. It'd be better if I could turn up, take some notes and leave without anyone figuring out why I'm there. And if Noah sees me and asks me, well, I'm Grace . . .

'Harper?' Hyacinth's voice.

I look up and around, everyone is staring at me.

'Yes?'

She gives a small smile and I realise she's about to repeat herself. 'You'll be a guinea pig with Nathalie, won't you?'

'Of course,' I say, no idea what I'm committing to, nor when, but maybe if I'm super nice and amenable she won't fire me if she hates my story. And I know that makes me sound annoyingly insecure, but we're all insecure about something. Usually the thing we think matters the most.

'Great,' says the girl who was just talking about perfume. Oh. So that's what I'm doing. 'I'll send you an invite.'

Then Hyacinth's gaze bores into me. 'Wonderful. So, Harper, pitch to me.'

Chapitre cinq

There are no white cloths over paintings tonight, and barely any room to move. I'm standing by painting number three, frowning down at my phone, pretending to type. What I'm really doing is pointing the camera lens at the canvas and snapping another picture. I took the first when I arrived fifteen minutes ago and uploaded it to Instagram with the hashtags: #LeVoltage #Paris and #rebel. The last of those refers to the fact that there's a big 'No photography' sign in both English and French by the door (inspired by moi?), but I don't have a choice. I need to leave before Noah arrives and I want to be able to describe a few of the images in detail for my article. Scratch that, I *need* to be able to describe a couple of his artworks in detail, otherwise my article will be pretty damned short.

Because, after the editorial meeting, Hyacinth handed me a black-and-white printout of my street art piece with a lot of red pen notes (*Why is this here? What do you mean? Reference other artists! Give the reader something to learn! Did you do any research at all?*). And so I didn't get that head start on my Noah X article after all. Instead, I spent the rest of the day reworking the street art piece, trying to ignore my smug inner critic. But after I finally pressed send at 5 pm, I devoted a good solid hour to researching Noah X, looking more carefully through his Instagram page, dissecting his website, and reading reviews of his older work. But all that left me with were rudimentary details ('born in Indiana' and 'attended Maryland Institute College of Art') and useless tidbits (his sister's name is Anna and she runs a gluten free bakery back in Indiana – this, I discovered by clicking on the handle beside an 'I miss you' on one of his Instagram posts). There are hardly any pictures of Noah X online and it seems he's at that stage of his career where he's 'emerging' enough to have a write-up in *The Paris Observer* but not quite famous enough to have a Wikipedia page or anything else that might make my job easier. He's not quite Banksy-level invisible, but the 'X' in his name is indicative of a strong and unusual branding choice: mystery. Which is all fine and good and probably sells paintings, but it doesn't help me.

I look around the gallery, making sure nobody is watching me. But thankfully Noah's model, the redhead, is here wandering around with her iPhone out, videoing people's reactions to the work. Everyone's attention is on her; lots of eyes darting to her nipples then back at the paintings.

But wait, there's a woman I recognise standing on the far side of the room.

The woman from that magazine article on Instagram. The one with the short strawberry blonde bob and fine features who 'discovered' Noah. *What was her name? It started with an 'A' . . .* She's chatting to a man with thick salt-and-pepper hair and black, square-framed glasses, and her body language says she's in charge. She must be Noah's agent or the real gallerist here. I should ask her some questions. But the moment she looks up and catches my eye, I instinctively look away.

Talking to her would be a bad idea.

It's just gone quarter past seven, Noah will arrive soon and I don't want to be trapped in conversation with his agent when that happens. It'll make it harder to slip out unnoticed.

I glance down at the photograph I just took: good, no reflections. The artwork has the same Marvel comics and the same model, but this time she's sitting up in bed, her legs barely covered by white sheets, her red hair brought forward over one shoulder. She's smoking a cigarette as she stares down at her phone. It's all in black and white except for her hair, the red string around her wrist, the red lighter beside her and the end of her cigarette.

I stare at it and consider what I might write about it. It reminds me of something, another work, but I can't quite figure out what.

'It's great, right?' comes a French female voice from beside me. I turn my head to see who's talking. *Oh fuck.* It's the woman I was just looking at.

Agnès, that was her name.

I nod and say, 'Yes,' as I take her in.

She's somewhere between thirty-eight and forty-five and smells refined. Expensive. She has the kind of translucent skin that

43

I recognise from the Fraxel leaflets that are handed to me every time I get a facial, and she's wearing a navy and cream lace pants suit, the sort that you just know didn't come from Zara. As for me, I'm wearing a black leather skirt (that *did* come from Zara), thick black stockings, black boots, a black V-neck, a gold necklace and a pair of dangly earrings I picked up from Topshop. I feel conspicuously inexpensive under her gaze.

She's watching me like she expects me to say something else. But I don't want to say something else, I want to leave, so instead I glance over her shoulder; the last thing I need is for Noah to walk in right now.

'Do you know much of his work?' she continues. My gaze snaps back to hers and she smiles. *God, she doesn't think I'm a proper buyer does she?*

'Not really,' I say, running polite reasons to excuse myself through my mind but the only compelling one I can come up with is: bathroom.

And then something truly wonderful happens. My phone starts vibrating in my hand. I look down and see 'Mum' flashing up on the screen. *Thank god.*

'Oh shit. Sorry, I have to take this,' I say, holding up my phone.

And that's true. My mother *never* calls me. And when she does it's never good. It means the wheels are falling off again and she needs me.

'Hey, Mum,' I say, 'just a sec.' I weave my way through the crowd, past the mousy-haired girl by the door who's greeting people and handing out champagne, and soon I'm outside in the crisp night air where it's quieter.

The sky is a rich starry-night blue and the yellow streetlights look gold against it.

'Mum?'

'Hi,' she says. Her voice cracks.

'What's going on?' I ask, moving away from the hum of the gallery.

'We broke up,' she says.

By 'we' she means her and Neville. This is not a bad thing, Neville is a shit – but of course he is, that's mum's type. She's been breaking up with men like Neville my whole life. And you'd think that would have taught me a thing or two about love but I guess there are some lessons that can't be learned secondhand.

'Okay, what actually happened?' I ask.

She starts sobbing. Then mumbling something – I'm pretty sure she just said 'took my car'.

'Take a deep breath,' I say into the phone.

She whimpers something back but I can't quite make it out because there are people spilling out of the gallery now, and they're talking loudly in French. I glance back at them: one is laughing; a man is lighting a woman's cigarette. I look around me: a row of parked motorbikes sparkling under streetlights and the red and white neon of a *tabac* up ahead. But just beside the gallery there's a narrow, cobbled side street. I duck into it. It'll be quieter in here.

'I just don't know why this always happens to me,' she says as I move into the alleyway. 'I try so hard.'

I lean against the cool bricks of the gallery. 'I know you do,' I say. She tries *too* hard. 'When did it happen, Mum?'

'Tonight.'

'Okay,' I say. She'll need a day or two. 'Mum, take a couple of paracetamol and get an early night. We can talk properly tomorrow.' Here's a life hack for you: on a purely physiological level, paracetamol soothes a broken heart.

'Okay,' she says. 'I love you, Harper.'

'I love you too,' I reply. 'Sleep well.'

And then we hang up.

The air smells sweet. Spicy. Familiar. But I haven't smelled that aroma in two years or so. Not since Harrison. I turn around, searching the cobbled street, up then down.

Weed. It's weed. And then I see him. He's just a little further down the alley, beyond a light, obscured by the shadows. He's sitting on the ground and leaning against the wall. He lifts something to his lips; the end glows amber in the dark.

Noah.

~

I look back down at my phone, pretending not to care whether he's there or not. In these sorts of situations, it's best to be the one in control. He needs to come to me.

46

And come to me he does.

'Well, look who it is,' he says, his teeth catching the light as he smiles and stands up. I take him in as he moves towards me: blue jeans and a white long-sleeved shirt with the top buttons undone. His expression is calm and his hair has fallen in front of one slightly pink eye. He's baked.

'Hey,' I say, sweeping my hair from my face. *Act cool.*

He's right by me now, leaning against the wall. I can smell his cologne, mingling with the weed, and my eyes move from his face to the joint.

'Want some?' His expression is open, like that of a small child offering up a sweet.

I look around. Nobody is here – it's just me and him. My insides are aching from that phone call with my mother, I'm stressed about seeing him, and yes, yes, I would like some.

I reach for it and our fingers touch. *Zap.*

'Might as well,' I say. 'We're all doomed anyway. This might take the edge off.' I take a deep inhale. The smoke singes my throat and moves into my lungs. My head grows light, my chest grows tight. I wait. Exhale. His eyes are still on me when I look back to him.

'Doomed?' he asks, with a small smile.

I narrow my eyes. 'Don't you read the news?'

'I didn't peg you as such a negative Nancy,' he says, reaching back for the joint.

I shrug. 'I'm full of surprises.'

He smiles and takes a drag.

'Shouldn't you be inside?' I ask, nodding to what I presume is the back door to the gallery.

'I should. But I need this first.' He nods to the joint. 'Makes the bullshitting easier.'

I think about yesterday and how he didn't tell me he was the artist, how he let me ramble on and just played me like some silly girl, some groupie. I glance over at him, there's something in his eyes, he's thinking, *She still has no idea who I am. Should I tell her?* And fuck that. Fuck letting him think he's smarter than me. Fuck letting him have control.

'Oh . . . yes,' I say, reaching for the blunt. The end of it has been stained pink-mauve from my lipstick. 'The bullshitting. You have quite a talent there.' I take another inhale.

'How do you mean?' he asks, frowning.

I hold my breath, my eyes on his. And then I breathe out a cloud of smoke.

'Why didn't you tell me who you were yesterday?' I ask. His features shift. He's trying to figure out what to say next.

Of course, I still haven't told him who I am either, so yes, technically that makes me a hypocrite but whatever. Nobody is perfect.

'How did you figure it out?' he says.

'Fun little tool called Google.'

His eyes are all sparks and flames. He's not used to being caught out. 'Well, I mean, I *am* your favourite French artist.' He takes the joint back from me.

'Not anymore,' I say.

'Oh, is that right?'

And then we stand there in silence for a moment.

'You wouldn't have told me the truth if you knew,' he says, his voice low and crackly from the weed. 'And I wanted to know what you really thought of it. The work. It's scary putting something new out into the world.'

The cool breeze blows my hair around as I look back to him. His face is fragile, childlike. But Harrison used to get that look, the tortured-artist-needing-validation look. It's that look that drew me in to start with. So fuck that look. I focus my gaze on the ground instead.

'So have you been inside tonight? Seen the rest?'

'I have,' I say.

'And?'

I look up at him. 'The one in bed is my favourite.'

'The one with the red.' He grins, nodding in agreement.

'Yes,' I say. And then I know what it reminds me of. 'It's very Berthe Morisot.'

He starts to laugh. 'What? *That* I was not expecting.'

'No, it is,' I say. 'It's like that painting she did of a man in a hat looking out the window at women outside. I think it's called *Eugène Manet on the Isle of Wight*.'

'Yes, I know the work. But Berthe was not really what I was going for.'

'No, you don't understand what I mean. I remember seeing that painting for the first time in the Musée d'Orsay and I had one of those little sound recording devices that tells you all about the painting. The guy on the recording kept talking about the light and the gauzy curtains and the greys and greens and all that. But I kept thinking, *She's having a dig at the status quo.* Because, at the time, femininity was all about confinement. Women were either stuck in the house, looking out windows, washing the femininity off them in the bath or in the garden close to nature. But the women in that painting are free. They're outside. It's the man who is inside, behind the bars of a picket fence and the barrier of a window. The roles have been reversed. I fucking love that painting.' I pause. 'And that's why I love yours. It's the girl ignoring the guy, not vice versa. A role reversal.'

I pause again for breath. But now my cheeks are getting hot in the dark. Insecurity is taking hold. Have I said something stupid?

'But then you're the artist.' I backtrack. 'Am I reading too much into it?'

'No.' He shakes his head. 'Not at all. I like the way you think.' Then he takes another drag and as he holds his breath he asks: 'How do you know so much about art?'

I shrug, watching him exhale as I think of all those galleries I wandered through while Harrison was fucking 'her'. All those long conversations with gallerists. But I don't want to get into that right now. So instead I say, 'I studied it a bit at uni,' and shrug. 'So who's the girl in the pictures?'

'Sabine? She's an artist's model.'

'Is that an actual thing? Being a model for a painter as a proper job?'

'Well, it is for her – now at least. She used to work here.' He bangs gently on the wall of the gallery. 'That's where we met.'

And that's when the weed hits. There's a blessed barrier between me and anything harsh in the world now. My lips feel big and tingly and my mouth is dry, and I'm very aware of the fact that Noah is standing close to me. That he's pulsing warmth and I want to giggle and melt into him.

'You must pay her well,' I say. 'Paris is expensive.' I don't really care what he pays her. I'm just filling the silence because it's thick with tension and I can't stand it.

'Not really, but she still lives with her mother. Cheap rent.'

The joint has burned down to his fingertips now, and so he drops it to the ground and stomps it out. And we stand there, both leaning against the wall, looking at each other. I'm toying with my necklace the way I always do when I'm a bit nervous or flirting, and I'm not sure which one it is right now. It's a gold coin pendant with my star sign on it: Virgo. Camilla got one for me before I left London. She has one just like it but hers is Pisces.

'This is cool,' he says, reaching for it. And we're standing even closer now. My cheeks are warm. 'What does it mean?'

'That I'm a Virgo,' I say softly, with a small smile. My voice is scratchy from the weed and it comes out like a whisper.

'And that means . . .'

'That I'm bad news,' I say.

He laughs – a big, real laugh – and says, 'What a coincidence, me too.' Then he lets go of my necklace and it jangles as it drops back to my breastbone.

And we're just standing here now.

'Shit. I really have to go inside,' he says, not moving.

'Yeah,' I say. And I don't move either.

One moment. Two moments. Three moments pass. Then he takes a deep breath and it comes out jagged; it breaks my train of thought. He takes a micro step back. And then he moves towards the door. I watch as he traces a cross on the keypad. The door buzzes. He pushes it open and a glittery white light spills out into the shadows.

'Good luck,' I say, before he goes inside.

And he looks back at me, hesitates for just a moment, and then says: 'Are you on Instagram?'

I nod, mentally scanning my new account – but there's nothing on there to identify me as 'Harper Brown'. No name. No work-place. And only a picture of the Eiffel Tower as my profile picture.

'@new.girlinparis,' I say. 'But there's a dot between new and girl.'

'Cute,' he replies. 'Well, I'll see you around, new dot girl in Paris.'

Then he closes the door and he's gone and it's just me and the treacle black sky and the yellow globe by the door. The air smells of fading weed and impending rain. But then my phone lights up in the dark: *@NoahXartist has started following you.* So I do the only polite thing . . . I follow him back.

Chapitre six

The Paris I used to visit with Harrison is not the same city I've lived in for the last five weeks. The former was all cobbled streets, picture-perfect cafés, neon signage, the sound of rain on tin roofs, the glittering lights of the Eiffel Tower in the middle of the night on our way back to our hotel room from his shows. It was an untainted projection of the Paris of my mind, a montage of movie scenes from *Amélie*, the golden hues of impressionism, that kissing photograph by Robert Doisneau and quotes like 'Paris is always a good idea'. It was pretty, poetic and romantic. But it was soulless, choreographed and two-dimensional compared to the Paris I live in now.

Because there's a grit to the real Paris I didn't see back then, an electric sort of madness that only opens itself to you once you've been here long enough to see beyond the varnish.

Yes, even in the 6th arrondissement.

Like, there's a homeless guy who poops on the corner by my flat every morning at the exact time I need to pass by to get to the metro. Nobody says anything. Nobody stares. Then there's the woman I see at the grocery store almost every time I go in.

She's perfectly coiffed, her makeup immaculate, and she wears her tabby cat in a grey baby-holder strapped to her chest. She just wanders the aisles in silence.

There's the ongoing battle not to eat an entire wheel of brie for dinner every night when it's only one euro at the supermarket and so clearly the most economical choice. And when I came across for my interview in August, there were thunderstorms, the hot pavement sizzling with summer rain. Sometimes I swear to god there were seagulls too, I could hear them from my open hotel window. It was eerie.

Real Paris is magic and grime and the unexpected all tangled up together like glittery wool.

But it's also rude commuters huffing and puffing over my shoulder as I shove my white paper *billet* in the metal slot and hurry through the gate to wait on the crowded platform. And it's stairs. So. Many. Fucking. Stairs. There are ninety-six of them leading up to my flat, meaning each trip to the supermarket or chemist requires a thorough cost–benefit analysis.

And last but not least, it's door codes.

The infuriating, can't-remember-them-all-because-I'm-not-Rain-Man door codes. Because in Paris, there's a door code for everything: two at the flat (one for the courtyard, one for the building), one for each yoga school I've trialled, one for anyone you visit, and one for work. In order not to go one hundred per cent bats, I've devised a system.

Like right now, I'm punching in the code for the downstairs door at work. Do I remember the numbers? Of course not. I'm as bad with numbers as I am with names; I'm a visual creature. But what I *can* remember easily is the 'shape' of the code: diagonals, middle lines, a square, etc. In this case, it's a big 'V' with a 'C' for cup at the end. If I were numerically minded that would translate as: 1-3-8-0-C. It's hard to explain but it works for me.

The door buzzes and I head for the lift. I can hear it rattle as it makes its way down towards me. Inside, the air smells of perfume — some sort of bruised flower — and I stare at my reflection in the mirrored doors as they close. I look tired. Wired. I was up late sending off Camilla's CV for a job at *Vogue* she'd be perfect for but would never have the confidence to apply for herself, and writing my article. My final draft landed in Hyacinth's inbox at around 3 am and by 3.01 I wanted to unsend it. But instead, I brushed my teeth, telling myself things like: *You probably nailed it.* And maybe I did. Hyacinth's feedback on my last story was certainly rattling around my head the whole time I typed: *Reference other artists! Give the reader something to learn!* And so I really worked the Berthe Morisot angle I spoke to Noah about in the alleyway.

Fingers crossed.

The lift doors open. Reception is empty and Claudia is sitting perched on her desk, talking loudly on speakerphone, while every-one around her pretends not to be annoyed. My head thumps, so I keep my eyes down and frown in a way that makes me seem unapproachable as I head to my desk. I drop my handbag on the floor, flop down on my chair and power on my computer.

It glows to life and I enter my password: *ParisObserver123*.

No, I'm not completely lacking in imagination, that's the same one I was issued on my first day, right before I embarked on that awkward introductory tour of the office.

I move to my inbox, staring at my screen, scanning through my emails for anything from Hyacinth. For feedback on my article. *Please love it, please love it, please love it.*

But who am I kidding, it's just gone 9 am and last time it took her more than twenty-four hours to get back to me. The best thing I can do right now is get a start on my next idea. But my head is thumping, my mouth is dry, and I either need an IV drip of caffeine or a defibrillator. Now. I glance up at the kitchen. There are people in there, milling around the Nespresso machine. One of them laughs loudly. I'll need to wait until they leave, otherwise I'll be drawn into the hell that is office small talk. Meanwhile, Claudia is still polluting the airwaves with her speakerphone call. It's interesting that there isn't more violence in the workplace.

But now the people are leaving. I stand up. I'm about to head to the kitchen when I hear a small voice say, 'Harper.'

I turn to look. It's Judy, the receptionist with her perfect short dark bob. She's wearing a cream knee-length dress that nips in at the waist and she is grinning a sweet grin. I smile back because she's the only person in this place I don't actively dislike.

But wait . . .

She's carrying roses.

Red ones.

I do a quick count: twelve.

I stand there, staring at her. *She's not bringing those to me, is she?* My breath is quick. Please be for someone else. Someone sitting right near me. Wesley?

My face is getting hot now because, nope, she's definitely coming for me.

'Lucky girl!' says Judy.

'Thanks,' I say, my throat constricting as she lays them down on my desk.

But my insides are all: *Fuck him.*

Because before I even reach for the card, I know what it will say: *H xx.*

Harrison.

I know this because today is the anniversary of the day we met.

And he always does something like this, always has, and it appears, always fucking will. Last year was a massive teddy bear which ended up finding its 'forever home' at Oxfam. I thought it was a one-off. A slip. A jagged end to a tradition. But here we are, a full swing around the sun later, and he's still being an arsehole. And don't get me wrong, I know it *looks* like a sweet gesture, but know this: anything Harrison does that seems 'sweet' has an ulterior motive. In this case he's trying to keep me on his hook. And I hate that, as hard as I try to break free, he's managing. I hate that I still google him. I hate that love is a bit like a prison: easy to get into but you have to tunnel your way out with a teaspoon.

'Those are pretty,' says Wesley from his side of the desk.

'Thanks,' I say, my voice deadpan. Because, no, Wesley, they are not pretty, they are twelve little Trojan horses full of poison. Treat them as such.

But this is partly my fault. I shouldn't have told Harrison I got this job. But when he dropped his last *just checking u r well* text it felt so good to say: *Actually all is great, I got a job in Paris!* It was the first time *my* news was the exciting news.

There's movement in my peripheral vision, the smell of bruised flowers I recognise from the elevator, and then there she is beside me. Leaning in to smell the roses. Claudia.

'Who are those from?' She grins at me. 'You've only been here, what – three weeks – and already you're getting flowers?'

'You can have them if you want.' I move back from them like they've been sent from Chernobyl. Because I'm thinking about those Instagram posts with him and Melody and that glistening pool beneath a perfect LA sky and screw him. He doesn't get to live in two hearts simultaneously.

Claudia looks at me, shocked.

'I mean it,' I snap, pushing them towards her. 'Take them. I don't want his stupid flowers.'

'Wow, Harper,' she says, picking them up. 'Whoever he is, he's just being nice. You know, it wouldn't kill *you* to be nice sometimes.' And then she walks away.

Statistically speaking, she's wrong of course. Being 'nice' absolutely *could* kill me. Being nice, being polite, is precisely how most women end up being pulled into a panel van by their killer. These are the helpful hints I used to write about in my 'How not to get murdered' column. If that magazine hadn't folded, I'd happily forward her the link. But I don't say that, do I? No, of course not. Because while the likes of Stan get to glare at Hyacinth and challenge her in meetings, I'm a woman, so I have to at least pretend to be likeable. Agreeable. Nice. That's the final frontier of feminism right there. You can be anything you want to be as a woman these days, but don't you dare be unlikeable.

Claudia is whispering to Nathalie now. The one who was talking about perfume in yesterday's meeting; the one I'm going to 'be a guinea pig' with. Probably about how fucked up I am. And she has a point: I *am* a bit fucked up.

But here's my point: so what?

Focus, Harper, focus. Because I don't have time to care about things like office bitchery right now. I have bigger problems, problems like Mum.

I need to make sure she isn't still in bed.

Chapitre sept

We're sitting in a bistro not far from work. It's the compulsory Friday team drinks thing. Except Hyacinth isn't here. She somehow got out of it the way people always do when they're in charge. The seats are covered in shiny red leather and there are a series of yellow-lit stained glass lanterns hanging from the ceiling. I'm nestled up against the exposed brick half-wall – lined with bright green fake plants – that separates us from the tables behind. The windows are all open, the sky outside is a deep navy black. My mother didn't answer the first four of my calls, and when she finally did pick up call number five, she told me to 'calm down' because she and Neville had 'worked things out'. That's code for: expect a repeat performance in a month. So now I'm four piña coladas deep and the world has shifted into soft focus.

Though I'm not sure my blood alcohol level can be blamed entirely on my mother.

Claudia tried to chat to me earlier; cornered me by the bar while I waited for my first drink to ask about my 'issues with roses'. I'm not making this up, those were her exact words. I escaped that in favour of a dull conversation with Helena about all the roadwork being done in Paris – a conversation that led to the skolling of piña colada number one and a swift ordering of number two. Next came a few polite chats with freelancers, another trip to the bar, and then a stressful half hour, nodding and smiling and staying mute, as I listened to two women talk first about an upcoming wedding (woman one) and then terrifying sounding birthing options (woman two). Halfway through piña colada number three, they paused for breath, turned to me and asked the question I'd been dreading all along: were babies in *my* plan?

Sometimes I wonder whether other people watch a different news channel to me. Because yesterday it was Matilde Beaumont. Today I learned that a multinational was being sued for knowingly selling a drug with undisclosed side-effects. Tomorrow there will be something else. We live in a world where for a great swathe of people, 'kindness' and 'empathy' are nothing more than hashtags used to atone between one hate-storm and another. How could I subject another being to all that? And given the transience of it all, what would be the point anyway?

But, even though all that is true, one of them was pregnant and that's not the kind of thing you point out to a pregnant lady. That would make me an arsehole. So instead I just said, 'Maybe if I meet the right guy,' and then suggested we pose for a photograph. By the time we'd selected which one to use, agreed on a filter and chosen the hashtags – #paris #bignight and #ifyoulikepinacoladas – they'd forgotten about me and were back to talking about complicated napkin folds and seating plans.

So now I'm sipping drink number four, talking to the person I wanted to talk to all along. Stan. The news guy. The guy who has the job I want.

But, honestly, he's pissing me off.

He's watching me pull my skirt over my knees with smug, light blue eyes, as he sips on a Guinness.

'It's important that we have people like you on staff,' he says. 'Not everyone wants to face what's going on in the world. Some people just want to go and see a good film. Talk about things like pretty pictures.' He takes another sip. 'You know what you should do?'

Oh good. Nothing I love more than a man telling me what I *should* do. Because, you know, he probably knows better than I do how I should live my life.

'You should cover more opera like Wesley. Elevate things.'

I want to throw my drink at him and tell him I have some pretty strong thoughts about what he *should* do too, but I don't. I just say: 'So tell me about this girl. The one that went missing.'

I've already read everything that was leaked to the papers – strangled, necklace missing, blunt force trauma to the back of the head, and damage to her wrist believed to have been caused by some sort of restraint – but Stan seems to think of himself as having the inside scoop. Maybe he knows something the papers don't and the Murderino in me is curious. Also, this seems like solid neutral ground. And Stan is the sort of person who needs to feel clever – so why not just give him what he needs?

'She worked as a secretary in a law firm,' he starts and then his eyes flicker and he grins. 'She looked a bit like you, actually.'

'Yes, you said,' I quip back. 'So what happened?'

'One night she left work and never returned. There was no sign of foul play so the police didn't follow it up. Everyone in France has the right to disappear, you know,' he says with a scoff, using his fingers to air-quote 'right to disappear'.

And he's right. I read that exact term in one of the articles about Matilde Beaumont, and googled it immediately. It spoke to some deep part of my imagination that, on a whim, you could leave everyone and everything and start anew without consequence. A few clicked hyperlinks later, I'd learned that, yes, it was true: in France, the police won't search for you unless there are clear signs of foul play or you're a minor. Which means that approximately one thousand unidentified bodies are found in France each year, compared with around sixty-six in Britain, which has a similar population. Most of the time the DNA from those bodies isn't recorded either.

Now, I know I've listened to a lot of true crime podcasts so my worldview might be skewed but all I thought when I read that was: what a perfect place to be a murderer.

'They're just fucking lazy,' Stan continues. 'It took finding her body for them to jump to attention. It always does. But nothing changes.'

'No CCTV footage?' I ask, like I don't already know the answer.

He shakes his head and I swear to god there's a flash of pain behind his eyes. A glint of humanity. And for a brief second I think maybe, just maybe, I've misjudged him. He clearly cares about female safety. But then he speaks.

'Look, if the police haven't solved it, I doubt you're going to.' His eyes narrow. 'Did you even study journalism?'

And, just like that, I'm back to hating him.

'Yes,' I say just a millisecond too quickly. It comes out defensive. Fake. *Shit.*

He noticed. He smells weakness. 'So where were you working before this, Harper Brown?'

Even the way he says my name is patronising.

'I was freelance.'

He exhales loudly as if to say: for fuck's sake.

'So, what, you had a blog?' He scoffs. 'Journalism was a noble profession back when I was starting out. It was all about truth. That's the problem with your generation – everyone wants a short cut. But there's no short cut to excellence. The only way to become truly great at this job is to do whatever it takes.'

I down the rest of my drink and clench my jaw. I need to keep my mouth busy with something, otherwise I'm going to say things like, 'I'm not sure two years of working for free every night can be classed as a fucking short cut, Stan.'

But saying things like that won't end well. I don't want to make enemies this early and Stan has already decided who I am. How I fit into the world. And he's spent too many years being told how clever he is, how right he is, to doubt those initial perceptions. And the worst part is I'm scared he's actually right. What if this is as good as it gets for me? What if nobody ever takes me seriously no matter how hard I try?

'I'm going to get another drink,' I say, crinkling my nose as I stand up and head to the bar.

I pull out my phone and refresh my emails. And there it is. Finally. A reply from Hyacinth.

Harper, what is this? We need less Berthe Morisot, and more about Noah. Who he is. What he wants. What makes him tick. We need zing. Dig deeper.

The first thing I notice is: no exclamation marks. This cannot be good. My cheeks grow hot. Maybe Stan's right. Maybe I do suck. Maybe I'm kidding myself thinking I can do this.

I click back to my inbox and glance down the rest of the subject titles. It's the fourth one down, a Google alert, that has me hanging onto the bar for stability as my downward spiral takes proper hold.

Harrison Daze to tour West Coast.

Fuck. Fuck. Fuck.

It's not that I want Harrison to fail as such (except for when I do). It's more that every time something like this happens I feel like maybe he was right to leave me, maybe I was holding him back.

66

I down the rest of my drink and look around for the bartender. But he's still busy, five people over, so I can't get another yet. I flick through to Instagram to distract myself, scanning through the list of people who've liked my photograph from earlier. When I first set up this Instagram account I had the naïve intention of becoming one of those Parisian lifestyle influencers: lots of balconies, bottles of perfume and paintings in galleries. That was before I realised how intense my new job would be, and how much work goes into maintaining an influencer account. But it's probably lucky I relinquished that dream. Because I've had seven likes. Seven. Fucking. Likes. But there at the top of the screen, amid all the other Instagram stories, gleaming from its technicolour halo, sits Noah's story.

I tap on it, expecting a still frame of a painting he's working on or a wineglass or, I don't know, the moon.

But up comes a video of what looks like an artist's studio, a crowd of people, then Noah and a girl with big white teeth. She's holding her wrist up to the lens and there's something drawn on it but then it's gone again.

My-my, how very interesting. The mysterious Noah X has posted something personal on social media for a change.

And just like that my pulse speeds up – the way it always does before I make a risky decision.

I glance back at our group: Stan is talking to one of the freelancers now, Claudia is holding up her vintage Hermès bag for someone to inspect, and the pregnant lady is stroking her stomach. I look back to the screen and play his story once again, taking in the surroundings. I think about Hyacinth's email – *dig deeper*; and my conversation with Stan – *whatever it takes*; and the Google alert about Harrison – and maybe it's all of those things, or maybe it's none, but it seems to me there's only one way this night should end.

And so I tap on 'send message' and type: *Hey stranger, can I come?*

Chapitre huit

I slam the door of the Uber and look around. There's an old Parisian streetlight covered in advertising stickers at the top of a set of concrete stairs that run between this street and the one below. Its amber glow reflects off the leaves of an overhanging tree and lights up the blue and white street sign: Rue Chappe. I look at my sat nav then down the stairs: Noah's building should be about a third of the way down. The Uber driver turns up his music – it's French hip-hop – revs his engine and drives away. And I'm left alone, on this empty cobbled street on the hill in Montmartre, wondering what the hell I'm doing.

I grasp the cool black railing and move down the steps, searching for a building number.

Number twenty-three.

It's cream and residential with those very-Parisian-shutters and, even in the dim light, I can tell that much of the paint is peeling off. The brown wooden doors are open, all the downstairs lights are on and the muted boom of drum and bass reverberates through the walls. I can feel it in my chest.

I stare at the entrance.

I'm here now, I should just go inside.

But I stay glued to the spot. My eyelids are heavy, my arms are covered in goosebumps beneath my denim jacket and maybe I'm sobering up now because I'm having some pretty strong second thoughts. I look down at the ground and it sways up towards me.

What precisely is my plan here? Just go in and ask him a bunch of questions and put the answers in my article? What exactly am I hoping he'll say?

I should go.

I reach into my bag, pull out my phone and go to the Uber app to order a car home. But just before I put in my address I hear, 'Are you just going to stand there all night?'

Shit.

I look up and around: left, right.

And then I see him. Standing right in front of me in the open doorway. Waving. I limply wave back and move towards him. He's wearing light blue jeans that are ripped at one knee and a black sleeveless T-shirt. His left arm is covered in tattoos. There's a big jagged speech bubble with the word *ka-pow*! on his bicep; he looks like he just stepped out of an Abercrombie & Fitch catalogue.

'Hey,' I say, swallowing hard as I get to him.

'Grace,' he replies, leaning forward and kissing one cheek and then the other. His skin is warm and his stubble rough, he smells just like he did on the day we met and my pulse is speeding up.

'Come,' he says, taking me by the hand and leading me inside before I can say anything else.

There are people in the hallway; a couple kissing against the wall to my right.

'This is Grace,' he announces as we move towards another door at the end of a hallway.

'Hi Grace,' everyone says in unison and I cringe. I'm good at lying, great at lying, but that doesn't mean I like it.

He pushes open a heavy black door and the room beyond smells like oil paints and turpentine and weed and dust. The music is loud, far louder than it seemed from the street outside. It's old-school hip-hop. The walls are lined with canvases all covered in the same white cloths I saw at Le Voltage, and the shelves are filled with a selection of paints. A general mess of newspapers and comics lies scattered haphazardly.

All around us swirl people I don't know – dancing, drinking, looking at us as we move through – but Noah keeps hold of my hand and leads me to a sort of kitchenette. He opens a fridge and pulls out a bottle of champagne as I lean back on a counter and watch him. He pours us each a drink and then hands one to me with a wink. 'I'm glad you came,' he yells over the music.

'Me too,' I yell back, taking a sip but not breaking eye contact, not even for a moment.

'Are you going to show me some of your work in progress?' I ask loudly, reminding myself that I'm here for a reason. But he frowns – *did he hear me?* – and so I point to the covered up canvases.

'What?' he yells, bringing his face in right beside mine so he can hear me.

But now I can smell his shampoo. Muted peppermint.

'Are you going to show me some of your work in progress?' I say into his ear.

He turns to me, and I can feel the warmth of his breath on my ear as he says, 'Hell, no. I still haven't recovered from being told I'm like Berthe.' Then he pulls away and he's grinning.

And I'm grinning too; my pulse is tapping fast.

He reaches for my wrist and pulls a Sharpie out of his back pocket. 'But I *am* going to brand you.' I watch as he draws something on my inner wrist: it's round on one edge and jagged on the other. It's half a broken heart.

'Is this some sort of warning?' I shout over the music, eyebrows raised.

'No.' He laughs, letting go of my wrist and leaning in close again so I can hear him. 'It's just so nobody asks you to leave. This is a *very* exclusive party, you know,' he mocks.

Then his eyes shift; he's looking past me, focusing on something over my shoulder. He smiles at whoever it is. Waves. And I turn to look: it's a guy of about fifty in a green velvet jacket.

'I'll be right back,' Noah says to me, touching me on the shoulder as he moves past me towards the man. So I lean back against the counter, sip my drink and watch him go.

That's when I see Sabine.

His model.

I recognise her immediately – the red hair, the pale skin, the vulpine face. She's wearing a pair of black jeans and an olive green netted top, and is talking to a guy with a long, limp brown ponytail.

Everyone else is either huddling in small groups or swaying on the dancefloor. I don't know anyone and nobody is talking to me. And even if I wanted to try to make conversation – which I don't, I hate small talk – they'd probably speak French and I'd get lost after the introductions.

So instead, I sip on my drink, pull out my phone, scroll through Instagram and wait for Noah to come back.

~

Twenty minutes later I'm getting annoyed. Noah has moved on from the guy in velvet to another guy of about twenty-two in baggy light denim jeans and now to a small group of girls. And I'm still standing here in the kitchen, trying to pretend I'm not watching him and feeling awkward. One of the girls he's talking to laughs. She's got long, pin-straight dark hair and it shimmers like onyx under the light. She looks like she's in a shampoo ad as she throws her head back in that flirty way girls do. I can feel myself wanting to go over, to try to pull him back to me, like he's some prize to be fawned over. I used to feel that way about Harrison too.

I shouldn't have come here.

So I down my drink, leave the glass on the countertop, set my eyes on the door and head in that direction. I'm almost free and clear when a hand reaches out, grabs mine and stops me.

'Hey,' comes his voice. 'Where are you going?'

'Oh,' I say. 'You seemed busy and I don't really know anyone . . .'

'I'm not busy,' he says, pulling me close so he can whisper in my ear, 'I've run out of weed. I was asking around.'

Goosebumps.

I can smell the booze on his breath and my skin is getting warm.

Then someone yells something and turns the music up louder. Tupac, 'All About U'.

'I love this song,' Noah yells over the music, 'come.' He takes my hand and leads me to the makeshift dancefloor.

Everyone is yelling and the walls spin around me as I sway side to side. There are four piña coladas and a glass of champagne pumping through my veins right now and I haven't eaten since a chocolate croissant at 11 am. I'm worried that if I don't hold onto something and keep moving around like this I'll topple over. So I drape my arms around Noah's neck and his hands land on my hips. We're barely moving, and that suits me just fine. I'm trying to remember what I wanted to ask him, why I came here, because right now all I can think about is the heat of his chest pressed against me. I look up at him, he's watching me and it puts my heart out of rhythm. I look away. To the side. And that's when I catch sight of his model again. Sabine.

She's watching me.

Watching us.

Wait, no, it's more than that: she's *videoing* us.

She's holding her iPhone at chest level, but it's pointed right at us and she keeps glancing down at the screen like she's checking her framing. This is just like what she was doing the other night at the gallery.

I don't want to be videoed.

A wave of heat flows through me. I need water.

I look back to Noah, he's grinning down at me.

'I'm thirsty,' I say, moving back to the kitchen. Noah follows me.

'Hey, are you okay?' He places his palm on my lower back as I reach for a glass, rinse it out and fill it with water.

'Yeah, I just feel weird,' I say. 'Dizzy.' I take a sip of water and glance back towards Sabine. I can't see her anymore. She must have moved on to someone else now.

'Come,' he says.

We move out of the studio, into the hallway and through a steel door that looks like it might lead to a parking garage but doesn't. Instead, it leads to a set of brightly lit cement stairs that smell of damp. He's already taking them two at a time.

'Where are we going?' I ask as I grab onto the bannister and follow him up.

'To get you some air.' He smiles back at me.

Soon we're at the top, I'm breathless and he's pushing open another big metal door. A gush of air as cool as a supermarket freezer hits my cheeks. He moves aside to let me pass and then the door clicks shut after us; the quiet is a relief. A single light glows from above the door.

We're standing on a small rooftop. There's a sturdy cement barrier in front of us and some sort of ramshackle tin shelter in the corner of the back wall. There's something underneath it, pushed up against the bricks: a couple of striped deckchairs. He flicks a switch and a series of small orange lanterns glow on the periphery.

A breeze catches my hair, and I hold it in one hand as I follow Noah towards the wall and look out at the view: the twinkling lights of Paris sprawl before us like a big black velvet blanket covered in sequins and glitter. I can see the glow of the Eiffel Tower in the distance.

'It's beautiful, right?' he asks.

I nod.

'Better up here?'

'Much better,' I say. We're standing close enough that our arms are touching. His hands on the railing are big and rough and his nails are flecked with paint. I gaze at his wrist. His forearm. His bicep. Without thinking, I reach out and trace the ka-pow tattoo with my finger.

'This is cool,' I say, as our eyes meet. Something changes behind his. I try to read it in the low light but I can't.

'I got it for my little brother,' he says, his voice cracking as he pulls a packet of cigarettes out of his pocket. He offers me one and

I take it. He lights his first, then holds it up so I can light mine off the end.

'He likes comics?' I ask, leaning in and touching the end of my cigarette to his. I inhale deeply and our eyes meet.

He grins and his teeth catch the light. 'He *loved* them. Was always asking me what my superpower was.' His Adam's apple bobs and he lets out a big breath. 'He passed away last year.' Then he takes a drag and looks back out towards the Eiffel Tower.

Shit.

'I'm sorry,' I say, my voice faltering as I reach out to touch his arm. When someone is in a lot of pain, you can almost see it pulsing off them. Like steam from a pavement in summer. And that's what it's like with Noah right now.

'It's all over, just like that,' he says, clicking his fingers. 'Puts things in perspective.'

We stand there for a little while, just looking out at the lights. The Eiffel Tower begins to twinkle the way it always does in the first five minutes following the change of the hour, and I wonder what the time is. Eleven? Twelve? My hair whips around in the cool breeze and I regather it to one side, trying to control it as my mind whirrs. I'm not sure what to say now. It seems insensitive to just change the subject but what if he doesn't want to talk about his brother?

'Is he why you started using comics in your work?' I ask eventually.

'Sure is,' he says, turning to look at me. 'You're quite the perceptive one, aren't you?'

'I have my moments.' I smile.

His eyes narrow and he starts to nod. 'I see what you do, you know,' he says. 'You ask all the questions but give nothing away. I'm onto you . . .'

'Or maybe you're just so self-obsessed you don't ask anything back,' I quip back.

He grins and stubs out his cigarette on the wall. Then I do the same.

'So tell me something. Anything about you,' he says.

'Ask me a question.'

'Okay,' he says. 'What would your superpower be?' And there's something flirty in his tone, in the flicker behind his eyes, but I don't bite. Not yet.

'Right . . .' I laugh. 'Well,' I say, taking a moment to think.

Say something cute.

'I can kind of read what people are thinking.'

'Really?' he asks, eyebrows raised.

'Yes.' I nod a knowing nod.

'So what am I thinking right now?'

'Hmmm,' I say, squinting my eyes and bringing my forefingers to my temples. 'Right now you are wondering if I can really read what you're thinking.'

He laughs. 'Impressive.'

'Right?' I say. 'Now your turn. Tell me something.'

'What do you want to know?' he asks, his eyes locked on mine.

I pretend to think about it but I've used this line many times before.

'What would I find if I looked through your search history?'

He starts to laugh. 'What kind of bullshit question is that?'

'You can tell a lot about a person from their search history.'

'That's probably true. But I'm an artist, Grace.' I flinch as he uses my fake name. I want to hear him say my real name. 'You can tell what I care about from my work.'

I think of all the paintings of Sabine. 'So you and Sabine . . .'

'She's just a model.' He smiles. 'A stand-in. Why, are you jealous?' His smile turns to a grin.

'No,' I say. 'A stand-in for who?'

'For someone I'm still looking for.' He winks.

'Right . . .' I say, breaking our gaze. Because now he's the one using a recycled line, one he's probably used a million times before, but my heart is dumb as shit and she's banging so hard against my ribs it's like she wants to jump from my chest into his.

'Any other questions?' he asks, his arm touching mine.

'Oh, just whatever you're most scared to tell me.' I smile, our eyes meeting again.

'Sure,' he says, and we both turn to face each other. 'If you think you can handle it.'

'Of course I can handle it,' I say.

He reaches forward and tucks a piece of hair behind one of my ears, and says, 'I think I like you, Grace.'

My breath is shallow and the dizziness is back.

'What are you thinking?' he asks.

His eyes are sparkling like the fucking Eiffel Tower and we're standing on a rooftop in Paris. And I may not believe in love, I may not *do* the love stuff, but that doesn't mean I'm immune to the rush. My brain pumps out the same lethal cocktail of dopamine, serotonin, norephedrine, oxytocin, and all the other things that shut down our critical thinking faculties better than a bottle of gin. The only difference between me and the rest of the world is I *know* I'm high.

And high people shouldn't make decisions.

I hear my voice crackle as it says, 'Nothing.'

And then I stand there, my pulse thumping in my throat as he takes a step towards me. And just like that I know what's going to happen next. He leans in and I lean forward too. His mouth meets mine and he tastes like metal and salt and booze.

His hands are in my hair and he's pulling me towards him; he's so warm. But then something cold hits my cheek. Then my forehead. *It's raining.* We both pull away and look up at the sky as the downfall starts in earnest. I squeal as he takes me by the hand.

'Over here,' he says, leading me to the shelter in the corner of the roof.

We stand there for a moment, under cover, leaning against the deckchairs, his arms around me as we listen to the rain pelting harder and harder on the tin above us. Both grinning like idiots. A bright 'ping' sounds in the darkness and he pulls his phone from his pocket, glances down at the screen and then places it beside us on a big metal barrel with an ashtray on top of it. Then he turns to me slowly.

'Where were we?' he asks.

And I could leave right now before this goes any further. Dash through the rain, run back down those stairs. Call an Uber. That would be the sensible thing to do.

But here's the thing: I don't want to.

So instead, I reach into my handbag, and feel around in the front pocket for a condom. I find one, place my bag on the floor, stand on my tippy-toes and kiss him. His tongue moves into my mouth and he pushes me against the wall. I can feel him under his jeans, pushing against my leg and I reach for his zipper but I don't pull it down. And all I can hear is the rain and our breath as his hands reach under my skirt, up to my hipbones and gently tug at the edges of my underwear.

Slowly, he begins to peel them down to my thighs.

'Is this okay?' he asks, pulling away for a moment.

'Yes,' I say, my voice croaky. Now they are down to my knees and he's crouching in front of me, and I'm stepping out of them. He stands up again, his hands on my face, his eyes looking straight into mine. I reach for his zipper and pull it down this time; it sounds out in the low light.

His eyes are still on mine as I press the condom into the palm of his hand.

'Prepared?' He smiles.

'Always,' I whisper.

I hear the sound of the wrapper tearing and wait as he puts it on. Then he leans in and starts kissing me again, lifting one of my legs up around his waist. He's touching me now and I can feel the tip of his tongue on mine; the rain has stopped and all I can hear is my heartbeat and his breath. And then he pushes himself inside me.

I inhale sharply; a split second of pain. But then we're moving, slowly. He lets out a small groan, my hands are in his hair, he's grabbing onto my hips, his stubble is on my cheek and we're moving together now. It's just his breath then mine, his, then mine, his, then mine. I can hear him moan in my ear, and then I can hear—

Wait. What was that?

A creak. A shuffle.

I turn my head quick, sharp. It takes a moment for my eyes to focus. For my brain to register.

Sabine.

With her iPhone.

Videoing us.

I flinch. Gasp. Pull back. Noah turns to look.

He squints at her. Frowns. 'Sabine?'

She lowers the phone, looking down at the screen. Checking her work.

'Sabine! What the fuck?' he yells, pulling back from me. I pull my skirt down to cover me.

Her eyes dart from Noah to me then back to Noah. '*C'est pour ta femme.*' Then she turns around and runs back to the doorway and down the stairs. My ears roar with blood: *pour ta femme*? You don't have to be fluent to know that means: for your wife.

I look down to his hands, searching for a wedding band – but no, there's no ring. Of course there's no ring. I'm not some rookie. I wouldn't have missed that.

'Fuck,' Noah says under his breath as he struggles to pull up his jeans.

'I'll be right back,' he says, turning back to me. His jaw is clenched and his eyes are so fucking blue and my heart is beating so fast.

And then I watch him jog across the wet rooftop towards the door while I'm left to try to piece things together.

What just happened?

He opens the heavy door to the stairwell and disappears. I can hear his footsteps fading and then bang. The door slams. And I'm alone in the silence, on a rooftop in Paris, amid glistening puddles.

Just me and my memories of Harrison.

All those times where he wouldn't let me go backstage after the show because he needed 'time to decompress'.

All the women I'd see leaving when I was finally allowed access.

All the lies I'd tell myself about how happy we were until he finally revealed that we weren't. All that pain.

Pour ta femme . . .

No. Married men are not my bag.

Do no harm, and all that.

My underwear is lying on the ground, a flash of white lace in the low light. I pick it up and slide it into my handbag. The air is cold and I'm shivering as I move over to the wall and look out onto the street. I can see Noah and Sabine arguing, moving down the stairs towards the road.

Fuck this.

I fumble around in the bottom of my bag, find my phone and pull up the Uber app. The time flashes back at me: 00.32.

I type my address into the app – *1 Rue du Regard* – and head towards the door. Halfway down the stairs, a notification flashes up on my screen: my driver's name is Khalid, he has five stars and he's four minutes away.

I rush down the rest of the stairs, tugging my skirt down as I go.

The hallway is empty when I get there, so I rush out the front door unseen and move up the outside stairs slowly. Carefully. I look down towards the bottom of the stairs; Noah and Sabine are right there, but they're too busy arguing to notice me. I try to make out what they're saying, but I can't so instead I focus on my feet, taking care not to slip on the rain-stained cement that glows orange under the streetlights until I'm standing by the tree where my Uber dropped me off earlier. A notification: *Your driver is seven minutes away.* I check the app – he must have got lost. Too many one-way streets to circumvent. I look left, then right. The street is silent. Nobody is here. And so I lean back against the cool stone of the building behind me and wait.

But seven minutes later Khalid is still not here and it's starting to drizzle again. I move through to the app to call him when a notification fills my screen: *Khalid is arriving soon.* I wait for his headlights in the dark. But all I see is a delivery guy on a motorbike and I'm shivering from cold.

I squint down at the app to see where he is, reading the names of the roads. *Shit.* My pick-up address has been set to the lower part of Rue Chappe. Just past Rue André Barsacq at the bottom of the stairs, not the top. I'm in the wrong place.

I'll have to walk past where Noah and Sabine are fighting.

Fuck.

But I have no choice. And so I brace myself and stumble down the stairs, but I can't see them now, they're gone. The breeze is chilly and it's starting to rain properly so I rush down towards where the pin has been set; halfway down that lower segment of the road.

I'm almost there when a white car ahead of me pulls out and speeds away. *Shit.* What if that was him? Khalid. I try to catch the number plate but I can only manage the last part of it: AA.

I stare down at my app, trying to focus on the car type and plate number.

Khalid is: WW 398 SG.

That wasn't him.

My phone lights up with a notification: *Khalid has arrived. He will wait for two minutes before charges begin.*

I turn around, searching the street for his car. Left. Right. Looking up towards the stairs and Noah's apartment. Did I walk right past him?

And then I see the glow of approaching headlights as Khalid drives around the corner.

Chapitre neuf

The sky outside is a bruised purple smudge and big fat raindrops catch the light as they splatter on the skylight. My cheek is still raw from Noah's stubble, the world is stained blue, the way it always is for me the morning after sex and a small piña-colada-shaped hammer is banging on the space behind my right eye. I'm sitting on the sofa, nestled beneath a beige blanket I found in the cupboard, staring down at my iPhone, just daring it not to recognise me hungover.

And all I can think as my phone unlocks is: *I need to fix this.*

I move quickly through to Noah's Instagram profile, tap on his followers and type in: *S-a-b* . . .

A flash of white and then there she is.

Right at the top: *Sabine Roux.*

But as I stare down at her profile picture – flaming red hair, statue-white skin, bare shoulders – I remember her phone lens catching the yellow light of the lanterns and then her voice saying, '*C'est pour ta femme.*'

I want to believe I won't be recognisable in the footage, that the light was too low or she wasn't close enough. But the light wasn't *that*

Pip Drysdale

low, and she wasn't *that* far away from us, and I have an iPhone too, so I know how good the low light camera is. That's why I bought it.

But still. There she is. It'll be fine.

All I need is an email address, a phone number, some means by which I can contact her and ask her to destroy it. Reason with her.

I tap on her photograph and go to her profile. She has almost two thousand followers. I scan the biography.

Sabine Roux. Video artist. Capturing the moments that make our lives. Video means 'I see' in Latin.

Shit.

This is bad-bad-bad. So much worse than I thought. Because the best way to get an artist to do something is to ask them not to.

What if she's uploaded it already?

I scour the thumbnails, searching for a rooftop, Noah and my silhouette in each frame. But they aren't there. In fact, she hasn't uploaded anything at all in fourteen hours. Not since a selfie at the bottom of a set of stairs. The sky is glowing indigo above her and behind her is a street sign: Rue Chappe. I vaguely recognise the surroundings; she's standing at the bottom of the stairs that lead up to Noah's building. Right near where Khalid picked me up. That must have been on her way to Noah's party last night.

The photo before that was taken in some sort of park – there are lots of miniature boats on a body of water behind her and a tonne of trees. The location is set to le Bois de Boulogne. And the caption translates as: *So lucky to live here.*

88

There's a link to a Vimeo page just below her biography. Maybe she uploaded it there. I tap on it. Hold my breath. And wait for it to load.

She has 1314 followers on Vimeo, joined three years ago and has uploaded thirty-eight videos in that time. I grip my jaw as I scan the details beside the most recent upload. It's from a month ago. It's entitled: 'Love Actually'. And it's had seventy-four views. I press play and sip my coffee as I watch the black screen fade to an image. There's a bridge with an apricot sunset reflecting off the Seine behind it. I recognise the buildings in the background; it's not in frame but the Louvre is right there to the left. Which means this was filmed on Pont des Arts.

The first time I stood on that bridge was with Harrison in the spring of 2014. We scrawled our names with a black sharpie onto a bronzed lock and then attached it to the fence beside hundreds of others just like it. But all those locks, like our love, have been cleared away now; the weight declared a safety hazard. But, from this video, it appears a few rebellious locks remain, catching the light wherever they can be attached, like ours was. I wince at the memory but then my attention is captured by a couple who are now standing square in the centre of the frame.

Because they're mid-argument.

The woman pushes the man's chest. The camera draws in closer. She's crying, wiping away tears with the back of her hand. Yelling something at him but there's no sound so I don't know what she's saying. The man is frowning, and using his hands a lot, like he's trying to explain. Tourists move around them, pretending not to watch. To notice. While behind them, another couple hold hands and blissfully stare out at the water.

The two moods of love caught in stark contrast.

The arguing man and woman both stand statue-still now, staring at each other while the world parts like a sea and moves around them. Seconds pass. Her eyes cast down. He steps towards her, takes her in his arms and they embrace. And the screen fades to black.

Two words in white font fade in: *Love Actually*.

I sit, staring at the screen, doing some quick mental arithmetic, adrenaline spinning through my veins. This video was only uploaded a month ago. But it was filmed while there were still green leaves on the trees in the background. We're mid-October now and all the leaves have long since turned to burnt amber and red and are gathering in gutters.

Which means Sabine takes her time cutting together her films before uploading them. So just because mine hasn't been uploaded yet doesn't mean it won't be.

She could be sitting in her apartment right now, sipping coffee just like I am, working on my video as she dreams up a white font name for the ending, something like: *La maîtresse*.

Fuck. I need to do something while I still have time.

I reach for my cup and take a sip of lukewarm coffee. My hand still smells of last night's cigarettes and as I stare up at the rain splattering on the skylight, I think of the Instagram message I woke up to this morning: *Hey, I'm so sorry about tonight. Catch up later? x*

Noah sent it at 2.33 am, but I was already asleep by then.

I could reply now and ask him what Sabine said. Ask him what happened. Whether he got her to delete the video.

But I don't want to.

And not just because he didn't tell me he was married, not just because he got my private bits caught on video, but because he ran off and left me there on that rooftop, and didn't bother texting for two whole hours.

Besides, it's his wife, his marriage on the line. If he *can* get Sabine to destroy it, he will. A message from me won't change a thing.

My head is thumping and my synapses are compromised. I get up and head through to the kitchen, pouring myself a glass of water. I'm thinking of Anne's bedroom now, of her ensuite, of her medicine cabinet: maybe she has some sort of strong painkiller in there.

I move through her room, into the bathroom, and open the cabinet. Rows and rows of toiletries and orange bottles of pills stare back at me. I reach for a couple and read the labels. There's a bottle of Ambien on the top shelf which has – I open the top and peer inside – three left. I take the bottle. There's a yellow box of Doliprane on the bottom shelf. That's the French version of para-cetamol. I grab that too and head back to the kitchen, popping two of the Doliprane out of the packaging. I drop them onto my tongue and take a sip of water, and it's as I swallow that relief finds me.

And not from the pills.

Sabine can't upload it!

Because I'm in France, the land of cheese, wine and next-level privacy laws. If she uploaded a video like this without consent she'd be fined, or go to jail or something . . .

But what if she sees that as a good thing? As free publicity to get more attention for her work? She didn't strike me as a people-pleaser.

What a fucking nightmare.

I head back to the sofa and plonk myself down, but as I sit there listening to the rain hit the glass in perfect sync with the throbbing of my head, I'm filled with a dark curiosity.

Who is this woman whose husband I had sex with last night?

Where was she last night? What does she do for a living? How does she wear her hair? What will she do if she sees that footage? Will she leave him? Will she try to fix it?

We never know exactly how we'll respond to these things until we're the one in the crosshairs.

My laptop is charging on the Louis Vuitton chest in front of me; I reach for it and fire it up. Pulling up a browser window, I type in *Noah X, Paris, wife, husband*. I didn't see anything about a wife last time I googled him, but I wasn't looking for things like that back then.

I imagine her young, naïve, adoring; maybe with some sort of tattoo to make her feel edgier. Perhaps a belly button ring.

My screen flashes white then up comes a list of links. Most of them are to various art blogs; all of them have the search terms 'husband' and 'wife' crossed out.

I move through to 'Images' and scan down through the thumbnails, looking for something, anything, I might have missed the last time I googled him. But most of the images are of Noah's old grey geometric work or links to articles I've seen before. There's only one that has him in it, and it's towards the bottom of the third page. It's of him and that woman, the one who discovered him. The one I spoke to at his exhibition . . . *wait.*

My heart bangs in my chest as I squint down at that little image. *Are they fucking holding hands?*

I click on it and wait for it to load. And then there it is, the image in full.

They're standing at some sort of black-tie event, him in a tuxedo, her in a long crimson dress with a string of diamonds glittering from her neck. It was taken two years ago. And yes, they're holding hands.

She's not his agent, she's his wife.

But wait, there's more. The caption reads 'International gallerist Agnès Bisset with husband, Noah X, at the opening of her Paris gallery, Le Voltage'.

The walls move in towards me. This is bad on so many levels.

Because Noah said Sabine used to work at Le Voltage; that's where they met. So if his wife owns that gallery, it'll be très easy for Sabine to send her that video of us . . . *they're probably friends*. Is that why she filmed us? Loyalty? But if Sabine and his wife were friends, Noah wouldn't have been dancing with me like that in front of her. And his wife would have been there too . . .

So what then? Only one thing makes sense: Noah lied to me; Sabine was *not* just a model. They *had* had a relationship and seeing him with me pissed her off. She wanted his wife to know.

And fuck, fuck, fuck.

Because I'm just starting my career as an art and culture writer. The industry is small. And Agnès Bisset is a gallerist; according to that caption, an 'international' one. From the fact that her name is listed first, she's also an important one. That means she's well connected. And, if the diamonds sparkling from her neck and her flawless skin are anything to go by, she's wealthy. Wealth means success, and success means clout. But more unsettling than any of that is something else: she's spoken to me. She's seen me up close. My cheeks flush hot as I remember her gaze sweeping over my cheap outfit at Noah's exhibition. If she sees that video she'll recognise me. I know she will. Which is all fine and good right now, while she doesn't know who I am, but what about when our paths cross again, which they surely will? Be it in six days, or six months, eventually it's bound to happen, and when it does, she'll know it was me, she'll realise where I work, and nothing good will happen after that.

The chances of me getting out of this unscathed and unidentified just got significantly smaller.

I reach for my phone, pull up Camilla's number and press 'FaceTime'.

Briiinnngg, briiinnggg, briiinngg . . .

'Bonjour,' Camilla says in an accent that's even worse than mine. I've caught her off guard. She's chewing a piece of toast at her kitchen table, staring into the camera lens. She's wearing a white She-Ra T-shirt under a turquoise satin kimono, her dark hair is back in a ponytail and her cheeks are shiny like she's just put on face cream. I can see her flat in the background and I'm filled with a pang for home.

'Hey,' I say. My voice comes out dry.

'Are you okay?' she asks, tilting her head to the side. 'You look weird.'

I shake my head in reply. 'No. I think I really fucked up.'

~

Three minutes and a short summary of last night later, Camilla has concurred that, yes, I definitely have fucked up. She's sipping peppermint tea, her eyes wide as she says: 'What are you going to do?'

'I don't know,' I say, taking a sip of what is now cold coffee while I stare at my own face in the little screen and adjust the angle so the bags under my eyes aren't quite so bad.

Pip Drysdale

'Well, even if that girl does upload it or his wife sees it,' she says slowly, like she's thinking as she goes, 'you're just some random woman, how will anyone know who you are? And if nobody knows who you are, they can't tell your boss, can they?'

'But I've spoken to her, the wife,' I say. 'If she sees that footage she'll definitely recognise me. And even though she doesn't know where I work right now, I'll bump into her again, I know I will.'

'Hmm,' Camilla says. 'It's a tricky one.'

'I'm so fucking stressed.'

'Okay,' she says, pausing. 'Just remember, you're not the married one. And it's not like you knew. Sex is hardly illegal. And you're in France. Doesn't everyone cheat over there?'

This is why I love Camilla. Even though she's the romantic one between us, the one who believes in soulmates and marriage and all that, she still has my back regardless.

'I'm not sure his wife will look at it like that and she's super connected. And I'm still in my probation period – Hyacinth could just fire me. God, I could lose my entire career over this before it even begins. It's a shitshow.'

'Hmmm,' she says. 'Right, this is what you do. Nobody knows your name, right?'

'No.'

'So you never talk to this guy Noah again. And you haven't contacted that Sabine girl yet, have you?'

I shake my head.

'Well, don't. Then she'll have no idea who you are either. If you see his wife out somewhere just dodge her. And if anyone asks what you did on Friday, you went home. You were never there.' She takes another bite of toast. 'And then just pray to all the gods and goddesses that Sabine doesn't upload it.'

And then we change the subject. She starts to tell me about the hot guy from work, the one she saw in the elevator, about how she's figured out he works on the fourteenth floor. And as she speaks, just out of view of the camera, I open that little orange bottle and take one of Anne's final three Ambiens.

Chapitre dix

I shake the rain off my umbrella at the door and then move into Franprix. It's bright in here. Fluorescent and vivid. While the sky outside looks like the gods dragged a dirty thumb over it. The contrast is startling and it takes a while for my eyes to adjust. It's ten past five on Sunday afternoon. I finished my revised article on Noah this morning at around 11 am. The rest of the day was spent watching Netflix, eating dark chocolate, squatting on Sabine's Vimeo and Instagram pages – nothing new has been uploaded – and googling a million variations on: Agnès Bisset, Noah X wife and Le Voltage. I'm not sure what I was looking for exactly – some sort of indication that things weren't as bad as they first seemed.

I found nothing of the sort.

Instead, while recent photographs of Agnès Bisset were almost non-existent, I found a splattering of images of a younger Agnès with numerous influential (though tastefully non-ostentatious) types, as well as a profile in a women's magazine from 2016. She was listed as number two in a piece called 'Ten most influential women in Paris'. Yes, brilliant. It didn't state her exact net worth but, from what it did say, I gather it's substantial enough to be deemed too vulgar to disclose. It then went on to talk about how she attended a famous finishing school in Switzerland, briefly dated the son of a famous socialite in New York, owns three galleries – in Switzerland, Vienna and now Le Voltage in Paris – and, despite being born into the upper echelon of Paris society and inheriting the means to rest on her laurels, has built a name for herself as the Mother Teresa of the art world, tirelessly launching the careers of young emerging artists like Noah X.

That last part gave me heart palpitations, as well as a pretty strong snapshot of both the nature of their relationship and Noah's flimsy moral fibre. He was using her. Using her, and cheating on her. Then came a scouring of Yelp, Google and Tripadvisor. Nothing but glowing reviews.

By 5 pm, my nerves were frayed and I needed a glass of wine. But when I went to pour myself a glass there wasn't any. There was no food nor (more concerningly) coffee either.

So here I am, wandering into the supermarket with a wet umbrella and jeans that are sticking to my legs from rain, wondering, as I pick up a shopping basket, whose idea it was to put fake greenery on the ceiling. The air is filled with the bright sound of coins jangling as they're dropped into the cash register, muted conversations, fridges humming and the squeak of soles of shoes sticking to a floor that smells of badly rinsed disinfectant.

To my right is an orange juice dispenser and a tray of day-old pastries, to my left is the cashier, standing in front of rows of liquor and stationery, today's newspapers laid out in front of her. Gone are the photographs of Matilde Beaumont and in their place lies a picture of a man with glasses and a big, bold headline I can't really understand. It's something to do with immigration. And in front of those papers, weaving a line, are three customers.

An elderly man with a walking stick, a woman in a short skirt and then, just behind her: Thomas.

Shit.

He's wearing dark blue jeans and a black long-sleeved jumper with a big white Endroit logo on the back – a not-so-subtle reminder that he works for a proper media company and I work for an online magazine and I should have just kept him as a contact and not fucked him.

I rush towards the safety of the baguettes; I never replied to his *just let me know you're okay* text, so I scuttle past, making sure he doesn't look back and see me. The last thing I want right now is to be drawn into an awkward conversation about how my parents have enjoyed their visit to Paris. But Thomas doesn't look up. He's too busy smiling down at his phone, typing, like someone just sent him the funniest text in the universe. This should make me happy – now I don't need to find a new laundromat – but for some reason it doesn't.

I grab a baguette and move past the chocolates, grab an apple, a tomato and a bunch of bananas from the trays of over-priced fruit and vegetables to my right, and then head down the alcohol aisle. I can see the lady with her tabby cat up ahead of me as I pick up a bottle of my favourite red and a few little bottles of Scotch. Then it's cheese, creamed spinach and coffee. I carry my heavy basket back to the front of the shop, peering around the corner to see whether Thomas is still there. Wondering whether maybe I should talk to him after all.

But he's not.

And here's the thoroughly illogical bit: something twinges inside me.

There's an emptiness.

This feeling happens sometimes, seemingly out of nowhere. Like a big black hole opens up inside me and all of a sudden I'm scared that the rest of the world is right to couple up and I'm the wrong one, even though every damned day I'm given evidence to the contrary. Let's all refer to exhibit A, Noah's wife, shall we?

But reason doesn't work in moments like these. In fact, I've only ever found one thing that does.

So I reach for my phone, go to my favourite dating app, and reply to Nicolas's last message with: *What are you doing tonight?*

~

Nicolas is pronounced Nee-koh-lah. He's already corrected me twice in the forty long-arsed minutes since we met. He's wearing black jeans and a blue button-up shirt, there are coins or keys in his

101

pocket that jingle with each step as we make our way down the rain-stained pavement towards his apartment. I was right, by the way: five foot eleven *was* code for five foot eight. But, whatever, he'll do. I'm not looking for a soulmate, I'm looking for a palate-cleanser. A distraction from the existential angst.

My breath tastes like the Malbec I just downed, the moment his hand awkwardly found its way to my knee and he finally, timidly, suggested going back to his place like I'd been in that bar for his conversational skills. And now here we are, en route, at 8.25 pm. I'll probably be home by 10 pm, which is perfect really. I'll be asleep by eleven. Nee-koh-lah isn't worth puffy eyes.

'Is it far?' I ask. This is the second time I've asked this question in the last three minutes. But Matilde Beaumont's killer is still out there and Nee-koh-lah's silence is making me jumpy. What if he's really a psychopath and trying to remember where he left his duct tape and plastic sheeting?

'Just on the corner,' he replies, saving me from myself. He has a thick French accent that could be sexy, but when you've done this as many times as I have you learn to gauge things upfront. Things like: Nee-koh-lah is going to have a hairy back. Mark my words. So the two cancel each other out.

I wrap my arms around myself – I need to start wearing a thicker coat – and listen to our footsteps on the pavement. They're just slightly out of sync: click-clunk, click-clunk, click-clunk. I hope the sex isn't like that: jarring, wrong, but I do pelvic floor exercises; I'll make it work.

'Here,' he says, smiling at me.

I wait as he punches in his door code – a flash of Noah, the joint, him punching in the door code that night at the gallery – and we move inside. His hand is hot on my lower back as he guides me down the hallway to a big white door.

He pulls out a metal key, inserts it into the lock, the door swings open and I move inside. He flicks on the light and I look around. It's sparse, there are books on a light wood bookshelf and a kitchen that looks like it is rarely used. But there's no Dexter-type set-up, just your stock-standard bachelor pad. I'm safe.

I can see the bedroom through an open door on the far side of the room – the characterless white linen of a bed, a pile of things on the floor I can't recognise from this distance, the legs of a chair. I'm guessing there's a big mirror in there too. Nee-koh-lah strikes me as a mirror guy. He'd probably be into handcuffs too, but I lost mine in the move from London and haven't replaced them yet.

I hear the door click shut and look back to him. His dark eyes are on mine now. He's wondering whether he needs to offer me a drink or if we can just do this thing. He decides on the latter. Reaches for me, his one arm around my waist, the other behind my head, and now his mouth is on mine. He tastes of vodka and his lips are tight. His tongue darts in and out like a lizard. Then he reaches under my skirt, pulls down my underwear and stockings – the air is cool on my skin – and then: slap.

His hand hits my bum.

It stings. Burns.

And as he rubs it and pulls his hand away, I think, *Oh, for fuck's sake.*

Slap.

Because twenty hook-ups ago this might have been exciting, it might have felt new, my heart would have been beating hard and my breath would have been fast. But now, it feels formulaic. Like every guy on every app gets his sex tips from the same forum.

Nee-koh-lah is just another short guy who thinks he's Christian Grey.

~

Twenty minutes later he's lying in bed, smoking a cigarette, as I pull on my stockings and then my skirt. I look over at him as I reach for my jumper and pull it on: he's on his phone. Scrolling. Pretending I'm not here even though ten short minutes ago he was pulling my hair and saying shitty things into my ear he thought I couldn't understand. I was right, by the way, there *is* a big mirror beside the bed; he watched himself the whole time. And he *does* have a hairy back.

I'm seriously considering a side-gig on the psychic network channel at this rate.

I glance over at him and he just keeps scrolling. If I were a different girl, this might hurt my feelings. But I'm keen to get the hell out of here within the next two minutes so the fewer distractions, the better.

'I'm going to go,' I say.

He grunts something in response. I reach for my bag on the floor by the end of the bed and say 'Bye'. Because, you know, politeness.

He waves but doesn't even make a move to get up. So I head through to the beige living room, picking up my shoes and slipping them on. My jacket is lying on the sofa, and as I grab for it, my gaze lands on my wrist. Peeking out from under my sleeve is that broken half-heart Noah drew on Friday night; it's still visible. I lick it and try to rub it off as I open the front door, close it behind me, rush through the security gate and head onto the cold street. I turn left towards the metro, putting my jacket on as I walk, then reach into my bag and pull out my phone.

As though telepathically linked to that drawing on my wrist, the one I'm still trying to rub off, there's an Instagram message on my screen from Noah.

We need to talk. Call me. My number is +1 (917) . . .

My heart beats quickly in my chest – she's such a little traitor – as I read the words again. But then it registers: his number begins with +1. He's given me a US number. *Of course he has.* He's probably got two phones, like every cheating husband in the history of the world.

So I don't care what he has to say; no way am I calling him back.

Instead, I put in my earbuds, scroll through to a murder podcast and press play.

The metro is right there in front of me – a red and white sign in the dark. The streets are relatively quiet, and the air is chilled as I move with a few other people down the stairs that smell of damp and urine into the fluorescently lit station. And as I push through the cold metal turnstiles and head to the platform to catch my train home, the narrator tells me the story of yet another woman who went missing without a trace.

Chapitre onze

My phone beeps as I rush down the stairs and the chandelier light flicks on. I'm carrying a bag of rubbish in one hand and my phone in the other. It's just gone 8.14 am so I'm late.

I press the release button and push open the door downstairs and head across the courtyard to the room with the bins.

The door is already open and, as I get closer, I can hear something coming from inside. A low mew. A kitten? I move inside and look around but it's not a kitten. It's my neighbour. The one with no curtains. She's wearing a big pink jumper, her wavy dark hair in a low bun. Her back is to me, her shoulders hunched forward. They're shuddering. She's crying.

Shit.

I start to back out quietly — somehow intruding on her crying feels so much more invasive, so much more intimate, than seeing her lie naked on her bed touching herself. And we've never had a conversation. I don't even know her name.

I hold my rubbish bag away from me so it doesn't rustle as I edge out the door. But then she lets out a proper sob. A desperate, gasping-for-breath sort of sob. And something twinges inside me. Because I know that kind of sob too well. I can't just leave her here like this.

'Bonjour,' I say, my tone unsure.

She turns to look at me; her eyes smudged with mascara. 'Bonjour.' She smiles, wiping her eyes with the back of her hand and sniffing loudly before turning away again.

She doesn't want to talk about it. I should go.

And so I lift the lid, drop my rubbish into the bin and quickly turn to leave but, just as I get to the door, the sobbing starts up again in earnest.

Shit.

'Are . . . are you okay?' I ask gently in French, turning back to her.

'Yes,' she says in English, sniffing loudly. 'I will be fine.' Then she reaches into the cardboard box beside her and pulls out some sort of white garment. There are clear plastic buttons down the front and they catch the light as she holds it up for me to see: boxer shorts. 'Fucking mens.'

She says it just like that: 'mens', plural.

Her arm moves and my gaze follows it. She's picking up a heavy duty pair of steel scissors that are lying on the recycling bin beside her. They make that shhhh sound as they open and then: snip, snip, snip. Pieces of pale fabric fall into the bin, but her breath seems to slow with the action and her shoulders noticeably relax.

Right.

This all makes sense now.

A breakup.

'Yeah,' I say, glancing down into the cardboard box beside her. There's a shirt in there too – light blue and white checks. This must be about that guy I saw with her a couple of times. 'Fucking men.'

Snip. Snip. Snip.

'He disappear!' she says, looking at me. Her eyes are big, dark and wild. And then her face crumples and she starts to cry again. Her cheeks flush pink. 'He didn't even say goodbye.'

I think about Harrison. And me, in those first weeks after he left. I've never felt so alone, so out of control, so weak.

That's when I learned what those sobs mean.

Because heartbreak is such a strange beast; to anyone looking on, it seems like no big deal. *Get over it,* they think. 'Your ex wasn't that great anyway,' they say. You can see the confusion in their eyes and it makes you feel pathetic. So you master the art of saying, 'I'm fine,' and then you go back to searching every crowded street for their face, every traffic jam for their car. But here's what I've learned about hearts: love makes them fragile. And when they snap, it's rarely a clean break. Those sharp and jagged edges lodge themselves between your ribs, they puncture your lungs, so even breathing hurts. It's crippling, humiliating, scary. And the damage lasts a lot longer than it 'should'.

Which is why I promised myself last time that I'd never go through that again.

So chop away, dear neighbour. Whatever gets you through. You'll get no judgement from me.

But now her cries turn to an embarrassed laugh and then comes a bravado I recognise. She's thinking, *I seem so stupid, so weak.* Like we aren't allowed to mourn. Like sorrow is not simply the watermark of being human; we can deny it as much as we like, but there it is, still visible, when held up to the light.

'But I don't cry. I cut!' she says.

I give her a small smile, pretend I believe her and then glance down at my phone: 8.21.

'I'm going to be late,' I say, giving her a you-will-be-fine smile. 'But if you need anything just knock on my door, okay?'

'Okay.' She reaches into her box again and pulls out the shirt. I can hear the fabric snipping as I head past the cars and across the courtyard and press the buzzer to get out of the enormous brown wooden door.

And as I rush to the metro beneath a perfect blue sky, ornate black balconies decorated with red pot plants set against it, I think to myself, *Thank god I'm no longer in love.* And then I check my messages.

There's one. It's from Camilla.

I just got a screening call from Vogue! *They want to interview me!*

~

The elevator doors open, and I walk casually across the office floor, over to my desk like I'm not the last one here and sweating from the jog from the station. But I'm feeling righteous, like a modern-day fairy godmother, what with Camilla's interview (I texted her straight back to tell her it was me who'd sent them her resume) and my being there for my neighbour. Not even the sight of twelve certain roses sitting on Claudia's desk can fuck up my mood this morning. Everything is well in the world. As long as I don't think about Noah, or Agnès Bisset, or Sabine, or that video . . .

I get to my desk, drop my bag on the floor, fire up my computer and sit down. Wesley is watching me with a smug I-got-here-before-you look on his face.

'Hyacinth is looking for you,' he says, a sort of glee in his eyes.

It's probably about my article. *Please let it be good.*

And then I hear, 'Harper?'

I look in the direction of the sound. It's Hyacinth, standing in her open doorway.

'Yes?' I ask, my voice coming out a lot more self-assured than I feel.

'You're late.'

Shit.

'Yes, I'm so sorry I—'

'Can I see you for a moment?'

Let me repeat: *Shiiiiiit.*

'Of course,' I say, heading to her office. *This can't be good.* If she loved my article she'd have just sent back a 'Great!' or 'Better!'.

My heart is beating double time as I move through her door while my mind sifts through the changes I made to Noah's article over the weekend: I spoke about his brother, his use of comics, his mysterious branding. I left out Sabine, of course. The last thing I needed was for her Vimeo account to blow up with new followers – if she posts that video of me and Noah I want as few people to see it as possible. But I'd cut my Berthe Morisot references in half, I thought I'd done well. Done exactly what she asked. So why is Hyacinth looking at me with an angry hyena glint as she sits down in her big black leather chair. 'Sit,' she says and so I do.

Oh god, I'm going to get sacked.

My legs are crossed, my hands clasped, my body leaning forward. I know enough about body language to know that I'm basically pleading, so I force myself to pull back and relax.

'I got your rework,' she says, her expression unreadable. She must get an inordinate amount of botox to keep her face that still.

'Yes,' I say, swallowing hard.

'It was good. *Much* better,' she says.

My shoulders soften. Though why do I feel like she's annoyed?

'But my question,' she says, leaning forward just an inch, 'is why didn't you do it that way to begin with?'

Oh.

'I was trying to fit in with what the magazine's demographic might want. Trying to match the tone of the section.'

She snorts.

Clearly the wrong answer.

'Harper, how many applications do you think we got for your job?' Her words fire out like irritated bullets.

'A lot?' I suggest.

'One hundred and seventy-six.'

'Oh,' I say. Why is she asking me this? Is she about to point out how replaceable I am?

'And of those about twenty-two were strong,' she continues. 'We interviewed three. And do you know why you were one of those three?'

'Because I had art knowledge?' I suggest, thinking of my interview questions.

'Yes,' she says slowly. 'That was *one* thing you had: real-life art knowledge. Not the sort you get from university, but the sort that people understand. That makes someone *want* to go to an art gallery. But that's not what I'm talking about. You had something else too. Something not everybody has. Something that can't be taught.'

I look at her, blank. I want to say the right thing but I have no idea what she's talking about.

'Balls, Harper. You had balls. Fire. I knew that the moment I read your piece "Why I hate John Lennon".'

Oh. The article I wrote about my breakup with Harrison. About how I'd lost myself and he'd ruined the Beatles for me forever. The article that started all of this.

'That's why we hired you, Harper. You're *interesting*. And you're accessible. So why do you keep trying to pretend you're not?'

I hold in a smile because I don't want to look smug but Hyacinth just complimented me.

'Understood,' I say.

'There's another show I'd like you to cover. It's on tonight at Galerie Nathalie Obadia. I'll forward you the invite.'

'Great, thank you, Hyacinth,' I say.

'That's it.' She smiles.

'Thank you,' I say again, standing up. And then I head back out of her office and over to my desk.

Wesley smirks as I sit down. 'Everything okay?' he asks.

'Great,' I say with a fuck-you smile. 'She just wanted to tell me how much she loved my new article.'

Chapitre douze

I stare at the triptych: three watercolours separated by two inches of stark, unblemished wall. Each is blue at the base for water, with trees or plants of differing proportions emerging with strokes of green, brown and fuchsia. Above them sits an orange and black all-seeing eye of a sun, in a grey and cloudy sky. The blue of the water drips upwards, while the trees and sun melt downwards, as though the canvases were rotated during production. I pull out my phone, balance it over the flyer I was given when I walked in and make a note: *The artist's representation of a cyclical and symbiotic relationship between earth and plants, air and sky, humans and planet, are deftly represented by . . .*

I pause. Searching for the right words. My eyes graze the room around me as I think. It's a large, cavernous space with high ceilings, exposed metal beams and concrete floors. There are about twelve of us here, all milling around, inspecting 'the work' of multiple artists, all with something environmental to say. I look back down at my phone and finish my sentence: *deftly represented by the way in which the medium drips and merges: that which goes up, comes down and vice versa.*

A full stop later I'm looking up and around again. There's an abstract marble statue balancing on a tall white stand to my right, but it's something behind that which has caught my eye, something on the far back wall. It's a sculpture – it looks like a seahorse. I move past a man in a grey suit who's enthusiastically sipping champagne to take a better look. Up close it's made of found objects, mainly bits of rubbish. The nose is constructed of an old plastic soft drink bottle and the rest is fishing nets and hooks and plastic bags and feathers. From a distance it's beautiful and sparkly and looks like it belongs in Bollywood. But up close, it's made of junk. I move back and take a picture then upload it to Instagram with the hashtags: #galerienathalieobadia #savetheplanet #beautyoutofrubbish. And then I move on to the next wall. There's a street sign there that reads 'Wrong way. Go back'.

I smile, take a picture of that too, and upload it with the caption: *Can I get one of these for my life?*

The gallerist – a tall, slender man of around thirty-five – is standing over by the desk near the entrance and I want to ask him some questions. He's towering over a fragile-looking woman of about seventy or so, who's craning her neck to look up at him as she speaks. As I move in their direction, I overhear her questions and his answers and I start taking mental notes. They're speaking in French but I catch the odd phrase. She's asking about things like where the artists grew up and where they trained and the gallerist is answering in good humour, smiling and nodding and, every so often, throwing me a glance to acknowledge that I'm there, a few steps back, and waiting.

Eventually she moves into the main room and the gallerist nods at me with a smile.

I speak in broken French. 'Hi, I'm Harper Brown, I'm from *The Paris Observer* and I have a couple of questions about the exhibition.'

He smiles. 'Of course,' he says, in perfect English, the way Parisians always do when they detect an accent.

~

Half an hour later I've done another lap of the room and I'm heading outside, making final notes as I walk. It's dark and the streets glimmer with the red and white reflections of restaurant signs and taxi headlights. The metro isn't far from here but it's been a long day so I scroll through my phone to order an Uber. I enter my address and wait for an estimate of the cost. A Deliveroo driver whooshes past me on a bicycle. I step out of the way. And then, seemingly from nowhere, I hear a voice: 'Grace?'

But Grace isn't my name so I don't turn around. I'm too busy double-checking the price of my Uber – *Why are they so expensive?* – and reconsidering the metro.

But then it comes again, louder this time, and closer too: '*Grace?*'

My heart recognises the timbre of his voice a split second before my mind does. It starts pumping double time. Then my breath follows suit as I swivel on my heel.

117

There he stands: blue jeans, white T-shirt, black leather jacket. His blue eyes watching me turn.

Noah.

My cheeks grow warm. 'Hey,' I say, a flood of incompatible thoughts and feelings downloading simultaneously. If I were a computer, right now, I'd crash. Because my body is happy to see him. My blood is speeding up. But my mind is pissed, hardening: *Why is he here?*

'How did you find me?' I ask.

'Instagram,' he says, unapologetically. He moves in towards me. He's close enough that I can smell his skin, his hair – metal, rain, peppermint – and a small electric shock runs through me.

'We need to talk,' he says. Serious.

I swallow hard. I don't want to talk. I want to go home before I make anything worse for myself. I know who he is now: an opportunist who married a woman ten years older than him to get what he could from her and then fucked around. With me. And probably with Sabine too.

'Noah, look, don't worry about Friday, it's fine,' I say, my eyes meeting his for a millisecond before glancing back down at my phone. It's not fine, of course, but no amount of talking it through will fix it.

I'm about to confirm my ride when he says, 'No, it's important, Grace. Let's go grab a drink. I need to explain what happened.'

I look up at him. 'There's nothing to say,' I reply, a little less blasé and a little more snappy than I'm aiming for. 'It's fine.'

He exhales loudly. 'Are you serious?'

I stare him down and say, 'Yes.'

His eyes narrow. 'So I chase you down like a fucking rom-com and you won't even talk to me? Not even for one drink? My feelings are hurt.'

I can't tell if he's joking or not.

My heart is banging in my chest and shit, shit, shit. Because I don't want to get further tangled up in this but I *do* want to know what Sabine said on Friday night when he went after her; whether she's deleted that file or what she plans on doing with it. I'm not a fan of surprises; I like to know how big my problems are upfront.

'Fine. One drink,' I say. Firm.

'Great,' he replies, nodding to the bistro across the street. It's pale pink brick with creepers in shades of red, amber and green lit up by the glow of yellow streetlights, and there's a row of tables outside looking onto the pavement.

A motorbike drives past, then a black Mercedes with a red taxi sign lit up on top. And as we weave between them, crossing the road, Noah reaches for my hand. His hand is big and warm and his fingers intertwine with mine. But when we get to the other side, I pull mine away.

He pushes open the door to the bistro and lets me go in first. Inside, it sounds like an easy-listening radio station. There's a dark wood table in a booth by the window, with a flickering candle in a jar in the centre. He moves towards it and we both sit down.

The waitress comes over. He orders wine. I order Scotch. And as soon as she's gone he leans in towards me.

'I'm sorry about how the other night ended,' he says, reaching for my hands again. I pull them away.

'Which bit? How you got me caught on video naked, how you didn't tell me you were married, or how you left me, mid-sex, on a rooftop and didn't even say sorry for two whole hours?'

'Fuck. All of it,' he says. 'I wanted to text you sooner but I just couldn't find my phone.'

A flash of that metal barrel on the roof, the ashtray and his phone.

'It was on the roof,' he continues. 'I must have taken it out of my pocket when we were—' He pauses and looks up at me sheepishly. 'But honestly even when I found it I didn't know what to say. I knew you'd be pissed off. Which is totally fair, by the way. And I couldn't cope with being around people so I just sat up there trying to figure out how I'd fucked everything up so badly until it started to rain again.'

'Right,' I say, my arms crossed. 'And your wife?'

His gaze moves to the table, the muscle on the side of his jaw twitches, then his eyes find mine again. 'Okay,' he starts. 'I'm in the middle of a messy divorce. That's what that party was for on Friday. To celebrate my freedom. Thursday night's exhibition was the last commitment I had to honour before I was free.'

I frown at him. The broken half of a heart he drew on everyone's wrist now makes sense. But something else just isn't slotting into place as seamlessly. 'If you're getting divorced then why would your ex care what you do with other women? Why would Sabine threaten to tell her?'

'You don't know my ex.' He scoffs. 'There's this side to her . . .'

This, right here, is my pet peeve: *every* guy says his ex is awful. But, mainly, women are not awful. Mainly, we're just fed up.

'Noah, don't do that. I googled her. I know she owns Le Voltage and is all old money and art connections. I also know that's probably why you married her so please don't spin some story about how it's somehow her fault. I won't buy it.'

He looks around at the other tables, like he's worried someone might be listening, the way people do when they've been doing bad things. Then he leans in a little closer and lowers his voice, inviting me to do the same.

'I didn't say it was her fault. There's a lot of good in her and I know she loves me.' He shifts in his seat. 'I owe her. And not just for my career. When my brother was sick and the insurance ran out, she covered it. But . . .' He's weighing his words. 'Look, just know it wasn't all me, okay?'

I narrow my eyes.

'Please don't look at me like that?'

'Like what?'

'Like I'm a total arsehole.'

I raise my eyebrows as if to say, 'Aren't you?'

'She put a tracker on my car, okay? And spyware on my phone. She's not some little victim here.'

I think of his US number. That makes a tad more sense now.

'Well, maybe she just wanted to see who you were fucking?' I suggest.

'I wasn't fucking anyone,' he says quietly.

'Oh, so I was the first woman you had up on that rooftop while you were still married? Is that what you're going with?'

'You *were* the first.'

I have to force myself not to roll my eyes. 'So, you never had an affair with Sabine?'

'I already told you she was just my model,' he says. 'Don't you listen?'

I lean forward, ready to go for the jugular. 'Then explain this: why would she want to out you to your wife? That seems a lot like jealousy to me.'

He shakes his head. 'It's complicated.'

The waitress places our drinks in front of us. I reach for mine and take a sip. It slows my blood just a little.

'Well, I'm a smart girl, try me.'

He smiles. 'Fine. Sabine *was* jealous, but not in the way you think. I wasn't sleeping with her.' He looks down at his drink then takes a sip. He's trying to figure out how to say whatever he's about to say. 'She . . . developed feelings for me. I told her I couldn't be with her because it would jeopardise my divorce. It seemed kinder than saying I didn't feel the same. I guess when she saw me with you, she got angry. I should have been more careful. But that's why she videoed us and made that threat. She was hurt.' He throws back the rest of his drink. 'But fuck me. I'm here, aren't I? Trying to do the right thing and be honest with you? Stop making it so hard, woman.'

He sits back in his seat and I sit back in mine and we look at each other for a few moments.

'So what did she say, exactly?' I ask, breaking the silence. 'When you ran after her?'

'Nothing,' he says, leaning in again. 'We argued for a while and I tried to walk her to the metro, but she was so mad at me. She just ran off and I went back up to the roof to look for you, but you were already gone.'

'Well, did you call her?' I ask. Because I'm here now. I want to know if she sent Agnès Bisset that video or not.

'Of course. But she won't answer.'

And then I ask the million dollar question: 'Do you think she'll do anything with that footage?'

His eyes meet mine, he gives a small smile and shakes his head. 'There's no chance of that. Not when she really thinks about it.'

I squint at him as if to say, 'How can you be so sure?'

'There's only one thing Sabine really wants in this world,' he continues, 'and that is to be an artist. It's a tightknit group here in Paris. If she fucked me over like that, she'd be a pariah. She'd never risk that.' He takes a sip of his wine and leans in a little further as if about to tell me a secret. So I lean in too.

'Agnès wouldn't thank her for it either. She'd pull her exhibition immediately. I mean, she doesn't even like Sabine's work, she calls it a Hallmark card on steroids. Getting Agnès to agree to an exhibition was a big win for Sabine. Agnès can *make* a career. So no matter what she threatens, no matter how upset she might be right now, there's no way Sabine's going to mess that up.' He smiles at me. 'So don't worry.' Then he reaches out for my hand again. And this time I let him take it. His eyes move to my wrist and his thumb traces the pale outline of that broken heart he drew on Friday night.

'Don't you shower?' he asks.

And I start to laugh.

Then he lets out a big sigh and our eyes meet again.

'Grace,' he says, in a tone that is so very serious.

'Noah,' I say, mimicking him.

'I need you to promise me something. You won't tell anyone about all this,' he says. 'About what happened on the roof. Agnès is a very private person and her image is everything to her. The one thing she asked of me when we decided to split was that we do it amicably. That I don't humiliate her. If she knew that footage was out there, that people could see it . . .' He trails off, shaking his head. 'It would complicate things. I don't know what she'll do if she's humiliated like that.'

And there we have it, ladies and gentlemen, the real reason why he's here. It's not about me and wanting to make sure I'm okay with things. He just doesn't want me telling anyone what happened between us and ruining his divorce settlement.

I pull my hand away. 'Who am I going to tell?' I ask like I don't care.

'I don't know,' he says, and something softens behind his eyes. The edges turn down in the smallest of ways, like he's sad. He opens his mouth to speak but it takes a moment for any sound to follow. 'That thing I said on the roof,' he says. 'It was true. I liked you. I mean . . .' He flinches slightly. 'I still like you.' His voice cracks as it hits the air. And my heart blips. If I were hooked up to a heart monitor in a hospital right now there would be bells and sirens going, nurses would be running to my bedside. And that means it's time to leave.

'Noah, I've got to go,' I say, standing up and hooking my bag over my shoulder. 'I'll see you around.'

And then I head to the door, my pulse banging in my wrists. I walk out into the street. And even though I want to, even though I can feel his eyes on my back, I don't look back. Not even once.

Because sometimes that's what you have to do in life: you have to bruise your own heart to ensure it doesn't break.

Chapitre treize

We're stuffed into a metro carriage; a sea of navy, beige and black sardines in trainers and shiny office shoes. The air is thick with body heat and damp umbrellas, and smells like cologne, stale cigarettes and wet newspaper. It's hard to believe that just two months ago, when I came across for my interview, the city was a ghost town; the whole of Paris having emptied out towards the south. I've never understood how people can go to the same place year after year. If I took a holiday I'd go to Japan. I'd go in the autumn and see the maple trees changing colour.

The doors beep and close and I grab onto the silver metal pole for stability and close my eyes. A flash of Noah's hand reaching for mine as we crossed the road. I push it away and think about the maple trees again.

A high-pitched metallic squeal pierces the air and makes me grimace, the carriage jolts and my eyes flick open. All around me people are listening to music with their eyes closed, pretending they're somewhere else; others try reading books, their necks craned at strange angles and elbows verging into others' private space; some glance at their reflections in the window, readjusting their fringe or tucking hair behind their ears; some are scrolling through messages on their phones; and then there's a man by the window. He's trying to read the newspaper but he doesn't have the space.

There's a guy of about seventy in mustard trousers, holding onto the same pole as me for stability. Music pounds from his head-phones and I can hear the beat, the voice. Hip-hop. This makes me instantly like him. Because I imagine the numerous marketing minds that defined that music's demographic core, and not once was mustard guy included. He's an anomaly just like me; a hip-hop soul in the body of a middle-class grandfather to my philophobe in the city of love.

Moments like this make me feel almost normal.

I'm still looking at him when I hear: '*Mesdames et messieurs*'. I look up and behind me a man with his hair scraped back in a ponytail, wearing a pale linen pair of pants and a shirt smeared with dirt around the cuffs, makes his way through the carriage. He's shaking a paper cup and telling some story at the top of his lungs. Everyone looks away. I reach into my pocket and when he gets to me I drop a euro into his cup. He smiles and moves on. It's only as I watch him move to the other side of the carriage that I glance down at his black trainers: a pair of black and white Balenciagas. It's barely 8.30 am and already I've been hustled. But now the train is slowing down; we're coming to a stop.

The brakes screech. I look out the window: cream tiled walls, a crowd of commuters and five plastic chairs all occupied. I glance up at the wall, it reads Hôtel de Ville.

People stand up and others sit down, someone presses the lever on the door and a crowd floods out onto the platform. There's usually wi-fi in stations so I reach for my phone to check for messages. There's one.

Camilla: *SOS!*

I type back: *What's going on?*

Typing bubbles.

Accidentally super-swiped guy on 14th floor! WTF DO I DO?

The doors close and we start to move again and before I can type back the wi-fi is gone and I'm just standing smiling down at my phone. I miss Camilla. I miss meeting for drinks after work and hearing about how her boss had done this or that. I miss the mid-date check-ins where she'd text to tell me what the guy was really like. She still does all that but it's not the same now that I'm not in London.

I drop my phone into my bag and look back at the man with the newspaper. Is that dandruff on his collar? He's fiddling around now, getting ready to leave. We're almost at Saint-Paul, the last stop before mine: Bastille. He closes his paper, grabs his briefcase and stands up. As the train slows down and he moves to stand in line to leave, I glance down at the front page of his newspaper.

It's folded in half, but I can see the whole top half of the page, the headline and the photograph.

My breath catches in my throat.

Another girl is missing.

She's young. Pretty.

Just like every other missing girl.

But this time it's different.

Because this time I know her.

Sabine.

~

By the time we arrive at Bastille, my mind is numb. Through the whirr of blood pumping through my brain I hear the doors beep – a foghorn – everyone spills out onto the platform and I'm absorbed into a swamp of commuters. I join the stampede towards the stairs that lead outside and tell myself, *I must be wrong, I must be wrong, I must be wrong.*

Because it can't be her, can it?

A woman in black stilettos moves slowly up the stairs, tottering as she holds onto the bannister for safety. I push past her and take my place in the slow-moving line. *Fuck. Fuck. Fuck. I need to check.* I reach for my phone and pull up Safari, but there's no reception yet. My hairline is damp with sweat and my pulse racing as I reach for my little white *billet* and push it into the slot, moving through the turnstiles, rushing towards the exit and up the stairs.

I'm met with a light mist of drizzle on my cheeks as I head out into the open and once again pull up Safari. I breathe in petrol fumes and shield my phone screen from the rain with my body as I tap through to *Le Parisien*. People push past me, muttering annoyance beneath their breath, as I scroll through the latest stories.

And then, there she is.

Staring back at me.

The same photograph I just saw in the newspaper.

Sabine.

The world swirls around me as I try to read the article. It's in French but I glean the basics: *woman's disappearance . . . last heard from on Friday night . . . didn't arrive . . . failed to respond to phone calls . . . reported missing . . .*

How can this be happening?

People are bumping into me, telling me to move out of the way. And so I reach for my umbrella, put it up, and in some sort of trance, I move towards the crosswalk. I'm shivering from cold or shock, but I cross the road with everyone else, and put one foot in front of the other until twelve minutes later I'm standing outside the office, stabbing the keypad with the code.

Bzzzz.

I push open the door and move inside. Time slows as I head towards the elevator and press the up button, then wait for the familiar sound of the lift tumbling down towards me.

There it is.

That blessed, familiar mechanical crunch.

The elevator arrives and I step inside.

My heart is slower now, as though it's scared to beat. And I'm telling myself shitty things like, *She's only missing not dead. Noah said she wanted more than anything to be an artist, maybe she's doing it for attention, some sort of messed-up PR stunt . . .*

And just as quickly as I think these things, I feel awful for going there.

Because this is how it happens. This is how victims get blamed.

The elevator doors slide open and I step out into the office. Everything is exactly as it was yesterday when I left: Judy smiles up from her desk as I move past her, printers hum, Claudia talks loudly on speakerphone, Stan is in with Hyacinth with the door closed, Wesley sits grimacing at his screen, Nathalie is in the kitchen and the rest of the office is quietly going about its business.

Nobody pays any attention to me as I move over to my desk, drop my bag on the floor and slowly, calmly, power on my computer.

'Morning,' Wesley snipes from his side of the desk.

'Morning.' I reply. Deadpan. I stare at my screen, waiting . . . waiting . . . waiting.

A flash of white and my computer is on. I pull up the browser and type in *Le Parisien*.

As I see her face yet again, I let out a deep, controlled exhale.

'Everything okay?'

'Fine,' I say without even looking up.

I need to know what else the article says. I need to know everything. And so I highlight the text, and copy and paste it into Reverso then press 'translate'. After a few moments the text appears in English. And, as I scan through the words, my vision blurs.

Woman's Disappearance Goes Viral

Sabine Roux, 22, was last heard from on her way to a party in Montmartre on Friday, 15 October. Miss Roux was a student at Parsons Paris and a small group of classmates began posting notices about her on social media on Monday morning after she didn't arrive at various sessions throughout the weekend, and failed to respond to phone calls. 'Her phone has been off since Friday and Sabine just isn't like that. She always answers her phone. And all she cares about is her work. She wouldn't just not turn up,' said the student who contacted Le Parisien. *'The police won't listen to us but something is very wrong. We had to do something.' Within 12 hours there were more than 3000 posts on various platforms asking if anyone had seen her. The police have not issued a comment but an informed source told* Le Parisien *that Sabine Roux has now been formally reported as missing.*

I pull up Instagram immediately, go to her page and click on 'tagged photographs'. Up come pages of pictures of Sabine – smiling, winking, blowing on a fake hand gun – all with loving messages beneath them. All with the hashtag #sauverSabineRoux.

A wave of nausea rolls through me.

She was last heard from on Friday night.

That was Noah's party.

I was there.

A flash of Sabine's phone lens glinting on the rooftop, just before she ran down those stairs. I look up from my computer screen and across to the white door of the bathroom.

Stan storms out of Hyacinth's office, slamming the door, and my mouth turns sour.

I'm going to be sick.

I stand up as calmly as I can and grab my bag. I avoid Wesley's eyes but can feel him watching me as I move across the room. I push open the bathroom door, move past the sink and mirror, pull open the cubicle, kneel on the cold tiles, hold back my hair with one hand and, as quietly as I can, vomit into the toilet bowl.

Sabine's voice echoes in my head: *'C'est pour ta femme.'*

My stomach contracts and bile fills my mouth and I vomit again. I grit my teeth and focus on the sound of my breath and the almost imperceptible hum of conversation coming in from outside.

I need to pull myself together. If someone finds me here there will be questions. Questions I'm not ready for. I reach for the loo roll and blow my nose. And, with the cool floor beneath me, I think of Noah and our conversation about Sabine in the bistro last night.

'She's not replying to my calls.'

This must be why. Has he seen the papers? Does he know?

I should call him. I fumble around in my handbag, find my phone, go to my Instagram messages and tap on his most recent message: his phone number.

133

My breath is quick and my thoughts fractured as I tap on it and listen as the line rings.

Ring.

Ring.

Ring.

'Hey, you've called Noah. Leave a message.'

Beep.

I speak before I really think it through, adrenaline making my words quick and jittery. 'Hey, Noah, it's me, I just saw the news about Sabine and Friday night and I—'

But instead of finishing the message, I hang up. Quickly. What was I thinking?

Because it was Noah's party. If it turns out something *has* happened to Sabine, the police will question him. They'll want to know who was there. And right now, nobody knows my real name. Nobody knows I was there. I can walk away and pretend it never happened. Without ever talking to the police. Without risking Hyacinth finding out. Because it's not like I know anything. It's not like I can help.

I push myself up and unlock the cubicle door. It swings open with a squeak. I move over to the white ceramic sink and splash my face with cold water. I take a deep breath. I reach for a paper towel from the dispenser above the bin and dab my face dry. Blot my mascara and reach into my bag for my lip gloss. As I trace my lips with vanilla, my mind calms. Because there's no need to do anything rash right now. It could be a false alarm. She could turn up tomorrow. The press probably wouldn't even be reporting this if it hadn't come hot on the heels of the Matilde Beaumont story. I can just ride it out.

You're fine, Harper. Fine.

Chapitre quatorze

Two blurry days later, it's a feeling of falling that wakes me up. Or maybe it's the incessant beeping of my alarm. I'm not sure what I was dreaming about, but as I pull my mask from my eyes, a hologram of Sabine standing in that doorway videoing us is branded on my mind's eye. I reach for my phone, turn off my alarm, and check the time. It's 7.20 am and there's one message from a dating app on the screen. Nee-koh-lah. *Hey beautiful, want to catch up tonight? X.*

Finally, a question I know the answer to: *No.*

I groan, pull out my earplugs, and try to stand up but my brain is fuzzy and my tongue is thick; I couldn't sleep last night so I took another one of Anne's Ambiens. Now I'm dizzy and late and as I move through to the kitchen, I can smell orange blossom coming from my wrist. Because yesterday I went with Nathalie to try out that perfume mixing place in Le Marais. It was four hours of pure hell: lots of smiling and nodding and pretending to care what oud smelled like while surreptitiously checking my phone while nobody was looking. Then last night was spent at the laundromat, listening to the whirr of my washing spinning around the dryer as

I scrolled through pages and pages of social media posts – the whole of Paris seemed keen to claim the missing girl now – and watched and re-watched every video on Sabine's Vimeo page, looking for god knows what. All I found were stolen snippets from her daily life: a busker counting his money in le Bois de Boulogne; a group of students huddling together and checking for onlookers, at what looked like her art school; Agnès Bisset talking to a tall, willowy potential buyer; and an elderly couple walking hand in hand outside Sacré-Cœur. But nothing to tell me what happened to Sabine.

Now today is Thursday, and she's still gone.

I flick on the kettle and stare out the window because I know what that means. Sabine has been gone since last Friday, that's six days, long past the seventy-two hours where the likelihood of finding her alive is high.

I swallow hard and warm my hands on the side of the kettle and my phone buzzes from the countertop: a private number. I stare at it: this happened yesterday too. But nobody calls from an unmarked number unless it's a telemarketer, so I press the red button and send it to voicemail.

The kettle boils. I make my coffee and take a sip. My tongue recoils. It's strong. And as my eyes return to the sky outside, I can't help thinking of what Camilla said when I called her to tell her Sabine was missing last night: *Come home.*

But I don't want to go home. Or rather, I do, but I can't. Because going home would mean going backwards. I'd be back in a mediocre job doing something I hate, going to bars that remind me of Harrison, with nothing but paying bills, consuming and dying to look forward to, telling anyone who'll listen about that one time I got a job in Paris but then left it because of something bad that happened. Something I had no control over. And bad things happen all the time, in every city in the world. I need to stick it out. I won't forgive myself if I leave now.

I take another sip of coffee waiting for the caffeine to work its magic as I look out the window. My hair is tangled from tossing and turning and I gently pull my fingers through it as I stare blankly at the space where Mr Oiseau usually sits. But he's not here this morning. And it feels cold and empty without him. My phone pings from the countertop and I glance down at the screen. Did the telemarketer leave a voicemail?

But it's not a voicemail.

It's a news notification.

I squint down at the screen, reading and rereading the words. It takes a while for the meaning to settle in my mind. Even Ambien can't protect me from this.

Woman's body identified as Sabine Roux.

No.

No. No. No.

I stare down at the words, needing them to morph into something else, anything else. How can this be happening?

Shit.

Shit. Shit. Shit. Now it's real.

She's dead.

I clench my eyes shut and hang onto the sink as a deep nausea washes over me. I scrabble to collect my thoughts. *Calm down, Harper.* But in the darkness all I can see is that headline: *Woman's body identified as Sabine Roux.*

My eyes flick open and I grab my phone. Because I need to know everything. Now. Where was she found? What happened to her? A flash: her face slightly purple, lying in a ditch. Who did this to her? I tap on the notification and move through to the article but it's in French and fuck other languages right now.

I pull the text through to Reverso and press translate.

A woman's body was found in the wood in le Bois de Boulogne by maintenance staff yesterday . . . confirmed to be the body of Sabine Roux, 22, the missing Parsons Paris student whose disappearance went viral on social media on Monday. Miss Roux had not been seen or heard from since the evening of Friday, October 15.

Le Bois de Boulogne was right near where she lived. Was she taken on her way home?

I imagine the red and white police tape cordoning off the crime scene. Was she buried or was she just lying there amid the autumn leaves?

My forehead tenses as images from that night flicker through my mind: Noah running after her, watching them from the roof, the empty hallway downstairs, the cobbled street, *Khalid is arriving soon,* the white car . . .

I can hear Noah's voice in my head: 'She just ran off and I went back up to the roof to look for you, but you were already gone.'

And now I'm thinking of his message, which came in on Saturday at 2.33 am. And his excuse: 'I wanted to text you sooner, I just couldn't find my phone . . . I didn't know what to say. I knew you'd be pissed off.'

Then a flash of Monday night at the gallery. He was so keen to find me he tracked me down via Instagram. It mattered *that* much. An echo of Noah's words: 'I need you to promise me something. You won't tell anyone about all this, about what happened on the roof.'

And then back to that message.

Two hours. He had two hours. I know what he said he was doing, but was he *really* sitting alone on that rooftop, contemplating life for two fucking hours?

My stomach twists.

My hands start to shake a little.

Then everything fades to silence.

Did Noah do this?

But he isn't a killer. I'd know, wouldn't I? I'd feel it. I'd sense *something.*

Still, things happen in the moment. One push. One slip. Another flash of that white car. Maybe that was his. Maybe he was driving her home and it all got heated and it just happened. He

140

panicked. Dropped her body in that park near her home. Went back to the party and pretended it never happened.

I'm the only one who knows exactly what happened on that roof on Friday night. I'm the only one who knows why he ran after her. Because, if he killed her, he would have destroyed her phone, which means nobody would ever see that video. Nobody would know he had motive.

Nobody except me.

That's why he came to talk to me.

He needed to sew his alibi in nice and tight. To make me believe him. So if anyone asked, I'd be a good little girl and corroborate his story. *No, Officer, he couldn't have been off killing Sabine because he was up on that rooftop looking for me. Yes, I'm certain. If he hadn't gone back, how else could he have known I'd left?*

Like it would never occur to me that Noah may have simply turned his head mid-argument and seen me make my way up those stairs.

My thoughts are so clear now, so rigid, they could snap if I moved too quickly. Because now I'm thinking of that first time we met, when he didn't tell me who he was, and how he didn't mention he was married. He doesn't seem to mention anything that's inconvenient to him.

He seems to think he can play me.

Well, fuck you, Noah. You picked the wrong girl to try to manipulate. Because I'm not like Sabine. I'm not scared of being a pariah.

I reach for my phone and google: *Paris police, homicide.* A few clicks later up come the words *Brigade Criminelle* and a series of pictures: an enormous, reflective, modern building beneath a perfect blue sky. A sand-coloured wall with big black words, *Direction Régionale de la Police Judiciaire.*

I imagine myself walking through those glass doors. But it's all the way out near Levallois-Perret, barely inside the Boulevard Périphérique. And today is Thursday. Our editorial meeting. I can't miss that.

I'll go straight after work.

Chapitre quinze

There's a blister on the back of my left foot and I'm thinking about whether I have any plasters in the bottom of my bag when the elevator doors slide open. Judy is standing behind her desk, staring at me, the red of the tulips in the vase to her right so vivid that she looks grey-white in contrast. If I were to squint she'd blend in perfectly with the walls. I wonder if she's ill? No. Wait. It's something else. Something is wrong. Her mouth is half-open and uncomfortable. Like she wants to say something but figures she'd better not.

This must have something to do with why she called me.

I was almost here, crossing the road by the station, when my phone began to vibrate and I saw the work number flash up. But what with struggling to control my umbrella against the wind, the blister on my foot, being drug-fucked on Ambien and the shellshock of this morning, I let it ring out. But now I'm worried.

Please, dear god, don't let me get sacked today too.

'Hi,' I say, dropping my wet umbrella into the metal bin provided and taking off my coat. It's good to be inside, away from the wind, the swirling autumn leaves and the rain coming in at impossible angles. 'Is everything okay?'

'Um, Harper.' She nods to behind me where there are four linen chairs. 'The police are here to see you.'

My pulse speeds up.

Fuck.

I turn around, and take them in. There are two of them: Batman and Robin. A big, attractive one – tall, thick dark hair, refined jaw, dark eyes, pink shirt – and a smaller, more ordinary one – around five foot eight, mousy hair, brown eyes, white shirt. They stand up.

'Ms Brown,' the attractive one says. He has a thick French accent.

'Hi,' I say, my brain whirring.

How did they find me?

'I'm Commandant Luneau and this is Brigadier Moor.'

'Hello,' Brigadier Moor says, reaching out a hand for me to shake. He has a perfect London accent. He was clearly handpicked due to his linguistic skills.

'We tried to call you,' Luneau continues.

The missed calls. The private number.

'We just have some questions for you.'

But how did they get my number?

'Of course,' I say. But Ambien is still slowing my mind. I need coffee just to be lucid.

'Is there somewhere we can speak privately?' Luneau asks.

'Yes,' I say, turning to Judy, whose mouth is still a little open. Her eyes are apologetic like she tried to warn me.

'You can take the meeting room?' Judy suggests.

'Thanks,' I say. 'I'm going to grab a coffee, can I get either of you something?'

'A coffee please,' says Luneau.

'Yes, same, thank you,' says Moor.

'Great, I'll be right back. Judy can show you to the room.'

Judy gives a small, scared smile, like she's never seen a policeman in such close proximity before. As I move towards the kitchen, I hear her say in French, 'This way, gentlemen.'

Wesley is in the kitchen when I get there, fucking around by the Nespresso machine, trying to decide whether he'd like a black pod or a purple one this morning. He looks up, sees me, and I swear to god he slows down just because I'm clearly in a rush.

I wait for him in silence, pulling three cups and saucers out of the cupboard and placing them on a black plastic tray. He finally decides on the purple one then makes his coffee, while I pour milk into a milk jug and pull out some teaspoons and a bowl of sugar cubes and run through what I'm going to say in my mind.

She videoed us. She threatened to tell his wife. Noah ran after her. I don't know anything after that.

Simple. I have nothing to hide. So why are my hands shaking? Is it the Ambien? Or is it the fact that once I say it, I can't unsay it?

They'll look for that video, and if they find it, Noah will become their prime suspect. And fuck my life, I kind of liked him.

Wesley finally leaves and I make the coffee, pick up the tray and head back through the open-plan office towards the meeting room, glancing in at Hyacinth's office. She's not in. That's good. I don't want to have to explain things to her yet if I don't have to.

The meeting room door is open when I get there and I quickly move inside. I put the tray down on the table then close the door behind me and sit down, passing cups across the table like it's a social visit. Luneau has a notebook open in front of him and is clicking a pen but he smiles with thanks as I pass him his cup.

I take a big sip of my own coffee and watch as Brigadier Moor adds milk and then four sugar cubes. The sound of his teaspoon clinking against the bottom of the ceramic mug fills the room. I can't stand it. I need this done, and quickly, before Hyacinth gets in.

'Right,' I say with a hospitable smile as I covertly take control. 'This is about Friday night, right?' I ask, taking another sip of my coffee. 'About Sabine Roux? I saw the news this morning. I was going to come and see you after work.'

'Yes,' Luneau says. He's watching me, trying to figure me out. 'We're asking questions of anyone . . . connected.' He clicks his pen. 'You called Noah Parker two days ago?'

Parker. That's his last name.

And I think of that morning in the bathrooms, the cold tiles beneath me as I left that message on Noah's phone: 'Hey, Noah, it's me, I just saw the news about Sabine and Friday night and I—'

All the police needed to do then was call my number back and they'd have heard: 'You've called Harper Brown at *The Paris Observer.*'

'Yes, I saw the news about Sabine going missing and I was worried.'

Luneau squints at me. 'Harper,' he says. 'Is it okay if I call you Harper?'

I nod, even though I sense I am not going to like what comes next.

'Noah claims to not know who you are?' It's posed like a question, the subtext being: please explain.

Right.

Even through the haze I can see what happened here. They went through Noah's phone when they questioned him. They listened to his voicemails and called me back. They asked who Harper Brown was and Noah said he had no idea. But that didn't quite make sense to Luneau: if Noah didn't know me, why was I leaving a message in an intimate tone on his voicemail about Friday night and Sabine? What was he hiding?

'He *does* know who I am,' I say, proceeding with caution. I don't want them to view me as unreliable. 'He just thinks my name is Grace.'

Luneau cocks his head slightly to the side. 'Why would he think that?' he asks. His English is perfect so I'm not sure why he bothered bringing Moor, who is all clinkety-clink-clink with his teaspoon then slurpy-slurp with his coffee.

'I didn't want him to know I was a journalist in case he was cagey with me. It was stupid but at the time it made sense.' This is the best I can come up with under pressure.

The sound of Luneau's pen pulling across the page fills the room.

'Right, but you *were* there on Friday night? At the party?'

I nod.

'Let's start at the beginning of the evening then?'

'Of course.'

'What time would you say you arrived?'

'I don't know, maybe ten thirty,' I reply.

He makes a note.

'Can you tell me more about your memory of the night?'

'Sure, I'd been out at a work do and saw that Noah was having a party. I was writing an article about him and wanted more information on him, to ask more questions, so I asked if I could come.'

He notes it down.

'And did you see Sabine Roux there?'

'Yes,' I say, 'she was videoing everything. She kept watching me and Noah. I was with him for most of the night, you see—' I'm getting ready to tell him about the video but he cuts me off.

148

'How well do you know Noah Parker?'

'Not well at all,' I say. 'I met him last week at his exhibition. But, like I said, I was there looking for more information for my article.'

He flips to a new page on his notebook and the sound fills the room.

'And Sabine, how well did you know her?'

'I didn't know her. I'd seen her in Noah's paintings and she was there at the exhibition last Thursday but we'd never spoken.'

'But you said she was watching you all night?'

'Yes,' I say, swallowing hard. 'Look, did Noah tell you that he ran after her? That they left the party together?'

'Yes. He said she was upset and he wanted to calm her down, but then she ran off and he went back to the party—'

'Did he tell you *why* she was upset?' I interrupt.

'He said she was jealous,' Luneau says and then waits for my input.

'Yeah. It was more than that,' I say. My stomach twists as I say the words. 'Like I said, she was videoing us. One of the videos was . . . intimate.'

Brigadier Moor smirks and throws Luneau a look. He's thinking, *And now we get to the real truth: she wasn't there to write a story, she's just some groupie who went there to fuck the rising art star.*

But screw Brigadier Moor. I will not be slut-shamed.

'It was of Noah and I having sex,' I continue, matter-of-factly. 'We were standing under cover, my leg was around his waist. Would you like me to draw you a diagram? It might help?'

Moor almost chokes on his coffee and Luneau shifts in his seat.

'Go on,' Luneau says.

'Sabine threatened to show that to Noah's wife. Well, I mean they're getting divorced but . . . That's why she ran off and that's why Noah ran after her.'

Again, the sound of Luneau's pen pulling across the page as he makes notes fills the room. My thoughts – *Noah did this* – and my feelings – *but I don't want him to be a killer* – are a matted mess. Moor takes a loud slurp of his coffee.

'Does anyone else know about this video?' Luneau asks.

'No,' I say. 'Just me and Noah. And Sabine.'

'Right,' he says, still writing. 'And what time did you leave the party?'

'Soon afterwards.'

'How long afterwards would you say?'

'About five minutes,' I say.

'And you didn't see Noah or Sabine on the street?'

'Yes,' I say. 'They were arguing at the bottom of the stairs when I first came outside.'

'What were they saying?'

'I don't know but it must have been about what happened. But they were gone by the time I headed down there.'

'What do you mean, by the time you headed down there?' Luneau asks.

'I went to wait for my Uber at the top of the stairs first. But I was in the wrong place – it was set to pick me up just past where Noah and Sabine had been arguing. But they were gone by the time I figured it out.' As I speak, a memory flickers in my mind. That white car.

And deep down I want to be wrong about Noah. I want to be told Sabine caught the metro and was attacked on her walk home. That he didn't do it. So I don't say this next bit outright, I pose it as a question.

'Do you know whether Sabine ever got to the metro station?' I ask.

Luneau frowns at me. I can tell he doesn't want to hand over any information about the case, but he also wants to know why I'm asking. He senses I know something more. 'This can't end up in print,' he warns and I nod. 'But no, she's not on any of the CCTV in the metro. Why?'

I swallow hard.

'It's just that there was a car. A white one. About halfway down Rue Chappe. It drove away as I got there. The number plate ended in double A.'

'Do you know what time that was?' Luneau asks.

'Ummm,' I say, reaching for my phone and navigating to Uber. 'Here you go. This was my ride. It arrived just after I saw the white car.' I pass it to him and he notes down the information and I log it in my memory: Khalid picked me up at 12.46 am.

'This has been very helpful, thank you,' Luneau says.

And then he stands up, Moor follows. I lead them back into the reception area. And as Judy watches on, Luneau hands me his card.

'Let me know if anything else occurs to you,' he says. And a moment later they're gone.

Chapitre seize

I'm hobbling back to my desk, the blister on the back of my foot stinging as my finger traces the edge of Commandant Luneau's business card when I hear: 'Harper?'

I turn my head. Hyacinth is standing in her doorway, hands on her hips. She's wearing some sort of woollen kaftan. She must have come in while I was in the meeting room and pried the morning's events, and the reason the meeting room door was closed, out of poor Judy. 'Can we have a word?'

'Of course,' I say with a smile, heading into her office.

'Take a seat,' she says.

I sit down, hearing the click of the door behind me.

She goes to her side of the desk and sits down too. 'Apparently we had a visit from the police this morning?' she says.

I swallow hard, trying to think of the least inflammatory way to tell the story. 'They had some questions,' I start, sombre. 'I was at a party on Friday night and a girl went missing. Sabine Roux. You might have seen her in the papers? There have been posts about her all over social media. They found her body yesterday.'

Hyacinth's posture stiffens. Thoughts flicker behind her eyes.

'Whose party was it?' she asks.

'Noah X,' I say. 'The artist I wrote about last week.' She gives me this look and I know I'd better explain. Fast. 'I went there to get more information for my story.'

She nods slowly, finishing my sentence for me. 'And the police are questioning everyone who was there that night? Trying to find out more information?'

I nod. But I fear it's a trap. They only found Sabine's body yesterday, why seek *me* out at my place of employment over everyone else at that party? I need to elaborate.

'Yes. Except they wanted to talk to me specifically,' I say, shifting in my seat. How to tell the next bit truthfully without screwing myself over in the process? 'I was talking to Noah just before Sabine Roux left. She came over, said something to him in French, and ran off. The police wanted to ask about that.'

'Well, what did she say, before she left?'

C'est pour ta femme.

'I'm not sure,' I say. 'It was in French. I think it was something about a painting.'

We sit there in silence for a few moments. I can hear her breathing. Her eyes are down. I brace myself to be told that going to that party was unprofessional. That having the police seek me out in my place of work is unacceptable.

But instead she just looks up, face blank, and says, 'Okay, thanks, Harper.'

And I head back towards my desk. Everyone is watching me now. Claudia is whispering something. Wesley is staring.

They all know the police were here talking to me.

They just don't know why.

Not yet.

And so I set my gaze on the large windows that look out onto the stormy sky, raindrops sparkling from the panes.

I sit down and fire up my computer. Wesley is shuffling around with papers on his side of the desk. The fluorescent light flickering above me is a little too bright. My computer sparks to life and I'm about to navigate to my inbox when Wesley stands up and says, 'Are you coming?'

Right. It's just before ten on a Thursday.

That means one thing: the editorial meeting.

~

Four minutes later I'm taking a seat at the meeting room table beside Wesley. I glance over at the sheet of paper in front of him. It's folded over, like he thinks I'm going to steal his ideas.

Hyacinth walks in and closes the door after her with a bang then sits at the head of the table.

'Right,' she says, 'dazzle me. Who would like to go first?'

'Me,' comes Stan's voice. Stern. Clear. We all turn to look at him. He's sitting at the end of the table, slouched forward so the buttons of his light blue shirt tug at the fabric.

Hyacinth hesitates for a split second. I think of him pacing around in her office on Tuesday then slamming the door as I ran to the loos to vomit.

'As some of you might have already read, they found a woman's body yesterday.' A vein is popping out the side of his temple like he's really fucking annoyed. 'The one I spoke to you about on Tuesday, Hyacinth. You'll be glad to know that she's officially dead now. And, bless the lord, she's pretty too. Will make perfect click-bait.'

The bit about click-bait is said with a dark and venomous smile. It's aimed at Hyacinth, at her moral compass.

'So, obviously, I'm going to be writing about that.'

I watch Hyacinth as she stares at him. Her fuchsia-painted lips are pursed, like her mouth just turned sour.

The room is as silent as the Notre Dame during mass as they stare each other down. Then Hyacinth speaks. 'No. Harper should write this,' she says, eyes to me.

Beat.

'What?' Stan's face gets so pink it's almost puce. 'Why the hell would Harper write it?'

He glares at me now and my stomach clenches.

'Because Harper was there,' Hyacinth says calmly. 'You will only be able to write exactly what every other reporter will be writing. Harper has an angle.'

'I have a source at the police,' Stan snaps.

Silence.

'What the fuck do *you* know about this case? About any case?' he snipes at me. 'And I don't mean what sort of cocktails they were serving. I mean what do you really know?' He's seething and my face is flushing pink and I hate him right now for making me feel so small.

Hyacinth continues, 'Harper will write it. And you'll tell her what you know.' Then she turns to me. 'Harper, we can feature it on the landing page tomorrow. I'll need it by 11 am at the latest.'

'Of course,' I say, a little stunned. I have no idea if I can do that but I'll figure out a way.

Stan is sneering at me. 'That's horseshit,' he blurts out.

'Stan,' she says, her voice a warning.

And he shuts up.

'Now, for the love of god would someone pitch me something that *isn't* about pretty dead girls?'

Chapitre dix-sept

Stan glares at me, like he's a horrible little schoolboy and I'm an insect, and the table between us is an enormous magnifying glass. If he holds it at just the right angle, maybe I'll burst into flames and he'll no longer have a problem on his hands. Well, bad luck, Stan, I'm here to stay.

All around us people gather up their things and head for the door. Claudia is telling Nathalie about some dress or other she just has to get and Wesley is stomping around even louder than normal because Hyacinth said he wasn't allowed to write about yet another opera and needed to choose something more accessible.

Wesley gives one last huff and closes the door – click – and now it's just me and Stan in here.

Stan shuffles the papers in front of him: a signal that he's more important than me and so isn't going to speak first.

'So,' I say, my voice perfectly congenial as I pick up my pen and reach for my notepad. 'What have you got?'

His jaw tightens. 'Nothing.'

I sigh and swallow my irritation. 'Well, what does your source at the police say? Do they have any evidence?'

'Nope.'

I try to control my expression.

'Well, they questioned me this morning so they must have questioned other people too. Someone must have said something?'

'I can't help you there, I'm afraid,' he says.

I give him an are-you-fucking-joking look and drop my pen to the desk as a punctuation point. Ching. 'Stan, you just sat there maybe twenty minutes ago saying you knew a lot more than I did about this story so you should be writing it,' I snap. 'So you must know something.'

He leans forward across the table. 'I know that Sabine Roux was murdered,' he says, batting his eyes. He's taunting me. Mimicking me. And he's not going to help. Not one bit.

Irritation bubbles up in my stomach. I could go and tattle-tale to Hyacinth but where would that get me? It won't change anything.

'Anyway, I'm so sorry I couldn't be any more help, princess,' he says with a smug smile. 'But I'm sure you'll do a fine job.'

Panic floods through me. I don't have enough for a whole story right now, just: I went to a party, Sabine saw us on the roof and ran out and Noah followed her. I can't mention the CCTV in the metro without pissing off Luneau and I'm loathe to mention the white car. As much as I want this story, I don't want to impede the investigation. But I need more. I need a spine for it. Something to make it stand out. A hook.

'Well, could I speak to your source?' I ask. 'Hyacinth did ask you to help me.'

'She asked me to tell you what I knew. I've done that.' He stands up. 'And no, Harper, I cannot reveal my source to you. But if you're so well qualified to write this story, I'm sure you'll figure it all out.' He heads for the door. 'Now, I've got to get back to work, I'm afraid. Good luck.' Then the door bangs shut after him.

And I'm left with an empty notebook, twenty-four hours to write my first feature article and the sibilant whisperings of my inner critic: *Don't fail now, princess . . .*

~

My phone beeps and my eyes dart to the screen.

Camilla: *Love you.*

I love her too, but I'm too stressed to answer. Because the time has just clicked over to 12.43 pm and the letters of my article are glowering at me like little black question marks against the blue-white light of my screen. I've been staring at this first draft for twenty minutes now, trying to talk myself off the ledge. Because at the moment it reads like a woman's magazine article, a slightly eerie puff piece. And that's not what I'm going for. Because this is my chance to show Hyacinth what I can do. I might not get another one.

My phone beeps again: *xxx.*

She's worried because after that shitty interlude with Stan I needed space to think. And so I hid in the loos for fifteen minutes, struggling to swallow, texting Camilla: *They found her body. She's definitely dead.*

Camilla called me straight away, of course. And I answered in a whisper in case somebody came in: 'Hey.'

'Come home. It'll be fine. But just come home.'

And that, right there, was the moment I knew I didn't want to go home. Not now that I'd been given this story to write; because you don't get that many chances to next level yourself in this life. It's all brick walls and work and struggle and work and struggle and then, out of nowhere, comes a trapdoor moment. A chance to get to the other side of that wall. This story is one of those moments.

'I'm worried about you,' came Camilla's voice.

But before I could reassure her, the bathroom door creaked open and someone moved into the cubicle next to mine. So I whispered, 'I have to go but I'll call you soon', with my hand shielding the mouthpiece, hung up and flushed the loo for authenticity.

And then I headed back to my desk. Which is where I am right now, staring once again at my blinking cursor at the end of my fourth paragraph, thinking, *How do I make this better?*

There's something missing at the moment and I don't know what it is.

I pull up a browser window and go to Sabine's Vimeo page, staring down at the clips I've already seen. I could talk about her being an artist in her own right, talk about her work . . . I move to

Instagram. She has almost four thousand followers now – that's two thousand more than when she was alive a week ago. My stomach twists: so few of those people actually know her. She's just another victim, just another hashtag, just another way to pass a mundane fifteen minutes before they head back to the safety of their cubicle or suburbia. Sabine will be forgotten within the week.

'How are you doing there?' comes Stan's voice over my shoulder. I close the browser window and glare at him.

'Going well,' I say. Deadpan.

He smirks and ponces away in his tight navy trousers and my stomach starts pumping out acid as I stare back at Sabine's Instagram page, at her follower count . . .

And then, I know. I know how to make this different.

Right now Sabine Roux is just another dead girl, the latest sacrifice for the media's altar. I need to make her into a real person, with hopes and dreams and life choices and, shock of all horrors, flaws. If she's a real person people will care about the night she died. Because, if she's a real person, it could happen to them too.

But I don't know where to look for more information. I could contact one of many people now claiming her as a friend on social media, but I have limited time and it's impossible to know where to start. Who she was *really* close to. What I need to do is to talk to her mother. But how can I find her?

Of course, there is one way I can think of . . . but it's risky.

Risky, but worth it.

I google Le Voltage, press the phone number into my dial pad and listen as it rings.

'Bonjour, Le Voltage,' comes a sweet, young voice.

'Bonjour,' I start then switch to English. 'Please could I speak to Agnès Bisset?'

A moment of pause.

'I'm sorry,' says the voice. 'Madame Bisset won't be back until tomorrow. Can I take a message?'

'No,' I say, 'it's okay. I'll call back then.'

And as I hang up, I think, *Perfect.*

Chapitre dix-huit

Rue Bonaparte looks different in the afternoon light: more ordinary somehow without the amber glow of streetlights; its stark grey pavements the same colour as the sky. Like all the magic of the Parisian night was wrung out with the dawn. I move past the little alleyway to my left, where I smoked with Noah. I glance down it and can almost see our ghosts there, laughing, smoking in the dark before all this happened. A flicker of warmth as I remember him reaching for my necklace. And then a chill as I remember what he might have done to Sabine. Why I'm here.

The door to Le Voltage is right in front of me now. I glance to the window: the poster for Noah's exhibition is gone.

I take a deep breath and step inside, reminding myself of the plan.

The gallery is empty. But it smells familiar now: like an old, dusty mansion that has just had its floors polished. Noah's paintings are still hanging on one wall, among a series of others I haven't seen before: a black-and-white Paris at night scene; a portrait of a young girl in rags sitting on the edge of a bed; a large, brightly coloured pop-art parakeet.

There is a jug of water with cucumbers swimming in it sitting on the right hand side of a big dark wood desk. In front of it sit two crystal-cut glasses, both upside down to signal that they've not been used yet. On the other side of the desk is a little wooden business card holder full of bright white cards. They read: Lors Carron, Gallery Assistant, Le Voltage. I reach forward and take a couple, dropping them into my bag.

I'll need those.

'Hello?' I say into the void.

A door at the back of the room opens, a mousy-haired girl emerges and locks it behind her. 'Bonjour.' She smiles at me, heading to the big desk with the water.

'Hi,' I say.

'Welcome to Le Voltage,' she says, switching to English and opening the top drawer. She drops a small plastic fob into it and my eyes trace her profile as she locks it. I recognise her. She was here the other night at Noah's exhibition, handing out champagne. She must have answered my call when I rang.

I clench my jaw, look at the floor and force myself not to blink so my eyes tear up a bit.

'Umm. I'm Grace.' I offer my hand, keeping it limp as she shakes it. A limp handshake means I'm not a threat. 'I was friends with Sabine?' I say, my voice cracking right on cue, like I'm hoping she mentioned me. 'I just—'

'You were here the other night, right?' she says. 'At the exhibition.'

Shit.

'Yes,' I say, smiling. 'I came with Sabine.'

'It's terrible, so terrible.' She shakes her head and her forehead creases to make that expression people make when they're scared they'll say the wrong thing but know they have to say something.

'I know,' I say. 'I want to send her mother some flowers,' I continue. 'I've been to her place before but don't know the delivery address. Do you have it?'

'I don't think so,' she says, cautious.

'It'll be the same as Sabine's address.' I smile. Helpful. 'She lived with her mother,' I say, preparing to ramble. 'I mean, I could just turn up in person but I don't want to impose. One never knows what to do in these sorts of situations . . .'

She looks at me a little startled. Hesitates. She's wondering whether she'll get in trouble but isn't sure how to say no. Should she say she's new and doesn't know where they keep that information? But I haven't blinked in a good sixty seconds and my eyes are burning with tears.

'It's right near le Bois de Boulogne,' I add, thinking of Sabine's Instagram page and that picture in the park.

Her eyes flicker with relief. I've won her over. She sits down and starts clicking on her keyboard.

'Sure. Of course.'

Click-click-click fills the empty room. Then she reaches beside her for a pad and pen and notes down an address. She writes in the big, round, bubbly schoolgirl way that should have a heart to dot the 'i'. She tears the page off and hands it to me.

'Thanks,' I say, glancing down at it and dropping it into my handbag.

But then: bang.

A door slams somewhere behind the dividing wall.

Footsteps.

The mousy-haired girl looks at me and says, 'Is there anything else I can help you with?' She wants me to leave.

'Lors?' comes a French voice. A female one. And a moment later a tall silhouette appears around the corner. She's wearing a pair of navy trousers and a cream silk shirt that gleams in the light. Her hair is tucked behind her ears and her lipstick is the colour of last night's wine.

Noah's wife. The person who's not supposed to be here until tomorrow morning.

Shit.

I glare at the mousy-haired girl – she lied to me.

'Hi,' I say, trying to act nonchalant.

'Hello.' She smiles, going about her business, but then she looks back at me, her eyes narrow just a little, there's a flicker of recognition, a hint of a smile and then: 'Have we met before?'

And even though there's no way she could have seen that video – unless Sabine sent it to her on Friday night before she died – my face flushes.

'Yes,' I say, grinning idiotically like I am happy she remembers, 'I was at Noah's exhibition last week. We spoke, actually. Right in front of that painting.' I point to the painting of Sabine with the red lighter. But, with art, everything is about context. That painting looks different now. Sabine no longer looks composed, now she looks wounded, and the red looks a lot like blood. Now it looks like a warning, a warning none of us read.

'Do you work here?' I ask. Because, you know, it would be weird if I already knew that this was her gallery from e-stalking her.

She laughs and her mouth makes a curve, but her eyes don't crinkle. It's as though the top and bottom parts of her face are disconnected. 'I own this gallery,' she says. 'What can I do for you?'

'Grace was a friend of Sabine's,' the mousy-haired girl explains, interrupting my thought process.

'It's so sad,' Agnès says. 'We all loved Sabine. She had a real spirit. Such a talent.' But all I can hear is Noah's voice in my head saying: *Agnès doesn't even like Sabine's work, she calls it a Hallmark card on steroids.*

Why do people only decide they like you, that you're talented, once you're dead? Still, at least this is safe territory.

'Yes, you were going to exhibit Sabine here, right?' I say, in an attempt to solidify my lie. 'She was so excited. Wouldn't stop talking about it.'

But something in Agnès's eyes changes. Like a match igniting. I've said something wrong and I don't know what it is. I need to leave before this goes badly.

'Yes,' she says slowly, her smile strained.

I give it a moment then check the time on my phone.

'Well, I should be going,' I say, with a small fake smile.

And then I head to the door. It's only as I step outside I realise I'm holding my breath and my shoulders are around my ears.

The door clicks closed behind me and I start to walk down the road. I pass the alleyway once more and glance down it.

And just above the back door, right where Noah and I were talking, is a CCTV camera.

Chapitre dix-neuf

Madame Roux returns with the flowers I brought her – yellow chrysanthemums – in a big white vase and puts them down on the large cream doily in the middle of the coffee table. Chrysanthemums. In France, those are the flowers you buy for people when somebody dies. At least, that's what the flower seller told me when I bought them on the way here this morning, but I'm not sure that's entirely true. Mme Roux didn't seem particularly thrilled when she saw them. But then I handed her that business card, introduced myself as Lors Carron from Le Voltage and told her why I was here. Her eyes softened after that. She let me inside.

She sits down and pours the coffee. A big silver pot and two tiny cups.

It's always strange to see where someone lives. It tells you so much about them. Often things you'd never guess from meeting them. Like Sabine with her bright red hair and enfant terrible demeanour seems misplaced in the leafy suburbia of Boulogne-Billancourt among the floral throw pillows and doilies. Yet that's where she lived. Right now, I'm sitting on the sofa she would have sat on many times: a light green and pink paisley. A shiver runs down my spine as though Sabine's ghost is here, right now, watching me lie to her mother.

The feeling is compounded by the fact Mme Roux looks just like her daughter: though her hair is grey and perfectly coiffed, not red and messy, and her movements are slower. It's as though she's weighed down or constricted by a heavy gauze of grief that has wrapped itself around her. A gauze that is bound to only tighten over time.

'Sabine was so excited about this exhibition,' she says, pushing my little cup towards me.

That's what I told her at the door: that we, at Le Voltage, were putting on Sabine's exhibition. That I needed some information for the flyers. Yes, I'm basically Satan's little helper, but it seemed like a good idea at the time. Because I don't know how she feels about journalists and I couldn't risk her not talking to me. So this was all I could think of. How else am I meant to do Sabine justice in my article?

'I wish I'd met Sabine,' I say. 'I only started working there after she had already left. Can you tell me about her?' I probe. Anything I can add to the eight hundred flimsy words I penned last night will do at this point. Because I can't even include the truth about what happened on that rooftop; to do so would open Pandora's box right up. Me being Pandora. And so instead I built on the lie I told Hyacinth and cited 'creative differences' as the fuel that sparked the argument between Noah and Sabine and had them leave the party together.

Mme Roux tries to smile at my question, but her eyes grow pink with tears and she looks down, clenching her jaw as if trying not to cry. 'She was brave,' she says in a small voice, nodding at her cup.

I glance up at the walls behind her: there are three large framed photographs I recognise from Sabine's Instagram page. Black-and-white prints of the same woman covering her eyes, her ears and her mouth: see no evil, hear no evil, speak no evil.

'She was such a talent,' I say gently and my stomach shrinks. This is a lot harder than I expected.

'With Sabine, everything was about her work,' Mme Roux says. 'Most girls are all about boys. Not Sabine. She fell in love with the camera . . .' Her eyes cast down.

Then she sets down her coffee cup, it clinks as it hits the saucer, and she gets up and heads off down the passageway somewhere. I look around the room: there's a big grandfather clock ticking away in the corner. The sort that looks like a little bird might pop out on the hour and say 'cuckoo'. A bookshelf filled with old books, the kind you know are old because the spines are all shades of navy, brown and burgundy with metallic type. There are silver frames with photographs, mainly of a little girl with dark blonde hair who I assume is Sabine.

Then there are footsteps and she's back. 'Here.' She hands me something black and square. 'Her work. For the exhibition.' Then she gives me a connecting cable too.

I don't want to take it, it feels wrong, but how can I refuse? If I tell her I'm lying now, she'll lose all faith in humanity.

I smile, drop it into my handbag and take a sip of my coffee.

She's sipping her coffee too but her hand trembles and the coffee spills out onto the saucer. 'Pardon,' she says, her cheeks flush.

That's it. I'm out. Enough is enough. Because even if Mme Roux knew all about the lie I'd just spun, she couldn't hate me any more than I hate myself right now.

'Of course,' I say. But my voice comes out strangled. 'I should get back anyway.'

'When do you think it will be?' she asks as we stand.

I look at her. My mind taking a split second to comprehend what she's asking.

'The showing?' she prompts.

'Oh, I need to look at the schedule and go through the work,' I say, 'but I'd like to get it in for late next month.'

She smiles and nods, and then she walks me to her perfectly suburban door, and lets me out onto her perfectly suburban street, and I leave. But as I watch her face disappear behind the closing door, I know deep within my marrow that some scars never heal. And so, as I head down towards the metro station, I focus on anything I can to shake the memory of Mme Roux loose.

My phone pings from my bag.

It's an email ping.

I reach for it and check the time: 9.38. Shit. My article is due in just under an hour and a half. And so I'm hurrying down the road as I move through to my inbox.

And there it is, right at the top.

Sender: Stan Dixon.

Subject: *Better luck next time, princess.*

My pulse slams against my wrists as I click on the attached link.

It takes me through to an article in a rival publication. The title translates as 'The Night Sabine Roux Went Missing: A first person account'.

A mix of shock and disappointment pulses through me as I read all about how Sabine and Noah X left arguing. How could this have happened? Nobody else saw them leave, did they? A flash of that empty hallway . . .

It's around two hundred words in that my suspicion first ignites. But by the end, by the time I've read 'creative differences', we have a small, semi-contained fire on our hands. Yes, these eight hundred words I am reading are *my* words, simply reinterpreted, re-penned, embellished. But how?

Images flicker on the cinema screen of my mind: the blue-white glow of my laptop screen late last night as I emailed myself my work in progress; the office; my work computer; and then: *ParisObserver123.*

The generic password.

Someone broke into my email.

Someone leaked my first-person account.

And I think we all know who that someone is.

I hate him. I hate him. I hate him.

Ping.

Another email flies into my inbox.

This one is from Hyacinth. I can hear her voice in my head as I read it.

Harper. I need you back in the office. Now.

Chapitre vingt

By the time I get up the ninety-six stairs that lead to my front door I feel as though I'm one hundred and seven, everything hurts and I want to cry.

The feeling scares me because I'm not what one might call 'a crier'.

I can't thank my mother for much, I'm afraid, but my ability to weather storms and self-soothe is one tool she did inadvertently endow me with. You can't have everybody simultaneously falling apart in a household, someone has to be the strong one.

I turn the key in the lock, push open the door and drop my bag on the kitchen counter as the door slams behind me. I grab two of the mini bottles of Scotch from next to the kettle and head through to the bathroom. Emotional pain is like any other pain: it requires anaesthesia.

Taps: on.

But all I can hear against the sound of water running is Hyacinth's brittle voice as Stan and I stood in her office: 'Harper, it's too late now. Stan, we'll run with your Femicide piece instead.' And his face, pathologically smug.

Shame pulses through me as I twist off the cap of one of the bottles and down it.

Hyacinth gave me a chance. A proper chance. And I blew it.

I should have just written what she asked. I would have been finished by 3 pm yesterday instead of heading off to Le Voltage. It would have been sitting in Hyacinth's inbox before Stan had a chance to break into my emails.

And I know that makes me sound ultra-paranoid but that's what happened.

Yes, I should have changed my password. I've changed it now, of course I've changed it now. And I'm so highly strung about it I'm not even going to tell you what it is. But I should have done it before. That was careless.

But as obvious as Stan's actions were to me, as I stood in Hyacinth's office, I had a choice to make. I could tell her the truth and risk looking like a hysterical woman trying to shift the blame instead of taking responsibility for her own stuff-ups. The sort of woman who keeps flimsy passwords and inserts lies about 'creative differences' into her article to avoid personal embarrassment.

Or I could swallow my rage.

Vow to never let it happen again. Apologise. And go back to my desk before it got any worse.

I chose the latter.

And then sat there all afternoon, paralysed by fury, a deep gnawing in my solar plexus as I stared blankly at my screen until the clock hit 5.30 pm and I could come home.

I strip off my clothes and leave them in a small sad pile beside the bath, choose a Spotify playlist, then step into the water. I let it submerge me, like that might cleanse away everything I'm feeling right now. But there's a deep, inky-black ache inside me. It's Friday today. One week since Sabine went missing. Thirty-six hours since I told Luneau what happened that night. And yet, a quick Google search while I waited on the metro platform revealed Noah hasn't been arrested yet. That means they haven't found Sabine's phone; they haven't seen the video that had him run after her.

There's a storm brewing inside of me and I need to get it out. And so I dry off my hands, pick up my phone and navigate to Harrison's band page. There it is, right at the top, their most popular song. The song he wrote for me: 'When She Sleeps'.

Play.

And then, as the acoustic guitar echoes off the tiles in that way he'd describe as tinny, I sit back against the cool porcelain of the bath, close my eyes, and remember the night he first played it to me – it was in the living room of our apartment, it was raining outside, and it was just before things turned around for him. In hindsight, I'm pretty sure it was his way of warning me. Hot tears stream down my cheeks.

Her eyes they burn, burn, burn me, She can see straight through me, So it's only when she sleeps, I'm the man she used to see.

It's still as derivative as shit. But it still makes me cry, even after all this time. I sniff back tears, close my eyes and sink deeper into the water, letting the warmth embrace me. It's just today. Tomorrow will be better. I'll get up, maybe go to yoga, maybe swipe through an app and find a date. There's a whole world out there. A whole life ahead of me. But then why does it ache like this? The song finishes but the tears keep coming, and I just lie still with my eyes closed, waiting for the song to start up again.

But then, from somewhere in the darkness, comes a different sound. The beep of my phone.

My eyes flick open and I reach for it, squinting down at the screen.

Camilla.

I wipe the tears away with the back of my hand as I read and reread her message.

But it makes no sense at all.

Surprise! I'm outside! Which one is your flat? Xxx

Chapitre vingt et un

I wake up to Lana Del Rey, the smell of coffee and a sour mouthful of hair.

A moment of confusion, some misfiring synapses, and then I remember: Camilla. I never knew I could be so grateful for an app like Find My Friends until I saw her there last night, on the street outside, with her little suitcase. I pull off my eye mask – it's bright, too bright for autumn – and roll over, pull out the one earplug still lodged in my ear and reach for my phone.

It's just after 8.30 am.

And I should just let it go, but I can't help it. I scroll through to *The Paris Observer* website and there, on the landing page, is Stan's article. Disappointment ripples through me.

I hate him.

I sit up. My feet hit the floorboards. I take a deep breath and then I drag my heavy limbs through to the kitchen. Camilla is by the sink, pouring coffee from a cafetière and biting into an apple.

'Morning,' she says. 'Want some?'

'Yeah, thanks,' I say. And then I wander over to the sofa bed we set up for her and sit down, hugging my knees to my chest.

She looks at me with narrowed eyes.

'You haven't been looking at his story, have you?' she asks. We agreed last night over a bottle of wine that I wouldn't look at Stan's piece. We'd pretend it never happened. But then, I agree to lots of stupid things when tipsy.

That was just before she told me all about Mr Fourteenth Floor and her screening call with *Vogue*, and about how everything was falling into place because her sun was conjunct something or other. I didn't argue that point like I normally would, didn't point out that it wasn't the sun who sent *Vogue* her resume. It was just so great to have her here.

'Maybe,' I say.

'Well, don't.' She brings my coffee over to me. 'Anyway, I have something that will cheer you up.'

I take a sip and watch as she reaches into her open suitcase and pulls out a pair of fluffy handcuffs, throwing them at me. They land on my lap.

I start to laugh. 'You found them?' I say, picking them up.

I stayed with Camilla for the week before I left for Paris, having given up my room in the flatshare.

'They were behind the laundry basket. God knows how they got there.'

She takes her coffee and sits down next to me and puts her hand on my arm. 'It'll be okay, you know,' she says.

And usually I'd make some quip about 'How do you know, is Mercury about to go direct or something?' But this morning I just smile and nod. Lana gets super sad and so Camilla reaches for her phone and changes it to something upbeat. But as she looks down at the screen her face breaks into a grin.

'What?' I ask.

'Nothing,' she says, putting down her phone.

'*What?*' I repeat, with emphasis.

'He texted me.'

'Mr Fourteenth Floor?' I ask.

'Yeah.' Her cheeks flush pink. 'It's nothing. Just: *Have fun in Paris!*'

I take a sip of my coffee. 'Well, maybe that guy on Etsy was right after all,' I say. 'Though I'd still keep an eye on my credit score if I were you.'

She laughs and I laugh, but my eyes are heavy. We are silent for a few moments and then her forehead crinkles and she says, 'I'm worried about you, Harps.'

'Why? Because I'm still attracted to narcissistic creative types after all this time?' I ask, stroking the fur on the handcuffs.

'You know what I mean.' She sips on her coffee, watching me. 'But do you have a picture of him?'

'Sure,' I say, feeling my insides get a little colder. 'Just google Noah X husband, Paris.'

And as Camilla scrolls through her phone, I reach for my bag on the floor by the sofa and riffle through it for a paperclip.

'I don't see anything,' she says.

'Third page. It's the picture right at the bottom. A man and a woman. Tux.'

As I wait for her to find it, I lengthen out the paperclip so it's a long piece of wire. I insert one end into the handcuff lock, bending it backwards so it kinks. Now I have a small 'L' shape at the bottom. I insert that under the lock pin like a tiny finger and lift it up. The upper teeth release and it clicks open. Still got it.

I wrote about this once: 'What to do if your Tinder date leaves you stranded'. It won me over three hundred likes.

'Is this it?' Camilla asks, turning her phone to face me.

'Yep,' I say, clicking shut the handcuffs again and putting them down next to me.

'But he's so hot,' she says.

'So was Patrick Bateman in *American Psycho*,' I say.

'Wait, is that his wife?'

I nod and take a big sip of coffee.

She's frowning at the screen. 'God, he just *really* doesn't look like a killer, does he?' She looks up at me.

'Nope,' I say. 'But people always want killers to be monsters. Nobody wants it to be the hot guy. But sometimes it is.'

She sighs, puts her phone down and looks up at me. 'Right. Enough of this. We have plans today, go shower.'

'What sort of plans?' I ask, eyes narrowed as I take another sip of coffee.

'I'm not telling. Just go shower.'

～

Fifteen minutes later I'm heading out of the steam of the shower, my hair in a towel as I head to my room to change. Camilla is still sitting on the sofa bed, scrolling through her phone.

I can see straight into my neighbour's window but she's not there today. So I drop my towel, pull on my underwear and an over-sized cream jumper, then a black pair of jeans. I pull my hair back into a loose pony and put on a pair of dangly earrings.

Then I head back through to the living room. Camilla is exactly where I left her.

'What are you doing?' I ask.

She looks up at me and I know immediately: something has happened. I head over to her. 'What are you looking at?' I ask, my pulse thumping like it already knows something I don't yet.

'I was googling Noah X and then I looked up Sabine Roux,' she says, her voice small and fragile.

'And?' I ask.

'I found this.'

She hands me her phone. It's an article. The first thing I notice is it's in English. I glance up at the URL. It's from a UK tabloid. And the headline reads 'Does Paris Have a Serial Killer?'.

I scan the text.

First a legal secretary, Matilde Beaumont, 28, was found dead in a forest to the south-west of Paris. Now, three weeks later, another body has been uncovered. This one belongs to a student at Parsons

Paris, Sabine Roux, 22. Both women were attractive and in their twenties, were French nationals, disappeared in inner Paris, and were found strangled and laid out in parkland. What other similarities are there between these two cases? More details as we have them, but for now we'll leave you with these terrifying questions: 'Is this the work of the same killer? And, if so, who is next?'

A shiver runs through me.

'What the hell,' I say, swallowing hard.

'What if it's true, Harps? You were right there. It could have been you.'

'It wasn't a serial killer,' I say. 'It was Noah. I'm not saying he did it on purpose but I saw him go off with her.'

'That doesn't mean he killed her,' Camilla says.

I frown down at the words. 'He had two hours, a shit alibi and a reason to kill her. It was him.'

She's wrapping her arms around herself now, like it's cold. But it's not cold in here, the heating is right up. 'I'm just scared for you,' she says.

'It's a tabloid. Last week they were probably announcing Jennifer Aniston and Brad Pitt had eloped before purchasing an avocado farm. Also, think about it: how many cases have you heard of where a girl was strangled and her body was left in a park? Tonnes, right? It's not exactly a niche method. They just want to sell magazines.'

She gives a small nod and I sit down next to her.

'So, what are we doing today?' I ask, trying to change the subject.

She smiles, reaches into her bag and pulls out two A4 printouts. 'We may or may not be going to the happiest place on earth.'

'Sephora?' I ask.

'Fuck off.' She laughs, putting down her phone. 'We're going to . . . Disneyland!'

Chapitre vingt-deux

Seven rides, one questionable burger, three lattes, two long train trips, two pairs of Mickey Mouse ears, and twelve hours later, we're in a bar not too far from home. Camilla has just ordered four more shots and my calves and feet are aching from walking around the theme park all day. I want to go home. The lights are dim and we're sitting on two stools at the end of the metal bar, trying not to get elbowed by strangers. The coloured glass of the liquor bottles – amber, brown and blue – refracts the lights that hang from the ceiling.

'Just these two more. Promise,' she says with an it'll-be-fun grin.

I reach for my phone and check the time – 10.02 pm – then go to scroll through my emails. But Camilla grabs it from me.

'You promised no work,' she says, squishing her face against mine and holding up the camera. We both smile and she takes a selfie.

'Oh, it's a pretty one. Send it to me so I can show him how amazing my life is?' she says. She's wearing a gold sequined dress she took from Anne's cupboard, with a big black blazer hanging over her seat back. I'm wearing a black lace top, the same black jeans I wore earlier today and my leather jacket is on the stool beneath me.

I send the photo to her, she forwards it to Mr Fourteenth Floor, and I resist posting it to Instagram – I already uploaded one just like it with #whatanight when we arrived an hour ago – then I put my phone face down on the bar.

The bartender delivers our drinks, Camilla grins at him, slides one towards me and we both pour a bit of salt on our hands. Then it's cheers, salt, drink, and a lemon wedge. Heat in my throat, my stomach, my veins and the room starts to spin a bit.

'Can we go now?' I say, putting my glass down. I don't even like tequila.

'No. We still have one more. We can't waste it,' she says. 'Ready.'

But then her phone screen lights up from the bar beside her. Her eyes get big and her mouth opens a bit then she looks at me: 'He's calling me.'

I look down at the screen. It's the sketch the Etsy-guy did. Mr Fourteenth Floor.

'Well, go answer it,' I say.

Camilla grabs her phone and pushes through the crowd, and just before she disappears behind a big guy in a dark blazer, she answers.

The bartender comes back to collect our empty glasses, a man in a grey coat pushes past me to get to the bar and I look back towards the door for Camilla. But I can't see her – she must be outside.

There are two more shots sitting on the bar and I do one of them alone, then reach again for my own phone. That's when I see it: a missed call. From a US number.

Noah.

My abdomen clenches: why is he calling? Did he see that first person account? Is he pissed because he thinks I went to the press? Or is it about the police? Is he worried I told them about that video? And why the fuck do I feel guilty?

I'm about to reach for the other shot, when a hand finds my arm and I swivel. It's Camilla. She's back. But her dark eyes are huge and her grip is tight. She leans into my ear and says loudly, 'We have to leave.'

'Sure,' I say.

But she's looking back at the direction she just came from, and her shoulders are hunched.

'What's going on?' I ask, putting on my leather jacket.

She's shaking her head as though she doesn't know whether to believe something or not.

'There's a guy out there,' she says. 'I want to show him to you.'

'Okay,' I say, as I grab my things and follow her through the crowd.

We're outside now and the wind is cold against my cheeks. She's looking left and right, scouring the street. And I'm not sure what she's looking for because there are just a bunch of people wearing navy and black with tasteful tailoring and well-cut shiny hair.

'There,' she says, pointing.

I follow her finger. There's a guy walking away from us.

'The guy in the cap?'

'Yeah,' she says.

I take him in: he's tall, broad shoulders. But soon he's gone and I can't really see anything else.

'What about him?'

'Harps, I know this sounds insane but I think he's following you.'

My face crunches up into an expression that says: 'What?'

'I've seen him before. He was outside your flat when I arrived last night.'

I look back to her. All colour has drained from her face.

'What did he look like?' I ask. Maybe it's one of the neighbours.

'Tall, dark, beaky,' she says. And I'm pretty sure this is just because of that article she read this morning, but she's scared. Really scared.

I look back towards the space where that guy was standing just a few moments ago, but he's well gone now. 'Hon, are you sure? I mean there are a lot of tall guys with dark hair around here.' I mentally run through the guys I've slept with while in Paris. *Please, dear god, don't let me have a stalker situation on my hands.* But none of them match her description. Camilla is gripping her jaw and I need to reassure her. 'I mean, look around.'

She glances back inside, over the crowd – and there are, indeed, many tall, dark-haired men among them. But then her gaze snaps back to me.

'I'm sure.'

~

I wake up breathless, my legs tangled in damp sheets. I was having a bad dream but I can't remember what it was. I pull my eye mask from my face and lie still in the darkness, my eyes fixed on a silvery spider's web in the upper corner of my window, until my breath slows down. I'd go back to sleep but I need to pee, so I tiptoe through to the bathroom in a daze.

There's a blue-white glow coming from the sofa. It's Camilla. I can just make out her face in the light cast from her phone.

'Mills?' I ask.

She looks up at me.

'Are you okay?' I ask. 'Can't you sleep?'

She shakes her head and I feel around on the wall for a light switch.

Flick.

We both squint against the light. She's huddled beneath her blankets, tears streaming down her face.

'What's going on?' I ask, moving over to her and sitting down.

'I'm just so scared,' she says, 'my heart won't stop racing.'

I take her hand in both of mine. 'What are you scared of?'

She takes a deep breath. 'What if something happens to you?' she says, holding up her phone.

I look at it. 'What have you been reading?'

'Everything,' she says. 'I can't stop reading it. I'm telling you, that guy tonight was bad news. I could feel it. I know it was the same guy I saw outside here. I just know. And as soon as I clocked him, he left. Why would he do that if he wasn't doing something bad? What if that article's right? What if there is some crazed killer on the loose?' It all comes out like a waterfall.

'Hon,' I say, squeezing her hand. 'Have you seen how many door codes are between me and the outside world? How many stairs? Someone would have to be pretty fucking committed to kill me.'

She starts to laugh. 'Don't joke about this. It's serious. It could have been you.'

'I'll be careful,' I say. 'I promise. But also, have you met me?' I smile. 'I'm the girl who writes about how to get out of duct tape. I'm the girl who told you to scratch a guy's face if you're ever attacked so he knows he'll have to answer questions about it if you turn up dead. I'm the girl who knows how to get out of a car boot. Good luck to any psycho who tries that shit on,' I say.

She squeezes my hand.

'I just . . .' she starts. 'I wish you'd just come home. I wish I'd never sent you the advert for this job. Then you'd still be living in London and you'd be safe.'

'But also, I'd still be miserable. A tabloid wrote that article. I'm not sure we should be basing our life choices on anything they say, you know?'

'Yeah,' she says, wiping her tears away. 'I'm just scared.'

'I know,' I say, gently. 'And if I could come home I would. But I've worked so hard to get here. And I finally have something of my own. I can't just run away from that.'

She sniffs back tears.

'Okay?'

She nods and I get up.

'So, I'm going to go pee, and then I'm going to make us some camomile tea, and then we are going to watch something super funny on Netflix. Yes?'

She nods again and I smile. I head to the kitchen and flick on the kettle, then go through to the loo. But as I close the door behind me, all I can hear is my pulse in my ears, and when I sit down my vision gets fuzzy. Because I'm great at calming other people down, defusing things with humour and keeping my shit together in a crisis. But sitting here with just my own thoughts, I can't help but wonder, *What if Camilla's right?*

Chapitre vingt-trois

'You're in early,' Wesley says, plonking himself down in his chair.

I glance up at him and give a small nod.

And as I watch him lean forward and stab his password into his keyboard, I can't help but wonder what his Tinder profile might look like. Is he smiling in his pictures? Does his bio say: friendly, kind, normal guy seeks kindred spirit? What would I do if I saw him on an app, the way Camilla saw her new guy?

What if I accidentally super-swiped him?

I shake the thoughts away and look back at the street scene on my screen. I've been in since 7 am, wading through footage on that hard drive Sabine's mother pressed into my hands on Friday. Needing there to be another angle on there somewhere; another way for me to write her story.

Because last week gave me a taste of what it might feel like to have the job I wanted. And it's hard to just let that go. But here I am, back to writing the 'accessible' pieces on art and cinema that give people like Stan intellectual superiority complexes.

But then, at least I still have a job. I might not be so lucky if Hyacinth knew what really happened on that roof with Noah;

if she knew how I got this drive, that I'd gone to Sabine's mother's house searching for a story without running it past her first. Of course, if that story had worked out the way I planned, going there would have shown 'initiative'. But it didn't.

So now all I can do is watch yet another boring, drawn-out street scene and pray.

Raw is an understatement. It's as though Sabine turned on her iPhone camera and then wandered around Paris, hoping something would happen by serendipity. Most of the videos are filmed either around Le Voltage, where she used to work, or Montmartre, presumably because that's where she'd sit for Noah's paintings. The one I'm watching at the moment is at least familiar, it's the clip from the bridge I saw on her Vimeo page, the one that video of the couple fighting was cut from. I've passed the part where they run through their sequence: fight, stare each other down, embrace. I've passed the part where it would usually fade to black and the words *Love Actually* would flash up in white on the screen. And now I'm watching the next bit, the part after that, the part where the arguing couple moves out of frame and the camera keeps rolling. It's as though Sabine didn't understand the weight of what she'd captured until she watched it back. There are two other couples on either side of the frame now. To the left is a girl with long, shiny dark hair so straight it looks artificial, who poses and reposes as her boyfriend takes her picture on his phone. She checks it, issues instructions and he takes another; just your garden-variety Instagram husband at work. And on the other side, a couple stands hand in hand, looking out at the water. She's small and wearing a sundress and the guy takes off his jacket and puts it around her shoulders like maybe she was cold. There's something painted on the back. I'm peering in at it thinking, *What is that, a tiger?*

Then, with no warning, no fucking footsteps, nothing, I hear, 'Whatcha doin', princess?'

My shoulders hunch and my body recoils as I swivel in my chair.

'Hi, Stan,' I say, minimising the viewing window as some pretty strong lower-octane thoughts bounce around my skull. Mainly variations on: *Oh fuck off.*

'Did you have a nice weekend?' I say, in that brittle way people do when they're being disingenuous. I hope he notices.

'Marvellous,' he says, his eyes flicking from me to the now empty screen to the hard drive. He's wondering what I was doing. Why I was so quick to close down the window. 'Yourself?'

'Fantastic,' I say, and then I turn away from him and look back at my screen, opening up a perfectly innocent Word document containing a list of pitches pre-approved by Hyacinth.

'Well, chin up. It's a new day, a new week!' And then fuckhead disappears off to the kitchen. A moment later the coffee machine whirrs to life and I take the opportunity to eject Sabine's hard drive and drop it into my handbag.

I stare at the list of pitch ideas. There has to be one here that doesn't make me want to shove a pencil up my nose.

If only I'd changed my password, none of this would have happened. As if on cue, Stan emerges with his coffee. I can feel his eyes on me as he moves over to his desk but I refuse to look up.

I hate him.

Instead, I try to ignore the heat simmering beneath my skin and focus on the screen. There's a photographic exhibition in the 1st arrondissement I could go to: a young German photographer with strong Saul Leiter influences. That would get me out of the office for a while, away from dangerous combinations like pencils and Stan.

Pulling up the gallery webpage, I press print on the address; the printer hums with industry.

I glance up at the time, it's just before nine. Hyacinth will be in soon. And if I can avoid seeing the disappointment in her eyes for a few hours more that would suit me just fine. So I pick up my bag, turn off my computer, grab my coat and phone, and head for the elevator door.

~

Twenty minutes later I'm on the platform at Bastille, standing back from the edge as the metro arrives. There aren't that many of us here now. The responsible people of the world are in their office cubicles by now. Doing their personal expenses. Seething as they reply to a passive-aggressive email from a colleague. Applying for another job. Sexting with the guy from last night while pretending to work. All the covert operations that allow the more superficial aspects of office life to hum along unhindered.

It's just me, and the artists, the retired, the unemployed and the young mothers with strollers. I press down the metal lever – it's cool in my hand – the foghorn sounds and the doors slide open. A man gets off, pushing past me in a mood, and three of us get on. I take a seat halfway between the doors, put in my earbuds and scroll through to the podcast I started this morning on my commute into work. It's just been revealed that the DNA evidence we've relied on until this point may not mean what we thought it did. Because DNA doesn't exactly stay put. We leave it on escalator rails, door handles, coins and public transport. It can then be transferred onto anyone or anything that touches it, travelling with them before being transferred again. So right now, each and every one of us has our genetic material on a hand we've never held, in a room we've never even entered. And that's scary as shit, because if you can't rely on the certainty of DNA, what the hell can you rely on in this world?

I look around the carriage as I listen to the narrator. Beyond her voice I can hear a baby cry and I look towards the sound. His mother picks him up, coos. A man nearby makes goo-goo faces at him. The train stops, a couple of people get on, a few get off, and then we speed up again.

A couple of girls in matching school uniforms are sitting together laughing.

Something twinges inside me and I scroll through my pictures, smiling down at the ones Camilla and I took on Saturday at Disneyland: our faces squished up together before the haunted house. Me looking fake terrified in the line outside *Big Thunder*. A selfie of us in sequined Mickey Mouse ears in front of Sleeping Beauty's castle.

The brakes screech and I look up at the board. A little white light flashes beside Hôtel de Ville.

The doors open. The foghorn sounds. People get off. Others get on. I watch them fumble around and take their seats. Glancing at their shoes – sneakers, ballet flats, brogues – and then their faces. We start to move again. The baby has stopped crying now and the schoolgirls are sitting silently scrolling through their phones. Behind them stands a man who's—

My heart stalls.

And my breath gets très fast.

Because it's *him*.

At least, I think it's him. He's wearing an unbranded navy cap but he looks exactly like what Camilla described: tall, dark, beaky and somehow familiar. It's like I've seen him before but I don't know where.

I pull my earbuds from my ears and stare at him as he looks down at his phone. The options run through my mind: was he at Noah's party? Or has he been following me for a while now and I clocked him subliminally?

I swallow hard and watch the windows, waiting, waiting, waiting for the black of the tunnel to turn to light. I glance up at the little lights on the wall – we're arriving at Châtelet. A soothing voice over the loudspeaker reminds us in French, English and then Spanish to take our belongings with us when we leave. I look over to the man, he sits still, staring down at his screen. People are lining up at the door, holding on for stability as we draw to a stop. I glance back at the man: still no movement.

It's now or never.

The doors beep and open. I wait for a moment to see if he moves. He doesn't. And so I stand up and rush over to the door and out onto the platform the moment before the doors close again.

I look around me. There's the woman with the stroller and a guy with grey hair, a couple of other people from other carriages all heading for the exit. And then . . . *shit.*

He's there too.

Standing between me and the staircase.

He must have seen me and used the other door.

The train starts to move again and the air swirls with dust. Everyone is moving towards the stairs except me and him. He's just standing still, doing nothing, staring down at his phone, frowning. The little hairs on the back of my neck are standing up on end now.

I'm going to have to move past him.

And so I look down at my phone like I'm texting someone and rush to join the crowd.

The air is filled with chattering, a text message beeping on someone's phone and the thud of footsteps as we move up the cement stairs, and I don't know if he's behind me or not and I don't want to turn around because then he'll know I've clocked him.

And what then?

But my phone is still there in my hands and, fuck this, I have an idea. I move through to the camera, rush to the top of the stairs and, when I get there, I turn around and start snapping photographs.

One.

Two.

Three.

Four.

The lens isn't specifically aimed at him, but he'll know he's in the frame. So the question is, what will he do about it? Here, in the midst of witnesses with CCTV watching?

But he does nothing at all. Just dips his head and moves past me. I swivel to watch him go. He doesn't look back but heads up the stairs and I'm left leaning against the cool tiles of the station, flicking through photos of a bunch of strangers wandering up the stairs. And as I swipe through the photographs I see him for what he is. Just some guy walking up the stairs in the metro station, wondering why some random girl is taking pictures.

And I realise: I'm losing it.

Chapitre vingt-quatre

Two days later, I'm staring up at a window. The light – right in the middle of the third floor – is glowing a soft amber. I can see movement behind the thin gauzy curtains; he's home. And so I press the buzzer for his apartment: number twelve.

Bzzzz.

A woman with a vape walks past me, she blows out a big cloud of smoke and now the air smells of maple syrup as I look in through the green metal and glass security door: mustard floor tiles, gentle lighting, brass letterboxes and a wide wooden staircase. I press the buzzer again.

Bzzzzz.

And I know I shouldn't be here. It's selfish and unfair. But I wouldn't be if there was anybody else who could help me. But there's not. And so here I am.

~

I awoke this morning, like any morning, to the sound of church bells – clang-ding-dong – pulled my sleeping mask from my eyes and reached for my phone. There were two messages. One from Camilla: *I have an interview on Monday!* And one from my mother: a picture of her and Neville on a jetty somewhere, grinning out at the camera, his arm wrapped tightly around her. This means she's right on schedule – they'll have another big row in about two weeks. Maybe three. It'll be over for good then. She sends me pictures like this when she needs to prove how happy she is, like if she can prove it to *me*, it might become true. And she only does that shit when the wheels are about to fall off. I've come to recognise the signs. I've also learned there's nothing I can do to stop it.

I trudged through to the kitchen, flicked on the kettle and scrolled aimlessly through Instagram as it hissed to life. Quotes. Selfies. And adverts for magnetic eyelashes, teeth whitening treatments, fillers, and dodgy-looking hair extensions – my morning reminder from the powers that be that I'm not quite good enough just as I am.

And then I did the thing I'm not supposed to do anymore.

Maybe it was out of habit, or maybe I just secretly hate myself, but something had me typing *H-a-r-r-i-* into the search bar and then clicking on his profile.

The room shook just a little as I took in the most recent post.

A bedroom. A view of the Hollywood Hills. Floor to ceiling windows and light wood floorboards. There was a big bookshelf filled with vinyl records and the brightly coloured spines of novels, a king-sized bed with white linen, a free-standing bathtub with big clawed feet and, in the corner, a piano.

The hashtag said: #wemoved

It was the exact room we'd dreamed of when we were together, down to the clawed feet of the bathtub. When we first broke up I had this theory that until I could paint him out of the imaginary future I'd created in my head for the two of us I wouldn't get over him. And so I got to work. But now I see: he'd erased me first. He'd taken my dreams and given them to her.

The kettle boiled and sang out, it switched off, and as I made my coffee, I dropped in a swig of whiskey. And then I waited for my blood to slow, tapped on the window to say hello to Mr Oiseau and told myself the day could only get better.

Judy was on the phone when I arrived at work.

'Morning,' I said as I passed her, still mellow from my boozy coffee.

She smiled at me in reply.

I sat down at my desk and powered on my computer as I looked around. The office was quiet, almost everyone was out except me, Judy and a freelancer wearing earbuds, working at a hot desk. I scanned through my inbox and a sense of calm came over me. Because it was okay. It didn't matter what Harrison did or did not do. This was me now: Harper Brown, Journalist. I had done it. And I needed to hang onto that. I was no longer that woman he cheated on, the woman who made excuses for him, who sacrificed everything for him. I was different now. I was stronger. And I'm not even sure this version of me wants that place in the Hollywood Hills anymore.

I pulled up the article I was working on – the Saul Leiter inspired German artist whose exhibition I went to see after that interlude on the metro – and read over what I'd penned thus far.

It wasn't half bad.

It wasn't going to put me on the landing page but that would come. I had to believe, *one day*, that would come. It's just one day felt so far away because I'd been so close.

My gaze moved to Satan's (whoops, I mean Stan's) empty desk then landed on my handbag. Sabine's hard drive was still in there and I needed to send it back to her mother. It wasn't fair to keep it. My stomach clenched as I imagined Mme Roux opening the envelope and reading the note, the expression on her face when she called the gallery to follow up on what had happened, and realised I'd lied to her.

Still, it needed to be done.

I went over to the stationery cupboard, pulled out a mid-sized envelope and went back to my desk, pulling out the drive – a flash of her mother's eyes as she pressed it into my hands. I copied the address down on the front of the envelope in my best version of round schoolgirl cursive, so she couldn't recognise my handwriting, even though there is no way in hell she'd be able to do that anyway. And I was just about to put the drive and the cord inside.

But something wouldn't let me.

Maybe it was Harrison and the clawed feet of his new bath.

The need to make something of myself. Something that would mean he was wrong to have left me. That I was worth something too.

Maybe it was the fact that it was Wednesday and Noah had still not been arrested. I'd told the police about the video, told them about the white car, told them about how he ran after Sabine and why. How could they have not found anything at all? What the hell were they doing with their time? Maybe Stan was right and the police *were* lazy.

Or, maybe it was guilt. Because every time I glanced across at that hard drive, I'd think of Mme Roux, of the way her hand trembled as she lifted her coffee cup, the way grief clung to the air around her. It wasn't fair.

I picked up the drive, glanced at the envelope and bit down on my lower lip. Maybe I could help move things along.

Because I knew what Noah had *told* me about the nature of his relationship with Sabine, but it wasn't like he'd never lied to me before. What if there was something else on that drive to prove they were having an affair? Something else she might have eventually threatened to show Noah's wife? Something to explain why she took that video of us in the first place.

Anything to show the police.

And the office was almost empty. I had the perfect opportunity.

So I reached for the cord and plugged it into my computer, attached my earbuds and started watching where I'd left off.

~

Fast forward half an hour and ten aimless Parisian street scenes, to the moment I clicked on a folder. It was named 'Untitled Folder' so my expectations were not particularly high going in.

It contained two video clips. Nothing new there.

I took a sip of lukewarm coffee, slouched into my seat a little deeper and pressed play on the first, bracing myself for another walk around Saint-Germain-des-Prés or Montmartre.

But up came a computer with some sort of document on the screen. The camera moved in towards it and Sabine's hand came into frame, pointing at a line of text. The camera lingered for a few more seconds and then it turned and Sabine's face filled the screen. This was new. She hadn't featured in any of her other videos, so why this one? Her mouth opened in a shock-horror gesture, her hand by her cheek like she was mimicking *The Scream*. There she was – still breathing, still hoping, looking exactly like she did in Noah's paintings down to her nose ring and the red string around her wrist – but now she was gone. Forever. Something twisted inside me and I closed down the window, quickly clicking on the second video because I didn't want to feel those feelings.

This one opened near the front desk of Le Voltage. The camera tracked towards the back room, the door opened and we moved inside. A small room with wooden crates the shape of canvases leaning up against the wall to the right and a sturdy metal set of shelves nestled into the left-hand corner. It was full of printing paper, boxes of pens, files and—

Of course that was the precise moment glum Wesley decided to return to the office. I felt him stomping across the floor before I saw him. I would have closed the video window if he posed any threat but his eyes were glued to his phone. Still, I kept my glance trained on him as he sat down at his desk and turned on his computer.

He saw me watching him and his mouth moved with what I am guessing was a begrudging: 'Hi.'

So I said, 'Hey,' back, and it was right after that that I heard it.

'*Je sais ce que tu fais, Agnès.*'

It was coming through the earbuds. It was Sabine's voice.

My eyes snapped back to the screen just in time to see Sabine blow a kiss at the lens and then the screen go black.

Shit.

I'd missed something.

I reached for the mouse and rewound the clip.

We were back in the small room. There were wooden canvas crates leaning up against the right-hand wall, and metal shelves to the left containing files, paper and stationery . . . but I kept watching this time. One of the canvas crates was open and the painting inside was fully visible. It was of a man at a piano with two women around him, and the whole thing was bathed in candlelight. As we moved in closer towards it, my breath caught in my throat. I stared at the image, tracing the outline, the colours, the form and holding it up to the light of my memory thinking, *What the actual fuck?*

Because, it couldn't be.

All I could do was stare at that painting and try to steady my breath, watching as the camera swivelled and Sabine looked straight into the lens and said, '*Je sais ce que tu fais, Agnès*,' before blowing a kiss.

That means: *I know what you're doing, Agnès.*

What was this?

Wesley was fucking around with the printer by then, his lips moving every now and then and I wasn't sure if he was talking to me, so I pulled my earbuds out to check.

'Is your system working? Mine's super slow,' he asked.

'Mine's fine,' I replied as snippets of memory from a long-gone conversation came trickling back – Austria, ceiling panels, SS, fire. It had been with a gallerist in Vienna, not long before Harrison finally gave me the shove. I'd had a lot of time on my hands by then. That was where I learned about that painting. Or rather, that's where I learned about the fire and everything it destroyed. I went back to the hotel room and while I waited for Harrison to finish 'rehearsing' I googled it, imagining a world where those paintings were still hanging on a wall somewhere.

And that painting of the man at the piano was one of them.

But I had to be wrong about this. It made no sense.

I was still staring at my screen when the elevator doors slid open and the sound of Stan talking on the phone snapped me back into the present moment. I looked back over my shoulder and he was watching me as he headed across to his desk. I turned back to my computer, set my face to nonchalant, opened my email account and sent myself those two videos, ejected the drive and dropped it back into my bag for safekeeping. Then I dropped the empty envelope in the wastepaper bin beneath my desk.

I put my phone in my bag, stood up and took it to the bathroom.

As soon as I closed the cubicle door, I pulled up a search engine and typed in everything I remembered about that conversation in Vienna: fire, World War II, paintings, destroyed, ceiling panels, SS.

Up came a Wikipedia page for Schloss Immendorf.

I scanned the details.

8th of May, 1945 . . . last day of WWII in the region . . . Schloss Immendorf set on fire by retreating German troops . . . Destroying . . ..

> *See also: Lost artworks.*

Click, scroll and then there it was: *Schubert at the Piano.*

By Klimt.

Destroyed in 1945.

I was right.

But what did this mean? Was that painting in Le Voltage a fake? Was Agnès dealing in fakes? It made no sense. And what was that document about? Why had Sabine sectioned it off in the same folder as that Klimt?

I put my phone on mute, pulled up the first video again and watched it play. As soon as the camera was close enough to the screen to read the text, I paused, took a screenshot and zoomed in.

Sabine's finger was pointing to a line that read: *Entered into by and between Hintos Holdings LTD (the seller) and LeKOR Corp (the purchaser, and together with the seller, the parties).* Right below that was a section called Recitals where the details of the transaction were listed. It was for a bond issued by a company named Genovexa. And it was worth 100 million euro.

Yes, 100 million euro. That's 100 million wheels of brie.

I focused on the name right above Sabine's finger: Hintos Holdings.

Why was she pointing at that?

So I did what anybody would do. I googled it.

And I found it immediately: Hintos Holdings belongs to a man named Philip Crawford-White. A philanthropist based in the Isle of Man. It was listed on his webpage along with a tonne of charitable activities. Nothing strange there.

But Sabine's words echoed in my mind: *I know what you're doing, Agnès.*

And I needed to know: what the fuck *had* Agnès been doing?

It felt like the contents of that folder were a cryptic message from the grave.

I wanted to find out what it all meant. And I tried to do it for myself. But by 7.30 pm, everyone else had gone home and I was no closer to an answer. I needed someone to decode that document for me. Someone who knew about finance. And there was only one person I could think of.

Which brings us back to me standing here, right now, outside Thomas's building, pressing his buzzer. And here I will stay, for as long as it takes for him to answer.

Bzzzz.

Chapitre vingt-cinq

I press the buzzer again and wait. Why isn't he answering? My fingers twitch as I stare at the numeric keypad by the door.

Because I know the code.

I saw Thomas punch it in the night we came back here and I gave him the flick. It wasn't on purpose. I was texting Camilla when it happened. I'd just pressed 'send' and looked up at the exact moment his fingers traced the corners of a square. And so I'm being polite right now. I could easily type it in, go upstairs, lie and say a neighbour let me in and knock on his door. And I absolutely will if he doesn't answer soon.

But wait, what's that? Is that the intercom crackling? I stare at the speaker.

'Hello?' comes his voice.

That's my cue; I use my cutest voice. 'Hey. It's Harper. Can I come up?'

The intercom goes silent but it's still crackling so I know he's still there.

'Harper?' he says. 'What are you doing here?'

He sounds a lot less happy to hear from me than I was hoping for. And while I could tell him the truth – that I'm here to use him for his skill base – I suspect a better way to get in the door is flattery.

'I just wanted to see you,' I say. 'To talk to you. Things ended so weirdly last time.' My voice comes out a perfect, fragile saccharine.

'Now's not a good time,' he says.

This is the problem with playing the crazy-girl card too well: they think you're crazy.

'Please, Thomas. I need you,' I whine. Yes, we're back to damsel in distress.

The intercom is scratchy and he isn't replying. I look up to his window in case he might be watching me and I could wave but he's not.

'Thomas? *Please.* I have no one to turn to. You have no idea what's been going on for me.' My voice is louder now. And I'm enunciating slowly so anyone walking past, any of his neighbours coming in or out of the building, might hear me. Because Thomas is a good guy. And so the best way to get him to let me inside is to make him feel very, very bad.

'I mean this girl I know was *murdered.* You might have read about her in the papers. I . . . I just don't want to be alone right now . . . please. I'm begging you.' I find myself throwing in a couple of fake sobs.

And then I wait.

Nothing.

Fuck.

'Please,' I try again, my voice a high-pitched screech.

The intercom crackles.

'Fine,' he says, finally. 'Just give me a second.'

And so I stand on the pavement, waiting for the buzzer to sound so I can go up.

And then, a few moments later: Bzzzzz.

~

I pull open the door and head inside, past the letterboxes on my left, towards the big wooden staircase in front of me. I take the stairs two by two, holding onto the thick, dark wood bannister all the way to the third floor.

I'm out of breath by the time I get to his door. The same door I slammed shut after me, right after I pulled my meet-the-parents stunt. But right now I need to win him over, which means acting extra 'normal'.

I take a deep breath, flick my hair over to one side and knock.

Tap-tap-tappity-tap.

A cute, seductive knock. The sort you want to answer.

I stand still, listening for sounds inside.

Footsteps.

The brass doorknob turns and the door creaks as it opens. Thomas looks just like he did over a week ago at the grocery store, but his tan has faded now and his caramel hair is the smallest bit longer, flopping over one brown eye.

'Hi,' I say. Breathy.

'Hi,' he replies, his eyes wide like he's trying to read me. 'Do you want to come in?' Then he moves aside and I nod and move past him. He smells like laundry detergent and cigarettes, and a moment later the door clicks closed behind us.

'Can I get you something to drink?' he asks, in typical polite British fashion, like he didn't just try to get me to sod off.

'Sure,' I say. 'Scotch?'

Then I sit down on the brown leather sofa and watch him pull a bottle of Scotch from one cupboard in the kitchen and two glasses from another. Ice clinks and drinks are poured. I look around the large room: the TV is on. Netflix. It's on mute. His computer, sitting on a desk against the wall, is on. His cigarettes and silver lighter are sitting on the coffee table in front of me beside his scarf – a multicoloured stripe. The bed in the corner is made this time and the candle beside it is unlit. But aside from those small details, everything else is exactly as it was last time I was here.

'Hot in Herre' starts playing from my bag and I reach for it: *Camilla is calling.*

Shit.

I stare down at the phone – I can't *not* answer, not after the weekend, she'll send out a search party – and then back up at Thomas, who is watching me from the kitchen. 'Sorry,' I say, screwing up my face a bit, 'I have to get this, my friend is super anxious.'

His jaw tightens like he's wishing he never let me in but I answer anyway and say: 'Hey.'

Maybe seeing me as a caring friend will soften Thomas up.

'Hey,' Camilla says, 'just checking on you. Any news?'

'Nope,' I say. 'I'm just at Thomas's house.' And then I give him a small smile. But, shit, that's veering into crazy-girl territory, so I add, 'A friend.'

'Wait, which one was Thomas?' Camilla asks.

But I can't exactly answer that with him listening, so instead I say, 'Yeah, okay, thanks, chat tomorrow?'

'Is he listening?' Camilla asks with a small laugh.

'Bye,' I say in a sing-song voice.

And then we hang up.

Thomas comes over and hands me my drink.

'Cheers,' he says. Our eyes meet and we clink glasses.

'Cheers,' I say and I take a sip.

He's trying to figure out what to say. I watch him grapple with the options. Should he start by telling me how he's met someone else, just in case I am here to win him back? Or should he do the kind thing and find out whether I'm okay first? I mean, I did say the 'm' word: murdered.

'So?' he asks, sitting down beside me.

What will he choose? What will he choose? What will he choose?

217

'Are you okay?' he asks. His face is a tightly knit ball. *Option B.*

I nod and take a sip of my drink. 'It was just such a shock,' I say. 'I mean one minute I'm at a party and the next I'm looking at her picture in the paper, knowing I saw her right before she died.'

'God,' he says. 'Who was it?'

'Sabine Roux,' I say, doing my best wounded bird impersonation. I need to get his sympathy, so he's amenable when I ask for his help in a little while. 'You've probably read about it in the papers?' I say.

'Right,' he says. 'It was that artist's party, right?'

'Yes,' I say, 'I was there for work. Talk about the assignment from hell.'

'God, I know those,' he says, eyes to the floor while he sips his drink.

I glance at his body language: his feet are pointed away from me and his hands are grasping his glass instead of reaching for my hand right now. It all screams: I want to be nice but also I want you to leave. Now is not the time to ask for help.

I need to soften him up first.

The man with the frilly neckline is watching us from the canvas, wondering why the hell I'm back. Why won't I just leave his owner alone? 'This is interesting,' I say, standing up and moving over to it.

This is strategic, the painting is right by the bed. Because I'm going to need to sleep with him. Then he'll feel like he took advantage of my vulnerable state and he'll do whatever he needs to do to make himself feel better about that.

'It came with the flat,' Thomas says, swigging down his drink. I hear the glass hit the coffee table, then his footsteps.

I reach out to touch the painting, like I'm inspecting the texture.

I can feel his heat behind me now. *Perfect.*

I turn and face him, our eyes meet and his pupils are huge so I know he wants me. I almost feel bad.

～

Twenty sweaty minutes later, we're lying naked, the sheets tangled around our legs, one of his arms slung over my shoulder and my head on his chest. I'm listening to his heart beating, staring at the ugly painting once again.

'That was great,' I say, snuggling into his chest.

And then I slowly, fluidly, pull away from him, reaching beside the bed for my (strategically positioned) handbag. I pull out my lip gloss first, unscrew the top and dip my finger into it, swirling it around and then running the tip over my lips as he watches. It smells like vanilla.

I look at him over my shoulder. 'Want some?'

He shakes his head and I drop it back into my bag and reach for what I really wanted all along.

My phone.

'What are you doing?' he asks, watching me as it unlocks.

'Just checking my emails. Work.' I smile back at him. 'You know how it is.'

I'm careful with the expression on my face; he's watching me and I need to seem calm yet confused.

I give a little frown at the screen and scroll a bit. Let his curiosity take hold. When I glance back at him he's still watching me. *Perfect.*

'What's wrong?' he asks.

'Nothing.' I sigh heavily. 'I'm just trying to figure something out.' I scroll past the video of Sabine and the Klimt to the photograph I took of the financial document and scrunch my face up again. 'Do you know what this is?' I ask, showing him.

I need to be careful here, it needs to seem like a spontaneous question, not the reason for my surprise nocturnal visit.

He reaches for my phone and takes a closer look. 'It's a convertible bond,' he says. 'Where did you get this?'

'I can't really tell you,' I say. 'It's for work. But . . . is this sort of thing legal?'

'Totally legal.' He shrugs.

'Even for one hundred million?'

'Harper, there are people in the world who trade bonds worth billions. But don't you write about art? What's this for?'

'Long story.' I smile, letting my eyes linger on his chest. I pause. Then my eyes click back to his like I've just thought of something. 'Thomas . . .' I start.

'Hmm?'

'I'm so sorry to ask this, I know you're busy, but do you think maybe you could point me in the right direction? I just know nothing about this stuff; I don't know where to start.'

He frowns at the screen then looks back at me.

'Sure.' He shrugs. 'I can try. Ask around.'

'Really?' I say, reaching for his arm. 'That'd be amazing, thank you.' I give a small smile, like it's an unexpected win.

'Send me the photo,' he says, rolling onto his back.

I hesitate for a brief moment, thinking of Stan and what happened on Friday. Thomas is a journalist too. What if he looks into it and finds something big and writes the story himself? But there's nothing in that image that speaks of Agnès Bisset or the Klimt, so I attach it to a text message and press send. His phone beeps from somewhere over near the computer and I lean across and kiss him on the cheek then pull away and sit on the side of the bed.

Mission accomplished. I can go home now.

The air is cold without him hugging me and my arms prickle with goosebumps. I look around the room for my clothes. My bra is on the floor so I slip it on and fasten it in silence. My knickers are right beside it, so they go on next. Thomas just lies in bed watching me move.

My skirt and jumper are hanging over the chair by the window and I get up out of bed and move towards them. Reach for them. I'm standing half-naked glancing out onto the street, scanning for anyone who might be looking in. But we're on the third floor, I'm pretty safe from prying eyes . . . except.

What. The. Fuck.

My stomach clenches and I step back quickly from the window, peering around the curtain.

'What's wrong?' Thomas asks.

I'm shaking my head, like if I say 'no' internally I can will it into falsehood. 'There's a guy out there,' I say, my voice cracking. I'm mentally comparing the guy outside with Camilla's description – tall, dark, beaky – and the guy on the metro on Monday.

It's him. I know it's him.

'He keeps following me,' I say. 'I don't know who he is. Here.' I scroll through to my photos. 'I took some photos of him on Monday.' I offer him the phone, but he's too busy pulling on his jeans to look.

'Are you sure?' he asks.

I nod. But I'm dizzy now so I hold onto the wall for stability.

'Okay . . . shit,' Thomas says, pulling on a thick jumper. 'I guess I'll go and see what's going on then.' He grabs his keys and heads for the door, pulls on some boots and then, bang, he's gone. And I'm just standing here not sure what to do. So I creep over to the window and, hiding behind the curtains, I peek out.

First, I see Thomas appear from the bottom of the building.

His arms swinging by his sides as he moves across the road and walks right up to the man.

The man is acting surprised.

Shit, I hope he's not dangerous. My insides twist.

They're talking now.

Oh wow, no, I think Thomas might be yelling.

The man looks up at the window.

Fuck.

I move back to the side of the curtain so I can try to peek through.

Thomas has the guy pinned up against a wall now, their faces really close. Then he lets go. The guy runs away. Fast.

I feel sick. God, I might actually vomit. I move over to the bed and sit down, trying to calm my breath.

Then Thomas is coming back inside.

The door opens with a creak. Then closes gently.

I look up at him and he smiles. 'He's gone,' Thomas says, dropping his keys on the counter with a metallic clang.

'Who was he?' I ask.

Thomas hands me a business card. 'A private investigator.' He sits down on the bed. 'I told him I was going to call the police if he kept loitering. That I thought he was casing my flat.' He looks proud of himself. All puffed up.

'Thanks.' I smile.

'It's pretty creepy though. Are you sure it was the same guy?'

I nod and scroll through the photos on my phone to the ones I took at the metro station the other day. 'Yeah,' I say. 'Look.' And then I show him my phone, hovering beside him to make sure he doesn't look at anything he shouldn't. He swipes through them slowly, taking them in.

'You can't see his face,' he says – and you can't, the man's face is well covered by his cap. 'But why would he be following you anyway?'

'I don't know,' I say, and a shiver runs through me. Because now 'whatcha doin' princess' is floating back. Then the way Stan was looking at my screen on Monday. The way he watched me today as he headed across the office to his desk. That envelope with Sabine's mother's address in the bin under my desk. Stan knows I was there the night Sabine disappeared. That I know Noah. Is he following me to see if I lead him to a bigger story? Would he really go that far?

The ping of a notification pulls me back to the present moment and we both stare at my phone screen. A message. From Nee-koh-lah via the dating app. Thomas saw it too and fuck, fuck, fuck the last thing I want to do is hurt his feelings while I need his help.

'Right,' Thomas says, handing me my phone back like nothing happened. 'Let's get you a cab. I'll come wait with you.'

Then he hands me my coat, I slip the card into my pocket and order an Uber home.

Chapitre vingt-six

Five minutes later I'm looking at Thomas through a rain-blurred Uber window as he waves goodbye. I wave too. He goes inside. And we start to drive.

'*Vous avez passé une bonne soirée?*' asks the cheery driver as I scan the streets for someone tall and beaky with dark hair. But all I see are a tangle of headlights, red tail lights and signage reflecting off the mirrored roads.

'*Oui,*' I say as I clench my jaw and sink back into the black leather seat and reach into my bag for my phone. The driver's hand finds its way to the volume knob and he turns it up. 'Bette Davis Eyes'. The whole of Paris seems to have an ongoing love affair with easy listening, as though everyone got together and decided nothing culturally valuable was going to happen on the music scene after 1995.

'*Aimez-vous la musique?*' asks the driver, smiling into his rearview mirror. He's trying to be polite. To get a good rating. But I don't want to chat, especially not in French, so I smile and nod and look down at my phone. I pull the business card from my pocket and take a picture of it.

The driver's eyes move back to the road. He's tapping along to the music on the steering wheel as I send the picture of that business card and the photographs I took on Monday on the metro to Camilla with one line of text: *Is this the guy?*

It's just after 11pm, which means it's 10pm in London; she might still be up.

The rain pelts down on the metal roof, the easy listening station continues to play and I rest my head back and close my eyes. A highlight reel from the past few days flickers on the back of my eyelids: *Better luck next time, princess*, Sleeping Beauty's castle, Camilla in that gold sequined dress, the tall creepy guy, the metro, him walking towards me, his face ... A flicker of recognition, a feeling of knowing in my chest ... I know him. I've seen him. His face in a crowd ... then nothing.

We take a corner and my eyes flick open. We turn left down Rue de Sèvres and head past the real estate agent, the pharmacy and Franprix. Then right, left and, before I know it, we're at my street and my pulse is thudding in my ears. I scan the streets outside but it's almost empty. I live on a one-way street so I'll have to walk the final few metres alone.

'This is okay,' I say. '*Ici.*'

The driver pulls to a stop, I take a deep breath, say '*Merci*', get out and run through the rain to my big wooden gate, my hand trembling as I punch in the code.

It opens, I push it and run across the cobbled courtyard, past the parked cars, and enter the next code. My hair is dripping and I'm shivering from cold by the time the light flicks on inside. And as I make my way up the ninety-six stairs, I feel for the cool metal of my keys in the bottom of my bag. I find them, put them into the lock, twist and exhale loudly as the door swings open and I go inside.

As I shut the door behind me and flick on the light, I subconsciously check the dark corners for a swarthy silhouette. I drop my bag on the counter, reach into my pocket, pull out that card and trace the lettering with my eyes. My phone beeps and I reach for it, expecting it to be Camilla. But it's not. It's a news notification.

Noah X questioned further over Sabine Roux murder.

And isn't it ironic how this morning that headline was exactly what I wanted to read. But now, just twelve hours later, I'm not so sure. Because now I've seen that video. Now I know someone else might have had a reason to want Sabine dead.

Chapitre vingt-sept

We're all sitting around the big dark wood table, an ominous silver light seeping in through the windows as we industriously fuck around with notepads and printouts in preparation for our weekly editorial meeting. My phone lights up from the table and I grab it.

A message.

Camilla.

I have a really bad feeling about this.

And she's not just talking about the PI card and the photographs I sent her late last night from the cab. That tabloid in the UK chose this morning to release its next instalment of fear, with news that 'inside sources' claimed both Sabine and Matilde's bodies had blunt force trauma to the back of the skull. Camilla's been texting about it all morning. And I've been cursing myself for sending her anything at all. It was supposed to reassure her but now, with this, all it's done is stress her out.

I let out a deep breath, put my phone down face up beside my notepad and look out the window: the clouds outside are the colour of deep dark bruises and it'll rain soon. I hope if Mr PI is lurking outside, he forgot his umbrella.

Hyacinth closes the door with a bang and then sits down at her spot at the head of the table.

'Nathalie, you're up first,' she says, without her usual fake-nice introduction. I can feel her bad mood seeping off her.

Nathalie looks down at her notes and her face goes a little pink.

'They're opening a new sensory-deprivation restaurant in—'

'The ones where you eat in the dark?' Hyacinth interrupts. I'm pretty sure if her forehead moved she'd be frowning right now.

'Yes,' says Nathalie, trepidatious.

'No,' Hyacinth says. Short. Sharp. Definite. 'It's boring. Too done. What else have you got?'

Nathalie's cheeks go from pink to red, as she looks down at her list.

'We could hire a Porsche or a Ferrari for a day and drive it through Paris, taking pictures . . . we could do a few things like that. Show how easy it is to fake an influencer lifestyle.'

Hyacinth shakes her head. 'No.'

Nathalie's voice is crackling, strangled. 'What about writing up a sober rave?'

Hyacinth thinks for a moment and the room rings with silence. We all feel bad for Nathalie but none of us want to end up in Hyacinth's crosshairs.

'Okay. But keep brainstorming.' Her gaze moves to me. *Shit.*

'What have you got, Harper?'

The words come out fast, 'There's a Charlotte Gainsbourg concert?'

'Okay,' she says. 'But find an angle.'

'Claudia?' comes Hyacinth's voice. I can hear Claudia telling her about how some celebrity or other is in town and rumoured to be staying at Le Meurice, about how she can get tickets to some sort of after party, but my gaze has moved to Stan. He catches my eye and smirks, and I look away. Down at my notes. Like I don't know what he's up to. I circle Charlotte Gainsbourg a couple of times and my phone glows with a message. My eyes snap to the screen. Maybe it's Thomas. Maybe he's found something . . .

But no.

It's another text from Camilla: *What are you going to do?*

~

I weave my way through the darkening street, my pulse all semi-quavers. I can see my destination just up ahead, past the traffic lights. According to my sat nav, that's where the PI has his offices. I'm not really sure what I'm going to say to him, but I want to walk through that door and have him see my face and know I'm onto him. It's that, or just let him keep shadowing me. I move past a grocer to my left, watching the little blue dot on my phone move towards the address. And then I'm here. It says I'm here.

I look around and across the street, frowning and looking up at the stone walls for a number. This is it: number 349.

And it's a nail salon.

There's a small woman watching me from inside. I pull the door open – it jingles with a bell – and smile at her.

'Hi,' I say.

'Bonjour,' she replies.

And so in French I say, 'I'm looking for this.' And then I show her the card.

She shrugs and her mouth does that French pfff thing, her eyes widening as she looks down at it and then up again. 'Is not here,' she says in English.

I look around. Is she lying? Is there a back room?

But all I can see are walls of nail varnish colours and massage seats with footbaths.

I smile at her and say 'Pardon', like I'm silly and made a mistake. Then I reach for my phone and call the number on the card.

It doesn't even ring.

He doesn't exist.

And if he doesn't exist, if he's not a PI, then Stan didn't hire him.

I stand statue still, my mind whirring.

Whoever has been following me, whoever was waiting outside Thomas's flat, is not only *not* a PI, but he had the foresight to make up some business cards in case he was called out. It's that last part that has my stomach twisting. Everything inside me is screaming, 'Leave', and so I turn left and head for the metro and walk as fast as I can.

~

Forty minutes later I'm emerging from the metro stairs, my stomach is growling and I'm thinking about the sushi I'm going to get for dinner when I reach for my phone to check the time.

One missed call from Thomas.

My heart speeds up.

Finally.

I keep step with the pedestrian traffic, and as I head past a real estate agency with photographs of well furnished, overpriced apartments in the window, I dial his number. It rings as I move past a *tabac*.

Briinngg. Brinngg.

'Harper?' he says, as I get to the road.

'Hey,' I say, pushing a finger against my free ear to block out the sound of traffic. 'Did you find something?'

'I did,' he says. 'Can we meet?'

Fuck. I don't want to meet up. *Please don't let him think last night meant something.*

'I can't right now, I'm on my way to a work thing,' I say, in a tone that says: I wish I could. 'Can you just tell me the basics?' The lights change and I cross the road.

'Well Genovexa is a company based in the Caymans.'

'Okay,' I say, as I get to the other side.

'Chances are it's a shell company,' he continues.

I stop and step to the side of the pavement, leaning up against the cool brick of a boutique as pedestrians move past me. This is exactly the sort of opaque situation I was hoping he'd come back with. Because I've read about shell companies before. They exist in name only and they have no employees. They're not illegal in and of themselves, but given *Je sais ce que tu fais, Agnès*, this could mean I'm onto something.

'Who owns it?' I ask.

Please say Agnès Bisset . . . Please say Agnès Bisset . . .

'Well, I had to pull a favour to find this out,' he says, taking his sweet time. He wants me to know I owe him now. 'But it's owned by a Liechtenstein foundation called Requiem.'

Shit.

'And who owns the foundation?' I ask, only thinly veiling my irritation: is he being intentionally obtuse so I *have* to meet up with him? All I want to know is where the buck stops.

'Foundations don't have owners, Harper,' he says. And there's an edge to his voice that tells me he's picked up on my inner dialogue.

My mind goes into overdrive. *That sounds illegal.*

'Okay,' I say, resetting my tone to sweet. 'But I don't understand though. So, some company with no owners issued a bond worth one hundred million. That doesn't make sense to me.'

'Companies raise money this way all the time. There's nothing strange about that part . . . but look, let's talk about all this in person.'

And there it is again.

'So, they just gave someone a bond worth one hundred million?'

'No, Harper, usually someone would have to invest capital first. The aim being to get one hundred million out of the deal when the bond matures and the company is worth significantly more. That or the equivalent in shares. It's speculative.'

'Oh,' I say. 'Okay.' That makes sense.

'Look, I want to help you with this. I'm guessing there's a reason you had that picture of the bond to start with, a reason you were looking into it?'

Oh. Right.

That's why he wants to meet up. He knows I'm onto something. He wants more information.

The fucker wants to steal my story.

He pauses, giving me time to speak up, but I don't bite. Instead, I start walking again, focusing on my footing because it's getting dark and there's dog poop. 'But I need all the information or I can't help you piece it together,' he continues. And then he pauses yet again and waits for me to crack.

But I'm not the kind of girl who cracks.

'I can't tell you,' I say in a small, fragile voice that says I'm cautious but maybe if you try really hard you can manipulate me.

'I'll get in trouble.' But I want to get off the phone now. 'I'm just about to head into the metro,' I lie. 'Chat soon.' And then we hang up and I can see the sushi place up ahead. I'm passing the laundromat – *I need to do my washing soon* – and I glance at my reflection in the window. But my gaze catches on the edges of the machines and I'm hit with a tidal wave of memories. That last time I was there my skin smelled of orange blossom and it was the night before they revealed they'd found Sabine's body. I was watching her entire Vimeo page . . .

Snippets of her videos flicker in my mind. A crowd . . . A tall man against the wall . . .

My hands are white with cold as I lean against the window and pull up a browser, going to her page. I scan down the videos, past the couple on the bridge, the busker counting his money in le Bois de Boulogne, the group of students huddling together and checking for onlookers and then, there it is.

The video I'm remembering.

I click on it.

I watch a group of well-dressed people swirl around each other in Le Voltage. Then the camera focuses on the opposite wall. Two people are speaking.

One is Agnès Bisset.

And the other is a certain tall and creepy fake PI.

Chapitre vingt-huit

My stomach twists as I reach for my phone, scroll through to my Instagram messages and stare down at my unanswered words: *Noah, can we talk. It's important.*

It's Friday morning – over 24 hours since he was taken in for questioning – and according to Google, that's the standard length of time to be *garde à vue*. So I know he has his phone back.

I also know he's seen my message. I know this as there's a little 'seen' beneath my words. Yet he has *chosen* not to answer.

And I *need* him to answer.

Because there are only two reasons Agnès Bisset would be having me followed. One of them is: Noah, jealousy, the usual suspect. The other is: she somehow knows I'm onto her. And call it a journalistic hunch, but I just *know* it's the second one.

Which means this is a real story.

The kind of story that makes a career.

She's following me because she's scared I'm going to expose her.

Which I absolutely fucking will. But I need more information. The sort of information someone like Noah might have. Because he was married to her. He must have seen something.

I reach for my phone and try again. I can't tell him what I know over text, it's too volatile and what if Ms Bisset has spyware on his US phone too, like she did on his other one?

And so I settle on: *Please.*

And then I take a deep breath, look back at the page on my screen and glance over the paragraph I've now read and reread ten times in the last thirty minutes. Hyacinth sent me back notes on my photography exhibition article this morning and she wants it in by 5 pm. Fair enough, I should be well and truly done with it by now but I can't focus. I don't care about an exhibition right now. I care about things like the fact that creepy fake PI was probably following Sabine too. He's probably the one who killed her.

I take a sip of cold coffee and bite on my inner cheek, but this is cup number three today and I'm already jittery as hell as I think about headlines like 'Does Paris Have a Serial Killer?'

Because I have a sick and twisted theory of my own.

Maybe that tabloid wasn't wrong after all. Maybe both bodies *did* share similarities like blunt force trauma to the back of the skull and strangulation. Maybe they shared *every* detail that was leaked to the press about Matilde's case. And maybe that wasn't a coincidence; Agnès Bisset could have just taken all the information about Matilde's murder available in the newspapers and had Sabine killed the same way. What a great way to cover her tracks.

It was a foolproof plan as long as nobody saw that video and heard: *Je sais ce que tu fais, Agnès.*

But I did.

And fuck, what if Agnès Bisset somehow knows that?

I stare at my phone. I need Noah to reply. Now.

'I know! What a beautiful day!' Claudia low-key screams from behind me, and I'm far too caffeinated for this shit today. I swivel in my chair. She's started up on a phone call. Judy got her a headset to try to shut her up, but for some reason she took it as a licence to be mobile. Now she's pacing around the office grinning at whoever is on the other end of the line. I glare at her, our eyes meet, and she moves in the opposite direction, then I turn back to my desk just in time to see my phone light up with a message.

Yes. Yes. Yes.

You have a message from @NoahXartist.

Yes. Yes. Yes.

I lurch for it, my blood thinned with relief.

Fuck you, Harper Brown.

Uh-oh. How does he know my real name? The missed call. In that bar with Camilla. He would have heard my voicemail message. Did he google me? Realise Harper Brown looked a lot like Grace?

Shit.

But this is ridiculous. It's a name – who cares?

Except: *The Paris Observer.* He knows I'm a journalist. How the hell am I going to get him to talk to me now?

I can hear Claudia screeching with laughter from the other side of the room. What if he won't talk to me? What then? If I can't write this story I'm going to need to go to the police. But every time I consider that my brain starts up a PowerPoint presentation of all the photographs I found of a young Agnès Bisset, her arms interlinked with the influential and well connected. She has friends in high places. People who can press mute on the truth. And even if the police decided I was onto something and followed it up, there would be a long lead time between an investigation and trial. Lots of time to destroy evidence. And what am I, if not evidence?

I have to get him to answer.

I scan my memory banks . . . tracker . . . spyware . . . common ground.

And so I scroll through to Sabine's Vimeo page and press play on that video of Agnès Bisset and the fake PI. I wait until his face is exposed, press pause and take a screenshot. And then I forward it to Noah with the text message: *Your wife is having me followed by this man.*

Seen.

Silence.

Answer.

And then typing bubbles.

They start. They stop. They start again.

And then: *Fuck. I knew she'd do something like this.*

Chapitre vingt-neuf

Two hours later the sky is the colour of denim and the leaves set against it are mustard and rust red. The bannister is cool beneath my hand as I head down the stairs, my eyes on the pale wood door of number twenty-three. An echo of the last time I was here moves through me – the vibration of drum and bass pushing through the walls, goosebumps on my arms, the piña coladas running through my veins – as I make my way down the stairs. And then I'm there, standing right where I stood when Noah found me last time and said, 'Are you just going to stand there all night?' As if by reflex, I glance up to the rooftop.

There's a rustle behind me and I swivel to look. I thought I made sure I wasn't followed. I snuck out the back of work and got an Uber from a parallel street to be safe.

But it's nothing.

There's nobody there aside from an elderly woman watching me from her open window, pretending to water plants.

I reach for my phone and text Noah: *I'm here.*

And then my glance is drawn, as if magnetised, to that bottom segment of Rue Chappe. I remember standing there, looking for

Khalid, seeing that white car speed away instead. A shiver runs through me: double A, that was the last part of the number plate.

Was it Agnès's guy in that car?

Bzzzz.

I push the door open and let it close heavy behind me. Click. I'm in the hallway now and I can see Noah's studio door up ahead. I move past the metal door that leads to the rooftop and his door opens and there he is, looking like he always did: tanned and blue-eyed. Except now he's wearing some old grey tracksuit pants with navy paint down one leg and a big white long-sleeved shirt. He looks drained. Greyscale.

Like a man who's been questioned by the police over a murder he didn't commit.

I move towards him. I can smell the muted peppermint of his shampoo.

'Hey,' I say, reaching out to touch his chest like I'm all trusting and vulnerable.

'Don't pull that cutesy crap with me,' he says as he pushes the door open and moves aside so I can enter. 'You lied to me.'

'And you've never lied to me?' I ask, as I move inside. It smells like oil paint and turpentine and old coffee, and it's almost too big without all the people. A vast messy space with one of the sofas I saw last time now converted into an unmade bed.

'Caffeine?' Noah asks as he closes the door and heads to the kitchen.

A flash of his party. Of him reaching for my wrist and drawing that half a heart. His breath on my ear.

'Sure,' I say, my voice thick.

I sit down on the other sofa and wait for him to bring my coffee. There's a canvas lying on the floor with only a rough outline on it. Noah walks towards me, hands me a cup and sits down.

'Thanks,' I say. The warmth between my hands is comforting even though I'm pretty sure if I drink the coffee I may have some sort of heart attack.

'So,' he says, his eyes on mine.

'So,' I reply. But I am thinking about his message.

'What did you mean by you knew she'd do something like this?' I ask. No point skirting around it.

'You went past the gallery, right? About a week ago.'

'So? Lots of people go there.'

'Yeah but you must have done something to make her think that we had a thing. Because she called me, said some girl named "Grace",' he inserts air-quotes here so I am guessing he's still pissed about the name thing, 'just came past. Wanted to know who you were. If Sabine had ever mentioned you.'

'Well, what did you say?' I ask, my mind a whirr as I try to recall our conversation from that day. Whether there was something I said to stir her suspicion.

'I said no . . . of course,' he replies. 'I know what she's like. I didn't want you on her radar. But it looks like I was too late.'

'Fuck.' The pieces are slotting into place. 'I told her I was Sabine's really good friend.' A flash of the CCTV outside the gallery. She would have seen Noah and me together. It would have raised a bright red flag when he said he didn't know who I was. She would have wondered who was lying: him or me? And why?

'But how would the guy in the picture have found me?' I ask. 'He didn't even have my name?' The subtext here is: did you tell her?

'He's always hanging around the gallery,' he says, reaching for my hand. I let him take it. 'But look, don't worry. She'll get bored soon enough. She's just possessive and jealous . . .'

And I might think that too if I hadn't seen what was on that video.

He's looking down at our hands and I'm looking at him. I sense he has no idea what Agnès has been really doing. And now that I have to tell him, I'm not sure how to start.

I take a deep breath. 'Noah, there's more to this than just jealousy.'

He tilts his head just slightly. 'Like what?'

'I found something.' I let go of his hand and reach for my phone, scrolling through my photographs to the still frame of that financial document on the screen. 'Here,' I say, handing it to him.

He frowns down at it. 'What is this?'

'That company, Hintos Holdings, belongs to Philip Crawford-White.'

'So?' Noah says. 'Agnès did loads of deals for loads of people. They all use company names. And Philip is a friend, she sells paintings for him sometimes to private collectors.'

'What kind of paintings?' I ask, slowly, thinking of the Klimt.

He shrugs. 'I don't really know. These people have extensive collections. It's a whole other world.'

'Did Agnès ever mention Genovexa or Requiem?'

'No, I don't think so.' He pauses. 'Why, what do *you* think is going on here, Harper?' He fully enunciates my name.

'I'm not sure,' I say, taking back my phone. 'But there was this too.' I pull up the video of Sabine and the Klimt.

I hand him my phone and watch his face as it plays.

His eyes get big. His mouth opens just a little bit. He frowns at the screen. And then Sabine says '*Je sais ce que tu fais, Agnès*', and blows a kiss at the camera.

His jaw clenches.

His face is pale when he looks at me. 'What the hell is this?' his voice comes out as an almost whisper. 'Where did you get it?'

'It was on one of Sabine's drives. I got it for a story I was working on.' I keep it intentionally vague.

He's looking from wall to wall, as though trying to get his head around it.

'I'm pretty sure Sabine was blackmailing your wife,' I say slowly. 'The painting in that video isn't supposed to exist anymore.'

He looks straight at me. I watch the thoughts dance behind his eyes. And when he speaks the words come out husky. 'Wait.

Do you think Agnès killed her?' He holds up my phone. 'Because of this?'

'I don't know,' I say, my voice small. 'But maybe.'

'Fuck,' he says, staring at a wall. 'I don't know, Harper, I mean she's batshit crazy, yes, but murder?'

'I know.'

'Except . . .' He pulls his hands through his hair.

'What?'

He lets out a big breath. 'This one time Sabine was talking all about her big exhibition. The one she was going to have at Le Voltage. And I wanted to prepare her for the fact that it might not happen. I knew how little Agnès rated her work. I was trying to be kind and soften the blow. So I told her, look the art world is full of disappointment and Agnès might pull it but it didn't mean she wasn't great.' His eyes are on mine. 'Do you know what she said?'

'What?'

'Just let her try.'

My stomach clenches and the room rings with silence.

An exhibition. Sabine was blackmailing Agnès for an exhibition.

Shit. Shit. Shit.

Because now the rest of our conversation from that day in the gallery is floating back. I'm thinking of how Agnès Bisset's eyes changed when I spoke about that exhibition. '*She was so excited. Wouldn't stop talking about it,*' I'd said.

I can almost hear Agnès's thoughts. She was wondering what *else* Sabine had told me. How close I was to the one person who knew exactly what she'd been up to; who had evidence to prove it. And whether if I dug deep enough, I might figure out *why* Sabine was killed.

This is why she's been having me followed.

And now my throat feels like it's closing up.

'Wait, she doesn't know you've seen this, does she?' Noah asks. He's looking at me and his voice is dark. 'You said there was more to it. That's not why you think she's following you?'

I shake my head. 'No,' I say. 'She couldn't know. I'm pretty sure she's just being careful.' And as I say it I pray I'm right.

'Okay, good,' he says, thinking for a moment. 'Hang on, what does Philip have to do with it all? What was that document?' Noah asks and I turn to look at him.

'I don't know exactly,' I say. 'But Sabine had them in the same folder. They have to be connected. Philip was the seller and I'm pretty sure it has something to do with how they moved the money around for the painting.'

'We should go to the police,' he says, turning his whole body towards me. 'They think *I* did this. That I killed her. They found the video,' he continues. 'The one Sabine took of us. It uploaded to her fucking iCloud and they think I had a reason. If they find one more shred of evidence against me I'm fucked. But this . . . this could change everything.'

Guilt courses through me. Because if it wasn't for me the police wouldn't have been looking for that video. They might never have even got a warrant for her iCloud. He might not be a suspect.

'We need more,' I say. Firm.

'Why? It's all there.'

I shake my head. 'If we take it to the police now, Agnès could just say it was a print. Or a fake. The original has officially been destroyed. And there's nothing on that document that is illegal. Her name isn't even on it. There is nothing other than the location to link that painting to Agnès even if they *did* believe it was real. And also, Agnès is basically the Mother Teresa of the art world. Nobody is going to bring her down without a lot more proof. And if she thinks we're onto her she'll have a chance to destroy everything. Then you'll definitely get the blame.'

The room is so silent that I can hear him swallow.

'You're right,' he says, holding his head in his hands. 'And she knows everyone. She'll be protected. I'm so fucked.'

He looks at me. 'But what other proof is there?'

'We need something linking her to it all. This is most likely not the first time she's done something like this, it's just the first one Sabine got on video. There must be documentation somewhere. Do you have access to Agnès's computers? Know any of her passwords?'

'No.' He shakes his head. 'But that wouldn't help anyway. A few months back she got paranoid as fuck. She wouldn't let anyone email her anything. Something about cyber crime.'

Or something about that video Sabine took of her computer screen. She'd been compromised and she knew it.

'Okay . . .' I say, thinking.

The room is silent and smells of coffee.

'Oh my god,' Noah says, his voice husky. I turn to look at him. '*This* is why she had that tracker on my car. The spyware on my phone. She was trying to keep tabs on what I knew.' His voice is feeble and his eyes are wide. Like he's seeing her clearly for the first time.

'Maybe . . .' I say and then I watch as he turns to stare at a wall. His jaw clenches and unclenches. His shoulders tense. But when he looks back to me his gaze is solid.

'There's a back room at the gallery,' he says slowly. 'That's where we need to look. Sabine said something once about that room being full of secrets. I thought she was just being Sabine. I mean she was a bit out there. Maybe she was trying to tell me something. Fuck. I can't believe this.'

I think of the fob in that top desk drawer. The one the mousy-haired girl put in there that day I went past the gallery. Then of the files and the shelving I saw in Sabine's video of that room. Then the back door. The code I saw him trace that night . . . a cross.

I could probably get into the gallery one way or another . . .

'Do you know the alarm code?' I ask, thinking of the sensors blinking red from the upper corners of the gallery.

'Our wedding anniversary,' he says beneath his breath.

I wait for him to elaborate and pull out my phone to note down the details. But he says nothing.

'Which is?' I ask, looking up at him.

He's frowning now. 'You don't think I'm letting you go alone, do you?' he asks.

'You're going to come along and protect me, are you?' I ask, eyebrows raised.

'No, of course not.' He gives the slightest hint of a smile. 'I'm going to come along and make sure you don't fuck anything up.'

Chapitre trente

So here we are, full circle. It's a Saturday morning and I'm back on my sofa, the rain tapping on the roof, the smell of Noah in my hair while I sip coffee and think about Agnès Bisset. Except this time the door is double bolted and there's no guilt pulsing through me. This time she's not the victim. This time she can't hide behind some pristine public image. This time I see her for what she is: the woman who had Sabine killed; the woman who deals in stolen art; the woman who is having me followed.

The woman whose gallery I will be breaking into tomorrow night.

Which would be why, right now, I'm feeling around the bottom of my bag for a couple of bobby pins.

I pull them into the light and adjust them so they look just like the ones on the screen.

I'm watching a YouTube video with corporate music in the background as a well-manicured hand demonstrates how to break into a desk drawer with just two bobby pins. Yes, these videos exist. I've already watched it once, but now that I have my tools at the ready I plan on rewatching it a couple more times so I'm ready when the time comes. I just need to somehow get the baubles off the ends of the bobby pins . . . Maybe a knife? Some pliers? My phone screen lights up from the sofa beside me with a message.

How's Paris, beautiful? H x

I put down the bobby pins, take a sip of coffee and glare at the message. You've got to be fucking kidding me.

Of course I get a message from Harrison today, just as I need to focus. The man has fucking antennae, I tell you. This is because I never called to say thank you for the roses, so now he's terrified that maybe, finally, I'm healing.

I should just block him. That would be one way to stop his fake-nice overtures. He wouldn't even know. He'd keep sending his Trojan horses, and never know why they stopped working.

And then it happens.

The way ideas always happen.

One thought links to another and boom.

My breath is quick as I reach for my phone, go to Notes and start to type before the idea deserts me.

That bond. 100 million euro. Klimt. Trojan Horse.

And just like that I know why Sabine had those two videos in the same folder. Philip Crawford-White *was* selling something, but it wasn't a bond. Not really. It was a painting. A painting that didn't exist. He just needed a solid cover story for why that money was going into his account.

A cover story like a bond worth about the same.

But is that sane? Would it even work?

Philip Crawford-White is an uber wealthy guy, so nobody would question the amount, but what about the buyer? What if one day he decided to collect on that bond?

My breath is quick as I reach for my phone and text Thomas.

What would happen if someone went to collect on a bond and the company had no money?

A split second later: typing bubbles.

Then they lose their money. That's the risk of business. But we can talk about all this when we meet. Tomorrow?

I can't do tomorrow, of course, because I'll be breaking into Le Voltage with Noah then. He's bringing the duct tape. I'm bringing the locksmithery. I wanted to do it tonight, but Noah said that was too risky. The gallery is closed on Mondays, like much else in Paris. So if we do it on Sunday night we'll have a twenty-four hour grace period before anyone realises the CCTV outside was compromised.

And at least now I know what we'll be looking for: something, anything, to link Agnès Bisset to Genovexa. And I know it was Agnès who set it up. Because, let's be fair, Philip would be pretty stupid to set up a company then issue himself a fake bond as a cover story. But what sort of evidence would prove that?

I imagine Thomas sitting there, on that brown leather sofa of his, waiting for my reply. I don't really want to see him unless I have to, so I give myself a wide girth and type back: *Tuesday?*

I'll know if I need any further information by then.

Typing bubbles.

Tuesday.

And then I close down the video and pull up my Word document. My article. Because now I know what to write.

I know not only what Agnès has been doing and how she's been doing it, but I understand *her*. Why her image matters so much to her. Why she's such a stickler for privacy. So terrified of scandal.

Because scandal attracts attention.

And if you're a criminal, the last thing you want is attention.

Chapitre trente et un

The sound of the upstairs neighbour drilling into a wall rips me from sleep. I pull my eye mask from my face and glare up at the ceiling: I couldn't sleep last night and it's a fucking Sunday. Even the church bells have the decency not to ring until just before 11 am on Sundays. But the drilling continues and I turn my gaze to the sky beyond the window. It's blue with a wisp of apricot and the air is Antarctic. What a beautiful day to become a criminal. I roll over, reach for my phone and squint at it through heavy lids. The screen is full of notifications but there's one right in the middle. A news notification. I blink hard and focus on it, translating in my head.

My breath catches in the back of my throat.

Noah X arrested over Sabine Roux murder.

I sit up, the walls pulsing in towards me as I tap through to the article and pull it into Reverso.

Noah Parker, 32, otherwise known as Noah X, has this morning been taken into police custody over the murder of Sabine Roux on 15 October. An informed source revealed this came after a white sheet of fabric traced back to Mr Parker was found near the crime scene . . .

tip-off to police from the public . . . seen entering the woodland at le Bois de Boulogne in the early hours of Saturday 16 October.

Shit.

I scan the article again: the white sheet of fabric. The ones Noah used to cover his work. I saw those in both his studio and at Le Voltage. How easily his wife could have planted that as evidence. And a tip-off from the public. *Please.* My bet is that call originated with Agnès Bisset or one of her cohort. But what made her frame Noah? Did she see me there on Friday afternoon? Was I followed after all? Was she worried about what he'd told me? And what does this mean she has in store for me?

Shit. Shit. Shit.

The air is icy so I reach for my jumper and pull it on then take my phone through to the kitchen and flick on the kettle. Mr Oiseau is sitting on the terracotta pots outside, like nothing bad has happened and I knock on the window as the hum of the kettle gets louder and louder. My eyes move beyond him and out onto the street: I search the crowd for a tall silhouette. Nothing.

Noah has been arrested.

What if he's charged?

I bite down on my lower lip.

My phone starts to sing from the countertop and I reach for it. Camilla is calling.

'Hey,' I say, spooning coffee into the cafetière with my free hand and spilling it on the counter.

'So which one?' Camilla asks.

'What?'

'Which outfit? For my interview on Monday?'

'Sorry, Mills, I just woke up,' I say.

'Oh, okay, I texted you some options. Fuck, I'm nervous. This is everything I've ever wanted.'

'You're made for this job,' I say, pouring the boiling water as the drilling from upstairs starts up again. Caffeine. I need caffeine. The air smells like coffee now and I reach for a cup from the drying rack by the sink. I'm aware of Camilla speaking but I can't focus, all I can think about is Noah behind big, steel bars and Agnès out there somewhere and the fact that I can't break into the gallery alone because he never gave me the stupid alarm codes. So I can't help him.

'It's the worst, right?' she says and I click to attention.

'What is?'

Silence rings down the line.

'What's wrong?' she asks. 'You aren't listening to me.'

'Sorry,' I say, 'I am, but I'm just making coffee.' Camilla is the only person in the world I hate lying to. But I have to. Because in my eyeline right now is the sofa where she sat in the dark scrolling through articles, tears streaming down her cheeks. And she needs to focus on preparing for Monday.

'Hmmm,' she says.

Shit, her bloody intuition is perking up.

'What time is your interview?' I say, moving the focus and taking a sip of coffee.

'Eight o'clock,' she says and then she lets out a little shriek.

'Okay, I'll be thinking of you,' I say.

'Let me know which outfit.'

And then we hang up, I take another sip of coffee, and move through to my messages to help Camilla pick an outfit as promised.

But wait.

There.

Just below Camilla's messages is one from Noah. It came in early this morning.

We were married on the third of November.

And all I can think is, *I guess I need duct tape.*

Chapitre trente-deux

I walk briskly down Rue Bonaparte, my hands deep in my pockets as I scan the street for a tall silhouette. But I've left my curtains closed, my lights on, snuck out the back and taken such a roundabout route that it would be the shittiest of miracles if he were here right now. But he's not. It's just after 10 pm and there are only five other people I can see on the streets. Their hair shimmers under streetlights. One of them smokes a cigarette. All of them are a long way away from me – without night-vision goggles they couldn't possibly see what I was doing even if they tried – but even so, I grit my jaw as I turn left, slipping into the alleyway beside the gallery. I'm not sure how much of the alleyway the CCTV takes in, so I skirt the far wall and keep my face angled down, until I'm past the camera and behind the stairs.

I reach into my bag, feeling around for the roll of duct tape I bought from the DIY section of Franprix as soon as I got Noah's message. There it was, all innocuous, right beside the mothballs, insect spray and little packets of screws.

I use my teeth to rip off a small piece of tape, step up onto the back of the stairs, and cover the CCTV lens. Then I drop the roll back into my bag and feel around for the locksmith tools I found in the bottom of my suitcase. Because what if she's changed the back door code? And what if that YouTube video is wrong: what if I can't just pop the lock on that drawer with a couple of bobby pins?

I make my way up the stairs to the back door, past the spot where I smoked with Noah, hold my breath and reach for the keypad and trace a cross, just like he did.

Click.

I push open the door and move into the dusty warmth, shutting the door behind me as I look around for the alarm. I expected beeping, but there is no beeping just the orange glow of a rectangular outline and some buttons up ahead on the wall. My heart bangs so loudly against my chest it feels like the vibration alone might set off the alarm. I rush towards that orange rectangle and punch in: 0-3-1-1.

The orange glow turns green, I pull my phone from my bag and turn on the torch, using it to light the way past a small kitchen and a bathroom, through to the main room. None of the windows have curtains on them, anyone walking past could see me and so, once I know where the desk is, I turn off the torch and crawl quickly in the shadows to crouch behind it.

Reaching into my bag I pull out the bobby pins.

I insert one at the bottom of the lock and, with a thumb, maintain pressure in a down and sideways motion. Then I take the second pin – already free of its little plastic baubles and pulled out into a wide 'v' (prepared earlier at home under the instruction of that YouTube video). I insert one end into the top of the lock and jiggle it up and down, up and down . . . Up and down . . . and then, just like on the video, the lock begins to turn.

Click.

Slowly I pull the drawer open, as though someone might hear me.

I reach inside and feel around: there. I have it. A small circular fob. I clasp onto it and crawl to the back room, lifting it to the pad by the door.

Beep.

Click.

I reach for the handle and let myself in, my heart ricocheting.

Closing the door behind me, I feel the walls either side of the door for a light switch.

Flick.

The room is flooded with light as I glance from one wall to the other.

There's a part of me that expected it to be empty. Or worse, for Mr Tall and Creepy to be waiting for me in here. But, instead, it looks exactly like it did in Sabine's video: a small, tidy room with wooden crates the shape of canvases against the wall to my right and a sturdy metal set of shelves in the left-hand corner. It's full of printing paper, boxes of pens and lever arch files.

I rush towards it and my eyes scan the labels. Invoices. No. Tax files. No. Client details. Invoices. Artist invoices. No. No. No.

I look around for a safe. Not that I will be able to get into a safe but I could try the codes I have . . . but there isn't one. There are just files upon files upon files.

And so I do the only thing I can, I pull down the first one and start to look through it.

~

It's half an hour later and I'm halfway through a file labelled 'Invoices', when a small, thin, purple file – the cheap kind you'd find in a supermarket – catches my eye. It's one level down and the spine reads '*Notes diverses*'. Loosely translated I'm pretty sure that means miscellaneous notes.

I reach for it, lay it down on the floor and open it up. It's a series of brightly coloured section dividers and I flip through them, scanning the first page of each section. There are stationery orders. Some sort of membership papers. And then, right in the middle, is a plastic pocket.

And inside are a set of papers.

They aren't the papers I was looking for. They don't pertain to Genovexa. But as I pull them from the plastic folder and leaf through them my breath catches. The top one is an invoice from a lawyer. It's for: *Liechtenstein Foundation: Requiem.* The rest are pages of correspondence – letters, emails – with words like 'appointees' and 'beneficiary' dotted throughout. I'll need to look through them properly when I'm at home. And then, at the bottom, there it is: a flimsy piece of paper.

A share registry for Genovexa.

One hundred shares owned by Requiem.

My hands are shaking as I pull out my phone and take a picture of each page, double-checking the focus. I can't come back. I need to get it right.

I put the papers and the folder back where I found them.

And then I hear it.

A noise outside.

What the hell is that? Have I tripped an alarm? Is it a security company? Are they shining torches through the window right now?

I hold my breath and tiptoe over to the door, flicking off the light. The room falls into darkness.

My heart hits the walls of its cage so hard I grit my teeth.

And then I just sit dead still, listening for movement, watching the thin crack under the door for light, for movement, frightened to even breathe.

But nothing more comes.

I need to get the hell out of here.

I edge open the door – a crack of grey light – and crawl over to the desk again. Opening the lowest drawer, I drop in the fob and close it again. And then I crawl to the back door. As soon as I'm out of sight, I stand up and set the alarm again. I take a deep breath, reach for the handle and crack the door open, peeking outside.

There's no one there. I move out into the cool night air, pulling it closed behind me with a gentle thud. Once I'm down the stairs, I hoist myself up onto the back of them and remove the tape from the camera. The only sound is water rushing into gutters and traffic in the distance as I skirt the wall and rush towards the main road. I turn right towards the Seine, reach for my phone and, as people walk past me, I hold it against my ear and pretend to talk.

Chapitre trente-trois

It's 7.48 am and the empty office echoes with the sound of the elevator doors opening. I step out into greyness and switch on the light. I'm the first one here. My head throbs as I make my way over to my desk, drop my bag on the floor, fire up my computer and take a sip of the coffee I grabbed on my way in.

My mouth is dry and my head is thumping. I barely slept last night. Every time I closed my eyes, all I could see was Sabine then Agnès then the tall and creepy guy then Noah then the photographs I took last night.

My screen glows to life and I feel around the bottom of my handbag for the memory stick in the inner pocket. There's my lip gloss. Some crumpled expenses receipts. Bobby pins from last night. My heart speeds up as I think of that desk drawer, the fob, the dark back room and the sound outside. What if someone saw me leave?

But then, there.

I've found it.

The memory stick.

The one I put my story on late yesterday afternoon. I didn't want to save it to Sabine's drive – I suspect that might be logged as evidence soon – but I've learned the hard way not to email myself a work in progress. The same way I've learned not to tell the likes of Stan what I'm writing about. And I like it, this feeling, like I have a little secret. A small flickering flame I need to protect. It's mine, all mine, until it burns Agnès's whole house of cards down.

I take another sip of coffee, click on the hard drive icon and open my article, scanning through what I've written so far. It's passable. And I now have proof that Agnès Bisset set up the foundation that owns Genovexa; proof that she is the one who issued that 100 million euro bond to Philip Crawford-White. But is that a crime? I'm not so sure about that. It sounds like the sort of white collar crime that's sectioned off from the rest of us with do not cross tape until it's made into a Netflix Original.

Because I might have video footage of that Klimt in her gallery but no proof that it isn't simply a fake. I might have a hypothesis that the bond was used as a cover, a way for Mr Crawford-White to receive funds from the buyer of his Klimt entirely legally, but again, can I prove it?

And as I sit here in the low light, all alone in the office, I realise this is how people get away with it. Not because nobody knows but because nobody can prove it.

But Noah will stand before the *juge d'instruction* soon. I can't just give up, he'll go to jail and I know he didn't do this. I need to do *something* with what I have. I need to help him.

I think of Thomas, if I were transparent with him, gave him everything I have, would he be able to help? And even if he could, *would* he help me? Or would he do exactly what Stan did?

~

It's an hour and a half later and Wesley is sitting across from me, sighing heavily, when my phone flashes with a message.

Camilla: *Just got out. Eeekkk! Xx*

Her interview.

Wesley crinkles a paper bag and takes a bite of a Danish, as his eyes dart to my lit-up screen. I don't want him listening in on a personal call, so I grab my phone and head past Judy. She's talking to someone at reception but smiles at me as I press the down button for the elevator. The doors slide open. Down. Down. Rattling down. To the foyer. And then, when I'm alone, I call Camilla.

It rings.

'It went so well. So, so, so well. I can't believe it,' she gushes.

It's great to hear her so effervescent after years of corporate servitude, spending all her money on suits she said did nothing for her silhouette.

'That's amazing, when do you hear?' I ask, moving to the back of the foyer.

'They said within a week,' she says. 'I so want this. I keep reading my fucking horoscope in case there's a prediction in there but god, Harps, I need this.'

'I know,' I say.

It's good to talk about normal things right now. I've missed her.

The clicking of high heels fills the little foyer and I turn around to see who's behind me. Hyacinth. I get a fright, push the phone against my ear and my earring hook digs into me. *Ouch.* But I give her a small smile. She gives me a tight-mouthed nod back then casts her eyes down.

'Thanks so much for your time,' I say, as Hyacinth gets into the elevator. 'Really, it's been so useful.'

'What?' Camilla asks.

The elevator door closes and I can hear the mechanical rumblings as it moves up to our floor.

'Sorry,' I say. 'My boss.'

'Oh.'

'I've got to go but well done.'

And then we hang up and I wait two minutes and then head upstairs.

I smile at Judy and make my way towards my desk and the tangle of information that is waiting for me there. Wesley is staring at his computer screen as he munches on his Danish and drops crumbs on his lap.

I sit down at my desk and wiggle my mouse so the screen comes to life. 'Harper?'

I turn and Hyacinth is standing in her doorway. 'A word?'

'Sure,' I say, standing up and heading over to her.

I step into her office and she closes the door behind me, moving over to her side of the desk. We both sit down and I wait for her to speak.

'What are you working on?'

'I have that Charlotte Gainsbourg concert coming up and a couple of galleries I still have to get to,' I say.

Her poker face is as strong as ever, but there's something in her eyes, something I haven't seen before, and her gaze doesn't flinch from mine for even a moment. Then she leans in a little way and says, 'Harper, what are you *really* working on?'

I swallow hard. *How does she know?* My cheeks are getting warm and I don't know what to say. Because what if I tell her and she shuts it down? But she'll have to see it eventually and I need help figuring this out. And she's the editor in chief.

'I know you're working on something,' she continues. 'You're the first one in, you leave late, you're distracted. I've been in this game for a long time. What is it?'

'It's to do with the Sabine Roux death,' I say.

'Go on.'

'I think there was more to it. A lot more to it.'

'Do you have a source?'

'I have evidence,' I say.

'Great,' she says. 'Send me what you have by tonight. I'll look through it first thing tomorrow morning.'

Chapitre trente-quatre

I move out of the shelter of the metro just as it begins to rain again. I reach into my bag for my umbrella and as dried out amber leaves swirl around my feet and buildings reflect off puddles, I put it up. All I can hear is the beep and whirr of traffic, snippets of distant conversation and the pitter-patter of raindrops on the fabric of my umbrella as I wrap my free arm around my woolen coat and stride towards my street.

But as I get closer to the corner my phone pings from my handbag. It will be Hyacinth. I sent her my story before I left the office. My stomach is tight as I pull my phone from my bag.

Hi Harper, you said you have evidence. I'll need that too. H

Fuck. I intentionally didn't include the evidence with my story; I wanted her feedback first. Because if she isn't going to run it, I want someone else to, and a scoop by definition means the information isn't already 'out there'. But now she's asking. And she's my boss.

A clear plastic bag dances in the wind as I stand still, staring at the screen, considering my options. But then my phone flashes with a low battery notification. I need to get home and plug it in.

The rain is heavier now and my shoes are getting wet. I rush past the row of parked motorbikes all sparkling with droplets, my fingers white with cold as I feel around the bottom of my bag for my keys. There they are, next to Sabine's hard drive.

But just as I get to the corner of my street, the moment before I turn, I see a parked car.

The occupant is looking down, doing something on his phone and his face is lit up by the screen.

There's no mistaking it: dark hair, beaky nose, big.

It's *him*.

My stomach clenches.

I stop.

I turn.

And I head right back the way I came.

Quickly.

My blood hurls through my veins like a rush hour metro through a tunnel as I head back to the main road thinking, *Did he see me? Do they know I was there last night? Do they somehow know what I am writing about?*

But then I've turned the corner and I'm out of view and the air is thick with danger as I look around me: left then right. I need to get out of here. Quickly. I rush across the main road, weaving through traffic, and as I get to the other side I glance down at my phone: it's already 7 pm.

There's only one place I can think of where I might be safe. One place he wouldn't want to go again.

And so I pull out my phone and text Thomas. *Heya, I'm free now. I'll come over.*

~

It's just as I head down Rue Vaneau and pass a *papeterie* that I realise he must have seen me. I glance into the shop window at the brightly coloured cards, a pile of Moleskine notebooks and a golden rabbit beside a rack of vintage pens. Then I focus on the pavement, huddling beneath my umbrella and as I pass a white van I glance at the side mirror. And there he is behind me, following on foot: tall, willowy, with a large black umbrella.

My stomach twists.

I look ahead of me and start to run, splashing through puddles, holding tight onto my handbag so nothing falls out. By the time I turn left onto Rue d'Olivet my lungs are burning from cold air and fear, but I can see Thomas's building just up ahead on the left. I reach for my phone to call him, to tell him I'm here, and rush towards his door. But just before I get there, I see there's a message from him.

Hi Harper, I'm not home. Deadline. Tomorrow?

I stop in the middle of the pavement. Pedestrians bump into me, muttering things under their breath as I look behind me.

Shit.

I look up to the third floor: to his dark window.

Shit. Shit. Shit.

But I can feel Mr Tall and Creepy approaching. I can feel it, even though I can't see him yet. And so I do the only thing I can: I punch Thomas's door code into the security pad. The four corners of a square.

Bzzzz.

I push the door open and, the moment before I go inside, I look back towards the corner and see him. I was right.

He's coming.

I quickly pull the door closed behind me.

Click.

And now I'm here, in Thomas's building, dripping water from my umbrella all over the mustard tiles by the letterboxes. And he's not here.

I look to the stairs and swallow hard, dropping my umbrella in the metal bin by the door. Then I take those stairs two by two.

I'm at the third floor now, and Thomas's hallway is empty. It's just me and the walls and the old carpet with the 1970s circular patterning that has probably seen far worse things than what I'm about to do. I move slowly towards his door, reaching into my handbag and feeling around for the leather case of my locksmith set.

The one I took with me last night.

The one I didn't need.

My pulse is thumping as I get to his door and look left, right and left again. I pause for a moment, listening for sounds – footsteps on the stairs – but all I can hear is my breathing. I zip open the case, pull out a tension wrench and my favourite pick, dropping the rest back into my bag.

These sorts of locks consist of five pin stacks of differing lengths. In simple terms, I need to lift all five simultaneously so none of them are engaged.

I push the tension wrench in first, applying the smallest amount of pressure. Just like I did with Harrison's door when I broke in to get my stuff back. Just like the YouTube videos I watched showed me. Next, I insert the lock pick and gently move it up and down.

I'm almost there. I can feel the lack of pressure from the centre pins.

I keep going.

But shit.

Fuck.

The middle pin stacks have unpicked now.

My hands are clammy and slipping; my heart is fast. What if someone catches me? I glance up to the ceiling and check for the blinking red light of CCTV. But there is none.

And so I take a deep breath, centre myself, and try again.

The middle part is picked.

The outermost pin is picked.

There's just one more to go.

I calm my breath, and slowly, gently, I twist the wrench ever so slightly as I work.

Then: click.

The final pin lifts and the lock swivels.

I reach for the handle and quickly move inside, relief pulsing through me. I click on the light switch, put the picks back in their case and drop my bag on the floor.

The door bangs gently behind me and I slip off my shoes, sliding off my coat and, as I look towards the window — *is he still waiting out there?* — I hang it over Thomas's on a hook on the back of the door. Then I head towards the window and peek out through the curtains. I can't see him but I know he's out there.

I look around inside. Everything is just as it was last time I was here: a brown leather sofa, a bookshelf, his bed, perfectly made with hospital corners, is in the far side of the room and that ugly painting sits above it, watching me. Judging me the way he has from the very first time he saw me.

Thomas's computer is sitting on a desk against the wall and there are a few wires around it. I search for a phone charging cord but there isn't one. *Shit.*

I reach for my phone and reply to Thomas. *What time do you think you'll be done? Should I come over?*

I stare down at the screen, waiting for typing bubbles . . .

Waiting.

Waiting.

And then there they are. They stop. They start again. And in comes his message: *It's going to be an all nighter.*

Brilliant.

I go to the kitchen, flick on the kettle and type back: *Tomorrow then. See you soon.*

And then, while the sound of the kettle humming fills the empty flat, I quickly go to my photographs and email the ones I took in the gallery last night to my Gmail account. I hear the whoosh of them sending. And then, with five per cent battery left on my phone, I pull up Safari and type: *How to reset the password on a MacBook Pro.*

Chapitre trente-cinq

Fifteen minutes later my tea has been replaced by the Scotch I located in Thomas's upper left cupboard, my phone is dead, Sabine's hard drive has been plugged into Thomas's computer and I'm typing the word 'evidence' into the subject field of an email. I reach for my Scotch and take a sip, waiting for the heat in my throat to slow my blood, then drag the files from the unnamed folder on Sabine's drive into the message body.

I've already pulled the photographs from my Gmail onto Thomas's perfectly organised desktop, and so I drag those in too.

Am I one hundred per cent comfortable sending everything I have to Hyacinth? No. It's a risk. But I don't really have a choice here. I'm being followed. I need this story out there so Noah is released; so Agnès Bisset has no reason left to silence me. And Hyacinth definitely won't publish it without evidence. So here we are.

I type: *Hi Hyacinth, here is the supporting evidence. Harper.*

And then I finally press send.

Then it's simply a matter of deleting the files from the desktop so Thomas doesn't know I was here, and double-clicking on the trashcan icon. Mine are the only files in there as I press 'empty'. The sound of it emptying echoes off the walls.

And then I just sit there, a little dazed, my blood diluted by equal parts adrenaline and Scotch. It's just me and the hum of traffic floating in from the road outside and that guy in the painting and Thomas's computer.

I think of the bond and the information he claims to want to share with me tomorrow night as the mouse arrow finds its way up to his search history. What if he knows something that could really help me? And what if I could learn whatever it is without having to see him again?

What if everything I need is right here?

Click.

I scan down through the list of sites but it's all just news. Nothing about a bond. Or Genovexa. Or Requiem.

I look down to the ribbon at the bottom of his screen, to the blue iMessage icon. Maybe there's something there. He said that he'd called in a favour . . .

So I point the arrow over it and click. Up comes the message window. I scroll down the left-hand column, scanning for anything that looks vaguely interesting.

But, again, there's nothing about the bond.

And strangely, nothing from me either.

Just random chats with a guy called Adam about a game of squash.

And then there, a little way down is a message that begins, *Thomas, please talk with me, is not fair that you* . . . It came in a week ago.

I can't see the rest of the text because it's too long for the preview, so I click on it to read the whole missive.

Is not fair that you disappear. We liked each other, no? Bisous.

Interesting.

I didn't think Thomas had ghosting in him. He always seemed more of the dumpee than the dumper to me. Which just goes to show, you never can tell. I remember him in the line at the supermarket, grinning down at his messages. Was he smiling down at a text from her?

I scroll through the many messages she's sent him. She likes him, poor girl. And he's ignoring her.

Tu me manques.

Baby?

Why you don't reply?

God, what a knob.

But then three messages away from that last one, I see something. It's dated just after Thomas and I met in that laundromat and it reads, *Don't you miss this?* I stare at an image of naked breasts exposed, back arched, head slightly tilted. Wavy dark hair.

But the words are not the reason I am frozen in place. The sexual nature of that picture is not the reason that my stomach is churning. Because I don't really give a fuck if he's sexting other people; we're not in a relationship. And I don't want to be in one either.

No, the problem is far bigger than that.

I recognise that girl.

It's my neighbour.

~

The little hairs on the back of my neck are standing up on end as I try to make sense of things. I picture my neighbour in the bin room, cutting up boxer shorts. Was it him? Was Thomas the guy? The owner of the boxer shorts? Snip. Snip. Snip.

I saw her boyfriend in her room a couple of times. I try to remember what he looked like. But it was through her window, from a distance, and I didn't really pay attention. It *could* have been Thomas. There was another time I saw them in the foyer downstairs but I rushed upstairs without making eye contact because I didn't want to be drawn into conversation.

I strain to remember: *tall, caramel hair.*

Was that him?

It feels like something is squeezing the air from my lungs.

But what does this mean? It seems unlikely that he would date two women from the same building, doesn't it? Or maybe it doesn't . . . things like that happen. In my experience of life six degrees of separation has always been more like three. I look around me, searching the room, like maybe there's something I've missed, some vital clue to explain what the hell is going on. Something to flood my veins with calm. But as my eyes graze over the furniture – from sofa to bookshelf, to kitchen to bed, to painting – I find no solace. My eyes linger on that painting, the stern-looking man with his air of disapproval, the frills around his neck. I turn back to the desk. There are two drawers to the left. I open the top one – I don't know what I'm looking for but I scour through the contents anyway. It's just a pile of envelopes neatly organised against one side, some coins in a shot glass, a few pens and bills with handwritten notes like *PAID* on them. I open the next one, but it's just more of the same.

Shit.

I look back to the computer. Think of the messages I've just seen. And something deep inside me screams: *Leave.*

I eject the hard drive and turn the computer off. I don't know how I'm going to avoid the man waiting for me outside, but I'm pretty sure I saw a back entrance. It probably leads to a garage. I can go that way. I can go home and he'll still think I'm here.

I drop Sabine's drive into my bag and slip on my shoes. Then I reach for my coat behind the door.

I hold it behind me, putting on one arm, then the other, my eyes on the floor as I move. It's only as I look up, ready to twist the doorknob, that I see it.

Or rather the side of it.

It was hanging under my coat, on the back of the door.

A bomber jacket.

With just the edge of a design visible.

I reach for it, holding it out in front of me, so I can see the painting on the back clearly.

A tiger.

The walls move in towards me as I stare at the brushstrokes. Because I've seen this jacket before. This pattern.

And the world stands still, all clocks ticking half time, as I reach back into my bag for Sabine's hard drive and move back to Thomas's computer.

I power it on. I enter his new password, the one I just set.

My breath is peculiarly slow and steady, but my hand is shaking as I use the mouse to navigate through the files on the hard drive, looking for the one I want. The video on the bridge.

When I find it, I fast forward to around three quarters of the way through and then press pause. I'm at the part where two other couples are standing by the railing. To the left is the Instagram husband. And to the right stands the other couple looking out at the apricot sky. The man has just put his jacket around the woman's shoulders.

And I'm staring at a tiger.

It's the very same jacket as the one on the back of Thomas's door.

Is that Thomas?

I take in his height, his hair, his shoulders. Maybe. It could be. But this guy has a beard.

But why would Thomas be in Sabine's video?

My pulse is thudding as I press play again.

He turns his face to look at the blonde girl with him.

It's Thomas. Beard or no beard, it's definitely Thomas.

And I'm not sure what I'm looking at or why it's there or what it really means, but something is very, very wrong.

It's only as the blonde girl beside him turns around that I know what it is. She's laughing, her mouth wide as she turns towards the camera. I only see her face for a split second.

But my breath catches and the world starts spinning a little faster.

Because I know that face.

The whole of Paris knows that face.

Matilde Beaumont.

Chapitre trente-six

My pulse thumps in my throat as Matilde watches me from the screen.

Matilde, Sabine's video, Agnès Bisset, Mr Tall and Creepy, Thomas, my neighbour. How is all of this connected?

I can hear the sound of traffic floating in from the street as conflicting thoughts compete for the microphone: Why didn't Thomas mention he knew Matilde? I gave him the perfect opening when I came here that night, I spoke about knowing a girl who'd been murdered . . .

But Thomas is a good guy. He ran outside to confront the guy who'd been following me. He tried to protect me . . . didn't he? I look back to the window, to the gauzy curtain I watched him through.

I need to get the fuck out of here. I reach for the hard drive but my gaze catches on a red '1' sitting in the corner of the mail icon. *Was that there before?* I can't help myself. I click on it.

And there, at the top, is one new email. It's from some sort of security system. The subject reads 'Movement Detected'.

Shit.

My breath is short and sharp as I scan the room: what does it mean by movement detected? Is he watching me? My eyes flit from the corners of the ceiling – there are no CCTV cameras there – to the bookcase, the closet, the bed, the painting, the window and then my skin gets icy cold.

Because there, in the corner of the room, attached to the lamp, glinting in the light, I see it.

A lens.

It's pointed right at me.

And I don't recall seeing it last time I was here . . . but fuck, fuck, fuck.

My heart is thudding in my chest as I conduct a quick risk analysis: Thomas is working, on deadline, not watching a live stream from his apartment right now. He probably hasn't seen that email yet, hasn't seen me. I need to leave. Now.

Adrenaline surges through me as I grab my phone, throw the hard drive into my bag and run for the door. I move out into Thomas's hallway, looking around. But it's empty.

I need to go to the police.

I get to the steps and take them two at a time, bile rising in my throat as I move.

I'm in the foyer and the door is right there. I can see the street outside.

But I can't go that way, the tall creepy guy is still waiting for me there.

And I don't know how it all fits together yet, who is the more dangerous of the two, or whether they're working together.

I look towards the other side of the foyer: there's the door to the garage.

I run towards it, pull it open and head down some fluorescent lit concrete stairs. There's a big, heavy metal door at the bottom of them and I reach for the lever, pushing down on it. It opens and I move out into a car park. There's strip lighting on the roof and rows of cars and concrete pillars. And on the other side in the corner is another door.

An exit.

I stop still. Listen for sounds, for footsteps, for a car, but there's nothing but the sound of my breathing.

And so I run towards it, my breath so shallow I'm dizzy.

I'm almost there.

I pass a concrete pillar and then bang.

A deep pain in the back of my head.

My ears ring.

Everything spins.

Then: black.

Chapitre trente-sept

My mouth is like sand and my head is throbbing as I try to lift my eyelids: a solid, inky black. It's hard to tell if my eyes are open or closed and I have to blink a couple of times to be sure. There's carpet beneath my cheek. And it's hot. So hot. The air is thick and smells like something familiar . . . What's happening? Where am I? I go to groan and sit up, but there's something on my mouth and my head hits something else and my hands . . . why the fuck are my hands bound? My pulse speeds up as I pull against whatever it is: duct tape. I try to move my lips. They're taped too.

And I'm inside something. Stuck. My breathing quickens as I push against the top, the sides. But I'm trapped. Fuck.

I go to scream but all that comes out is a little high-pitched squeak.

But wait. I know what this smells like.

A car.

I'm in a car boot.

The carpet, the purr of the engine, the heat, the sound of gravel beneath tyres.

Yes.

We hit a bump and my teeth clatter together. *Ow.*

I blink hard, trying to remember how I got here.

The jacket on the back of the door. The tiger. The video on the bridge. Matilde. The stairs. The doors that led outside. The garage. The exit sign. Pain. Ringing. Spinning.

Darkness.

Someone knocked me out.

Who the fuck is driving?

Is it the creepy guy who's been following me? Or is it Thomas?

Those text messages to Thomas from my neighbour come flooding back. Thomas was dating my neighbour. He was dating her when he met me.

A flashback to the day we met in the laundromat. He was checking me out. That's why I talked to him – was he looking at me because he recognised me from his girlfriend's building? Or did he come looking for me?

A shiver runs through me and tears burn in my eyes. But I need to stay calm. I can't make a noise. The worst thing I could do would be to make a noise. Because if I let him know I'm awake, he might come back here and do whatever he's going to do early. I don't want him to come back here.

But I can do this. Because I know about car boots. I've written about them. There's an emergency release catch somewhere. I squint in the dark searching for something that glows: nothing. I lift my hands to feel along the perimeter. But I can't see anything and beneath my fingertips is just carpet.

Panic grips me as I feel around some more but I can't find it.

Where the fuck is it? What good was my fucking column?

The tail lights.

That's my other option.

I can push out the tail lights. Wave to an oncoming car.

Or I could, if I had use of my hands.

I can't even reach for the jack near the spare tyre beneath me.

My breath gets faster and faster and my lungs burn.

And it's hot. It's so fucking hot. So much hotter than I thought it might be. Did those YouTube videos I watched ever talk about how fucking hot it is in a car boot?

Panic rushes through me like a volt of electricity. Realisation hits.

He's taking me to the second location.

My stomach turns to oil and my ears roar like the ocean.

Because everybody knows the second location is where everything bad happens.

I clench my eyes shut. How can this be happening?

I'm never going to get to go to Japan and see the maple trees. I'll never see Camilla again, or have sex with another beautiful stranger in the rain on a rooftop. I'll never have my heart broken in that way that only sounds like a good idea when you know it's already happened for the last time.

Who will tell Mum?

What will they think happened to me?

I struggle for air.

In. Two. Three. Four. Five.

Out. Two. Three. Four. Five.

In. Two. Three. Four. Five.

And then I go limp. Denial, shock, something pulsing through me. Like it's not really me in this car boot. It's somebody else.

This can't be real.

Think, Harper, think.

I wrote a column once on how to get out of duct tape – hands over your head, pull down hard to your hips and back. I even tried it out with Camilla. It wasn't that hard.

But I can't do any of that lying in a car boot. I can barely move and hope is slipping from my grasp.

But Camilla. Find My Friends. Maybe she will check it when I don't reply, see I'm . . . where the fuck am I? I do some mental calculations. He knocked me out. How long have I been unconscious? It could have been two minutes or two hours. How far are we from Paris now?

How close to the second location?

And I realise: this is it, this is how normal women like Matilde, like Sabine, like me, end up on the front page of a newspaper. How we end up just another dead girl in a murder podcast.

My breath gets faster and I'm sweating. *I don't want to die. I don't want to die. I don't want to die.* My eyes burn with tears and I'm going to pass out from the heat.

Uh-oh. We're slowing down.

I swallow hard, shake my head to cover my face with my hair in case I blink and force my limbs to go limp.

And then I lie and wait for the boot to pop open.

Click.

A cool rush of air. It smells of soil and pine needles and rain – we're in the countryside somewhere – and the sound of some sort of insect fills the air. Arms reach in and grab me. Forcefully, I'm hoisted over his shoulder. I crack open my eyes to look around and he slams the boot shut. It's Thomas. I recognise the scent. He's holding a torch and the light sweeps across the number plate. The last two letters are AA.

It's the same number plate as that car I saw speeding off on the night Sabine was taken.

My pulse thuds in my ears and I struggle to stay limp as we move to the passenger seat of the car and he reaches for the handle. Who is in the passenger seat?

What are they going to do to me?

But when the door opens and the car's interior light flicks on, all I see is a big black bag. Thomas reaches for it and then slams the door and we move away from the car.

Something isn't fitting together properly. Because it's just me and him here.

And he was dating my neighbour. And I know from his number plate that he was there the night Sabine died. And he was on that bridge with Matilde.

291

I think back to his iMessage. There was nothing in there from Agnès. Nothing about me. Nothing about Le Voltage. And if Agnès Bisset had decided I knew too much and it was time to get rid of me, I'd be dead by now. There would be no value in keeping me alive.

No, something about all this – the car boot, the countryside, and every murder podcast I've ever listened to – tells me Thomas did this alone.

My brain struggles to recalibrate.

If Thomas did it alone then it was him who planted the white covering near the crime scene not Agnès Bisset. *Him* who was trying to frame Noah. Was he covering his tracks after that article about Paris having a serial killer came out? I think of the evidence in the most recent instalment: blunt force trauma to the back of the head. And my own head is throbbing right now . . . And Noah was the perfect person to frame because he was already in the papers as being questioned . . .

But how the fuck did Thomas get that white sheet of fabric to begin with?

We're walking up steps now. Thomas's footsteps are heavy with our combined weight and the wood creaks. A door opens and we move inside. It's dark aside from the torchlight then flick. The light switch. A yellow buzzy glow fills the room. I'm facing the door and I can see the windows. They're covered in thick black fabric, duct taped to the walls. The same sort of duct tape I got at Franprix for the CCTV at Le Voltage.

He drops me on a bed and I lie there as though still unconscious, watching through cracked lids and strands of hair as he takes the big black bag over to a small kitchenette. There's a rusty-looking sink, one of those gas hotplates for camping, an old kettle and a dirty looking bar fridge. To the side of the fridge is a long wooden counter with three plastic trays on it. There are some metal tongs. Some sort of equipment I vaguely recognise, a drying rack and a small sort of washing line with analogue film hanging from it.

It's a photographic darkroom.

He's brought me to a darkroom.

When I saw those books on Henri Cartier-Bresson and Man Ray on his bookshelf, this is not how I saw things playing out.

He moves to the big black bag and the sound of it unzipping echoes in the silence. Every murder documentary I've ever watched, every podcast I have ever listened to, flickers in my mind. What the fuck does he have in that bag?

And I don't know why he's doing this. I don't know what's going to happen.

But I do know this: I must not cry.

I must not scream.

I must not show fear.

Because men who kill get off on one common thing: control. And so the best way to stay alive a little longer is to not give him what he needs.

Then he'll keep trying to get it. And that will buy me time.

Chapitre trente-huit

I never realised how big Thomas was before now. You could fit three of my biceps in his. Maybe four. And he's tall, too. Looming over the rusty sink, having to bend himself in half just to put a litre of milk in the buzzing bar fridge. And where the hell did he get milk? Did he stop at a corner store while I was bound and gagged in the boot to buy that? Or did he calmly grab it from the fridge at work when he saw me on his security app and knew he was in for a long night?

But still, a litre of milk is good. A litre of milk means he thinks he's going to be here for a few days. He'll need multiple cups of tea. That means he's not going to kill me tonight.

These are the things I am consoling myself with.

I watch as he turns on the tap to wash his hands. My wrists are sore from the duct tape and the hair over my eyes is tickling my face. But I lie dead still and focus on not moving. I can't let him know I'm awake until I have figured out how to play this.

I piece together the room from what I saw when we came in and what I can see now through the thin veil of my hair. Because there's a way out of everywhere, if you look hard enough. I just have to find it. A window to be broken, a heavy object to use as a weapon, something. I could probably use the thick fabric covering the windows to protect my arm while I break a window, if I could just get free. There's nothing I could use as a weapon around me, but there are three flickering, dusty globes, buzzing from the wooden ceiling. If I could somehow reach them, maybe I could break them, use them . . .

I look down at the lumpy bed I'm lying on. It has sheets and a duvet cover with pale yellow daisies and that has to be good. It's not a bare stained mattress. Sheets are humane. Sheets are hopeful. But also: it looks like a girl's bedspread and that makes my stomach twist. Who did it belong to? Matilde? Some other girl they haven't found yet?

But still, the milk.

The tea.

I watch him wash his hands, like germs are the most danger- ous thing in the room, and think back to last Wednesday night: me watching Thomas through those flimsy curtains. A flash of him grabbing Mr Tall and Creepy by the throat. It seemed so protective back then, but now everything looks different. Because he wasn't protecting me. He was protecting himself. He wanted to know who the hell I'd led to his house: the police, a journalist, who?

He didn't want to get caught.

Shit.

The taps turn off and he moves back to the door and outside. I can hear him opening the car doors. Shutting the doors.

Oh god, what the hell is he doing out there? What's he getting from the back seat?

A flash of the apricot sunset reflected by the Seine behind that bridge. That jacket. Matilde's blonde hair shining. All caught on camera.

Was that why Thomas killed Sabine?

But how did he *know* she had caught him on video?

And my neighbour . . . how does she fit into all this?

And Agnès Bisset? Everything she's been doing.

And Hyacinth. Will she run my story? Will they arrest Agnès? I think of the evidence I sent through. Everyone will think Agnès killed Sabine.

And so nobody will be looking for Thomas.

And nobody will be looking for me.

And, even if they are, they sure as shit won't be looking for us out here.

No. The first seventy-two hours that are so vital in a missing person case will tick past. Soon it'll be too late. And when they find my body, the media will do what the media do and I'll be famous for a few days if they can even tell it was me.

But if they can't, if Thomas makes me unrecognisable, or harder to find, the French police won't take DNA and if they do they won't bother to match it to me. Because I will be diluted on that ever expanding list of people who disappeared this year.

My heart is beating loud in my ears and tears threaten to fall, but I won't let them. I need to figure this out.

I have to get out of here.

A car door slams loudly. Footsteps.

Boots scraping over gravel. They get louder and louder as they approach. The floorboards squeak with his weight outside, then the door creaks open and all my cells recoil simultaneously.

But I know what I have to do.

'Thomas?' I try to say, but it comes out like a mew. I'm moving slowly, like I'm just waking up, looking over at him through confused eyes. His face is the colour of cement and he's carrying my handbag over his shoulder. The video is in my bag. All the evidence I have. Nobody will see that video of him with Matilde if I die.

He stares at me and shuts the door. I look around, like it's the first time I'm seeing things, and try to talk again.

I look down at my hands and fake-notice they're tied up. I look up at him, eyes wide as I struggle to sit up.

My breath is quick now, just like it should be, given the situation. But I'm not freaking out quite as much as I might be if this were the first I knew of what he'd done. Of course, I could get out of this. I could hold my hands over my head and pull them down and break the tape, but then what? No, I'd best save that party trick for later. Make him think I'm helpless.

'Thomas?' I mew again from beneath the tape.

'Harper, you need to stay calm,' he says, in his polite way.

I nod. And he comes over to me, reaches for one corner of the tape and pulls it off my mouth.

'What's going on?' I ask as he watches me. I need to humanise myself. Maybe I can negotiate with him.

But he ignores me, and instead just empties my bag onto the table. The clattering sounds of plastic and metal hitting wood: Sabine's drive, my lipstick, a tampon, some wrinkled receipts, a couple of pens, the bobby pins, my article on that memory stick, Anne's bottle of pills and my locksmith tools.

But every cell within me clenches, because all I really notice is: no phone. No way for Camilla to find me.

I bite back tears. I will not cry.

'Please let me go,' I say to him. Sweet. Kind.

He ignores me, picking up the hard drive, putting it in his pocket, then the locksmith tools.

'Please?' I try again. 'This isn't you.' But he just ignores me. And so I change tack. 'Thomas. The *least* you can do is tell me why I'm here.'

'Shut,' he starts slowly, 'the fuck up.' He's yelling by the end of that sentence, his jaw set, like I just said something terrible. And his face is almost purple it's so red. There's a little vein popping out of his left temple, spittle flying from his mouth. Then he turns to face me. Rabid. Like he's spitting out the truth and I need to hear it. 'This is all your fucking fault. None of this is how it was meant to go.' I've never seen him like this. Not even when he was on the street, yelling at that guy Agnès had sent to follow me.

I don't know how to react, I don't want to make it worse.

So I just sit there, watching him, digesting the phrase 'how it was meant to go'.

None of this is random. He had a well-laid plan. A plan he'd used before.

An echo of Stan's voice: *You look just like the dead girl we aren't allowed to write about anymore.*

Matilde Beaumont and I are a 'type'.

My stomach twists as I think, *Is this how he does it?* He approaches a woman in a safe space. With me it was a laundromat. Where was it for Matilde? A supermarket? Did he ask her about which brand of coffee he should get? Strike up a rapport? Take her for a walk on that bridge? Is that what he gets off on? Making us trust him and then watching the horror in our eyes when we realise what he *really* is?

And then what? Does he always sleep with us, or was that just me? Does he do it then and there, or does he offer to drive us home, sedate us with a drink, drive us out here . . . to this? Or does he do it a few days later? Grab us in the dark?

Whatever the plan, it worked with Matilde.

But what about me? If he'd picked me out, chosen me, why didn't he kill me?

And then my throat burns with bile because I know the answer.

He didn't kill me because he couldn't.

I'm thinking back to that night in bed with him, when I told him I'd sent a photograph of him to my mother. No wonder he tensed up. He knew what he was planning, but now my mother knew what he looked like . . .

He needed to reassess. Take a beat. Create some distance between us first. Take me from somewhere that couldn't be linked to him.

I'm biting back tears; there's heat on my cheeks and I can taste salt.

And then, as quickly as it came on, his face relaxes and goes back to a normal colour.

He moves over towards me, a small kind smile on his face. 'I'm going to have to go out,' he says. 'But you should get some sleep.' And then he pulls back the daisy duvet cover for me to get in.

And the sheet is white, but there's a stain. A streak of brownish red.

Blood. Is that blood?

My skin burns hot.

And even though nobody can help me, I do the one thing I wasn't going to do: I open my mouth and scream.

Chapitre trente-neuf

I wake up with a mouth that tastes like the barrel of a gun: metal. No, not metal, blood. My head throbs and my face is sore and swollen. My eyes crack open: there's a trickle of red on the pillowcase.

A flash of memory: his hand coming down hard to silence me.

I lie still, controlling my breath as I listen. But there's nothing, just the hum of the bar fridge. I slowly, cautiously, glance around the room.

He's not here.

My wrists aren't taped together anymore, which on the surface sounds like good news, but it's not, because I knew how to get out of duct tape. But now one hand is free and the other is attached to the bedframe above my head with a handcuff. I sit up, inspect it. It's your stock-standard-buy-it-off-eBay type and I could get out of it easily, if only I had a paperclip, a bobby pin, anything.

But I don't.

I glance across at the wooden table. He's taken my bag and everything that was in it, bobby pins included. Not that I could reach it from here anyway.

My glance flickers around the room, searching for a means of escape. There's a thin crack of grey light coming in through the space under the door, and the insects outside have been replaced by chirping birds. It's morning.

And I don't know when he's coming back.

There has to be a way.

I look back at the handcuff and try contorting my hand, pushing my thumb up against my palm, and pulling. But it's no use. My hand is too big and now it's red and there's a bruised mark around my wrist from the pressure. I think back to the details about Matilde in the paper: *damage to her wrist believed to have been caused by some sort of restraint . . .*

Shit. Shit. Shit.

But think, Harper, think. Even if I do get out, what then?

I look across at the covered windows, to the locked door and then the rusty kitchenette: there must be something, somewhere in here, that I can use.

I close my eyes and steady my thoughts. I can do this. I *will* do this. I cannot just sit here and wait for him to come back with his special collection of Dexter knives, or whatever he's gone to get, and kill me.

I edge over to the side of the bed and look down at the floor. There's a Tupperware with a note: *if you need to pee.*

It seems like an oddly humane gesture all things considered, but then a mattress full of urine would require more of a clean-up.

I *do* need to pee, but I don't want to pee in that.

I push the Tupperware aside and look under the bed. There might be something I can use hidden under there. But no, just: dust, hair and an old tennis ball.

Nothing thin and bendy I could use to pick this lock.

I look back at the Tupperware.

Fuck it.

Two minutes later I'm drip-drying, negotiating the awkwardness that is being cuffed to a bedpost while trying to pee.

And then I hear it: tyres pulling over dirt. The whirr of an engine. My heart speeds up.

He's back.

The engine stops. A car door slams outside and I lie back down, pretending to be asleep. The room is filled with the metallic clicking of him unlocking the door . . .

The door creaks and opens: a gush of cool, sweet air. The crinkling of plastic. I open my eyes just a crack: he's carrying a small bag of what look like groceries and my handbag. I watch his caramel hair gleam in the light as he moves inside.

He ignores me, going over to the counter where he starts unpacking things: a newspaper, some chocolate, orange juice and plastic cups.

And as I watch him, I realise how alone I am out here. Nobody is going to find me. I'm not going to get out of this.

Of course. Of course this is where it ends. The how-not-to-get-murdered girl gets murdered.

Thank you, life, for your sardonic wit.

But I can't just sit here and wait for it to happen. If he's going to do it, if he's going to kill me, I need to at least make sure he gets caught. I need his DNA all over me. So I need to trigger the side of him I saw last night.

'Thomas?' I start. My heart banging in my chest. Because this could go either way.

He doesn't look at me. He just keeps slowly unpacking things.

'Thomas?' I yell at the top of my lungs, my throat burning.

His eyes close, like he's trying to calm himself. I think of those books on his bookshelf beside the photography collections, and imagine him saying some positivity affirmations in his head – *I am happy, I am calm, I am stable* – but I can't afford for him to be calm, happy or stable right now. Because calm, happy and stable people are rational, and rational people don't make mistakes.

And so I let rip.

'You need to let me go now!' I scream. And then the tears start for real. I'm howling, heat on my cheeks, my nose running. 'You'll never get away with this.'

'Yes, I will,' he says, too calm for my taste. '*If* the police investigate, and that's a big *if*, they'll blame someone like . . . Nicolas.'

Shit.

That message that came in from Nee-koh-lah while Thomas was holding my phone.

And he's right.

I think of Nee-koh-lah's sparse apartment and hairy back. Everyone will totally believe he's a killer.

I need to up the ante.

'You're a fucking monster,' I scream, going for the cutting frequency of crying babies and telephones. 'A monster!'

His face is getting red. Almost puce, really. 'I hope you burn in hell.'

The idea is to just keep screaming. He will only be able to stand it for so long.

He looks over at me. His eyes blaze.

Here we go.

'Shut up,' he seethes.

But I just keep on.

'You shut up!' I scream. 'How do you look at yourself in the mirror?'

He closes his eyes and takes a deep breath as though to centre himself again.

'You're a fucking monster!' I scream. I need to rupture any sense that might be finding its way into his psyche.

'No,' he says, his eyes flicking open. 'I'm not.'

'You are!' I scream.

He stares at me and I know something's about to happen. My pulse thuds, my breath is quick.

He's looking around the room now, his eyes wild. They settle on my handbag and he reaches inside it then pulls out Anne's pill bottle. He goes to the counter, opens the packet of plastic cups then moves to the sink. The sound of water hitting metal fills the room and then he pours a cup of water.

Is he seriously going to take a fucking Ambien?

But he doesn't, he hands me the water. He's thought of everything. If it were glass I could hit him with it. Then he twists off the top of the pill bottle and I know what he's planning. He's going to try to give that last pill to me. To sedate me.

But I have a better idea.

He drops the last of Anne's pills onto his hand and then reaches for my face as though to force me to take it like I were a dog.

But I turn my face just before he grabs my jaw and I bite.

Hard.

I get the fleshy part of his hand.

I taste blood. His blood this time, not mine. And he lets out a yelp, his eyes wide.

And now his blood is in my mouth and he's going to have to explain away having a bite mark on his hand when he goes into work.

I let go. And keep my eyes trained on him as I put my fingers of my free hand straight into my mouth. His DNA is under my fingernails now. On the tissue inside my mouth. He raises his hand, his bloody hand, but before he swings, he stops.

He steps backwards.

He heads out the door.

And I don't know whether he's suddenly developed a conscience or whether he simply didn't want any more of his DNA mingling with mine. Or whether perhaps he just wants medical attention. But no matter the reason, he's retreating.

The door closes with a bang and I hear it click as he locks it. His engine starts. Tyres over gravel fade to silence.

And now it's just me, the taste of his blood, and the certainty that I need to figure something out.

I turn my head quickly, looking around me. There has to be a way.

And it's as my head swivels that I hear a jangle.

A blessed fucking jangle.

~

I'm wearing earrings. Earrings with hooks. Wire hooks.

Wire hooks that bend, baby.

My hands are trembling as I reach for the left one and slip it from my lobe. I don't know if this will work. I don't know when he'll be back. But I have to try.

I straighten out the metal wire and insert it into the lock on the handcuff, bending it backwards so it kinks, just like I did with that paperclip when I was sitting on the sofa in my apartment.

My forehead is covered in a thin layer of sweat as I take a deep breath, insert it under the lock pin and lift it up. I expect it not to work. But, in the silence of that big and sparse wooden cabin, I hear the sound of hope.

Click.

I swallow hard and slowly pull the two sides of the cuff apart.

And now I'm free.

I stand up, my pulse thudding in my inner wrists, my eardrums, my neck, and run to the door. I reach for the handle and pull. Then push. It's locked, of course it's locked, and a door lock is not the sort of thing you can crack with an earring.

'Fuck,' I say out loud, moving over to the windows. I'll break one with my elbow.

I tear the black cloth from the window at the rear of the cabin and get ready to shatter the glass.

But there is no glass beneath it.

There are wooden slats.

They're screwed into the walls. A hundred little screws sparkle back at me.

My gaze snaps to the kitchen.

I may not be able to get out of here, but at least I'm free. I can fight.

I run over to the sink and open the cupboard beneath it. I'm looking for a weapon. Any sort of weapon. Maybe the chemicals he uses for developing film. But all I find are a bunch of sponges, some insect spray and a big bottle of bleach. I hold onto the counter as the room swirls around me, because bleach is what killers use to mask the smell of blood. To get it out of things.

I swivel, look to the drawers and pull them open one by one –

a couple of plastic spoons, some small packets of wasabi and soy sauce, a few napkins. I pull open the next one, it's filled with damaged and marred photographic prints.

I reach for the top one and look closer. A curtain takes up a fifth of the frame and it's not entirely in focus but I can still make it out. Because I know that building, I know that window. I know that room.

And I know that girl.

It's me.

It's me taken from my neighbour's window.

That's how he found me. How he chose me . . .

My hand is trembling as I leaf through the others. The second one is an old, worn-out, black-and-white print of a girl I've never seen before. She's around seventeen or eighteen, blonde, sweet looking. She's wearing a white T-shirt and a pair of dark shorts. The focus is slightly off but she's very clearly smiling down at the camera. Who is that girl? Where is she now? I flick through to the third photo and I only glimpse it for a split second before I drop them all to the floor. Because it's of Matilde.

And she's sitting on the bed in the corner of this very room. She's tied to the frame. And she's crying.

I need to get the fuck out of here.

I pull open drawer number three and all I find are little packets of sugar and tomato sauce. But beside them lies a blunt butterknife.

I grab it. I can't stab him with it. But there is something else I could do.

I run over to the back window, insert it into the groove of a screw. And then I twist. And twist. And twist. And soon my hand is sore but one screw is out. There are five more on this one slat and I don't know when he'll be back. *Shit.*

Adrenaline zings through my veins as I move onto the next screw . . .

Chapitre quarante

Around ten minutes later I have one wooden slat sitting on the dusty floor beside me, and am starting on the next. But then, in the distance, I hear the crunching of gravel beneath car tyres. It gets louder and louder, the engine idles for a moment and then nothingness. Silence.

I hear a car door open and close. Then another one opens. I don't dare look through the space in the window I've just created. I quickly stick the black fabric back on and pray he doesn't notice the missing slat from outside. I imagine him out there, and wonder what he's doing. What he's pulling from the back seat? A shovel, knives, rope? There are no good options here.

I pick up the piece of wood and move to the door.

The car door slams. I can hear the creak of the boards outside as he steps onto them. Then the clinking of keys as he puts one into the lock. My legs are wide and set so I don't fall over. I'm ready.

The door opens, I see the back of his head, and I swing.

Hard.

He stumbles, almost falls. But he stops himself and turns towards me. I hit him again, and his arms don't move in time to protect the side of his face. He falls to his knees, drops the bag he's carrying and holds his head. His cigarettes and lighter fall from his pocket and scatter across the floor. But he's between me and the door now. *Shit.* He pushes the door so it closes and turns to me and fucking smiles.

My heart is wild but my mind is clear. I grab his lighter and then run to the kitchen and open the cupboard beneath the sink.

He's standing up now and running for me as I reach past the bleach and pull out the bug spray.

He's four steps away from me.

Three steps.

Two.

I make a low guttural sound, flick the lighter, aim the nozzle and spray.

A stream of fire hits him in the face and he steps backwards, holding his face. His hair is singed and the collar of his shirt is on fire. He trips. Falls.

I can see the door, right there on the other side of him, and I need it to get out. So I flick the lighter again, aim the nozzle again, as though to threaten him. It's not my fucking fault that he lurches at me. That I spray. There are proper flames now and the can is so hot. I drop it.

My pulse is one continuous beat.

I pull open the door, stumble outside and slam it behind me. The key is still in the lock and with shaking hands I twist it.

And then I run.

I don't know where I'm going, I just run.

Past the car.

And down the path the car drove up. I can still see its tyre marks in the mud. *That must be the way to the main road.*

By the time I get there, and see the smooth tar and the promise of traffic, my lungs are burning and I'm trembling with adrenaline. I stand in the middle of the road and look around me. Left. Right.

I have no idea where I am. I have no phone. I have no money and no identification.

Left. I choose left.

I take two steps in that direction and *boom.*

A big, big bang behind me.

I turn to look.

There are flames and smoke and embers. And it's coming from the cabin I left Thomas in. My mind puts together the picture quickly: gas cooker, fire, wood.

Oh god.

I'm still standing, staring at the smoke, my eyes wide, when I hear the hum of an engine and look behind me. A black car is coming down the road and I raise my hands and wave to it manically. It slows down and stops behind me. I can see the driver peering through the windscreen, his wide eyes focused on the smoke coming from the cabin behind me. He gets out of the car and rushes over to me. He's speaking in French and pulling out his phone and I don't really know what's happening or what he's saying, all I can hear is the beating of my own heart and the chattering of my teeth, but I do recognise one phrase: 'Mon dieu'.

He's talking very quickly on the phone now. He hands me his jacket. And I just stand still, staring at the smoke. Seconds melt into minutes and soon there are sirens.

Chapitre quarante et un

The offices of 36 Bastion des Orfevres look the same in real life as they did on Google: a big modern building with hundreds of windows reflecting the sky, on the edge of the 17th arrondissement. The same but bigger. And more menacing. Those were my first impressions as I pushed my way through the glass door and went inside. I gave the man at the desk my and he rode with me up an elevator, led me down a few, and opened the door to a small room.

That's where I'm sitting now. Waiting. Trying to keep my eyelids open. Because I'm that wired kind of tired; where your brain knows the threat is gone but your body refuses to let down its guard, to sleep. Just in case.

It's Thursday now, forty-eight hours after that big boom. I spent the first twelve hours in a hospital, having all sorts of people come in and ask me questions and then all sorts of other people tell them that they really should wait. But from that hospital bed, with the smell of antiseptic in my nostrils, the sound of sirens still ringing in my ears and still in a mild delirium, I told them everything.

I gave them Thomas's name, his address, told them what he'd done, showed them my wrist and the marks from the handcuff. I told them all about that video of Thomas and Matilde on the bridge; about Sabine and the numberplate. From the looks on their faces, 'everything' did not make much sense to them, but notes were made in notepads all the same.

A policeman drove me home when it was time to leave the hospital. I'm pretty sure he thought I'd suffered some sort of concussion when I asked him to come upstairs and make sure there was nobody tall and ominous waiting for me.

But he came. And he looked. And there was nobody, of course.

Hyacinth hadn't, and still hasn't, published my article. When I checked my emails, there was a message from her saying, 'Great, let me run with this, I'll do some digging.' Nothing since then but I didn't care. I was too busy scouring the streets outside every time I boiled the kettle and spoke to Mr Oiseau. Too busy lying on the sofa beneath a blanket, my eyes trained on the door just in case someone broke in.

I didn't leave for food. For anything. I just ate and drank what was in the house until I got the call this morning.

And then I ordered an Uber and came here.

The door swings open and Luneau walks in. He's carrying an iPad and some papers. And Brigadier Moor is trailing behind him.

'Harper,' Luneau says, pulling out a chair and sitting down opposite me.

'Hi,' I reply as Moor sits down too.

'How are you feeling?' he asks, his eyes on my bruised face. But his expression is uncomfortable, he's thinking, *Please don't go into too much detail*. I don't suppose police are hired for their bedside manner.

And so I keep my reply succinct. 'Shit.' My stomach twists as my eyes meet his.

He gives a small nod, reaches beside him and flicks on a black, square recording device, and a little light glows red. He runs through the date, time, location and people present all in French, pulls out his notebook, and then his eyes return to mine.

'Harper, when did you meet Thomas Jamison?' Luneau asks, all business.

'In early October,' I say. 'It was in the laundromat.' But now I'm thinking of that picture of me through the window. 'I think he found me before that though. I think he was watching me.'

He nods. 'Yes, he was. We found these.'

He fiddles around on his iPad, then pushes it towards me so I can see. I expect it to be another picture of me through my neighbour's window but it's not.

It's an image of me standing outside my building, entering the door code, waiting for that big brown wooden door to swing open.

I frown down at it and then look back up at Luneau. He touches the screen to flick through to the next one.

Me, in the laundromat, texting someone. It's taken through the window.

'That's it,' I say, pointing to the laundromat. 'That's where I met him.' My voice is dry and scratchy from lack of sleep and god knows what else.

'This was taken late September,' Luneau says.

I nod.

'We also found some videos on Sabine's iCloud,' he says, slowly, reaching for the iPad and scrolling. 'I'd like you to take a look at them and let me know what you can tell me about them.'

He swivels the iPad and pushes it towards me, and I brace myself to see the video of me and Noah having sex. But when he presses play I realise it's not that at all.

'That's Le Voltage,' I say, looking up at him, and he nods. I look back down and watch the stream of images. It's the night of Noah's exhibition. I recognise his paintings on the wall, the people in the crowd – there's the guy with the thick grey hair, Agnès Bisset and the mousy-haired girl by the door handing out champagne. The camera moves through the crowd. Now the camera moves to the doorway and heads outside. A long, unbroken shot. It scans the street. Focuses on the sky. Then a streetlight. Then a figure in the dark, looking down the alleyway where Noah and I were smoking. The camera creeps towards him – I recognise the jacket, the tiger – and then comes a giggle and '*Coucou!*'. The figure swivels, his face in a state of shock. And Sabine says in French, 'Wait, I know you.'

'No, you don't,' Thomas replies in English.

'I do. From the bridge. I know you.'

318

The camera is still rolling, Thomas's eyes are wide. And then he says, 'You're wrong.'

'Here's my card, I'll send you the footage, it's cute,' comes Sabine's voice. And then the screen cuts to black.

I look up at Luneau. 'That was the night of Noah's exhibition. I'd seen Thomas just the night before and I'd posted about it on Instagram. He must have followed me there.'

Guilt pulses through me as Luneau makes a note on his pad.

Because poor Sabine. She really was the wrong girl in the wrong place at the wrong time . . . he got rid of her because she recognised him. He feared she could link him to Matilde.

My stomach clenches.

Luneau reaches for the iPad, scrolls through and presses play then pushes it back towards me.

'This is from the next night, on the fifteenth.' He says.

I watch the images of the crowd in Noah's studio. I can almost smell the turpentine and dust in the air. She's videoing, people are dancing. And I'm there. Noah leads me onto the dancefloor and my hands reach around his neck. I blink hard as I watch. My face is clear as I look over to the lens. Then I go to the kitchen and Noah follows me. Sabine keeps videoing, she wanders through the crowd, turning in circles in a way that makes the footage hard to watch without getting dizzy. And then she stops and simply films. I'm watching people move around, talk to each other. The guy in the green velvet jacket is in frame now.

Luneau presses pause.

I glance up at him, then back down at the screen. His finger points to a face in the background.

My breath catches in my throat as I take in the features.

'That's Thomas,' I say, almost a whisper.

And now I'm thinking of the white fabric found at the scene of the body. Thomas was there, at the studio. There were sheets of it covering all of Noah's paintings. How easy it would be to take one. To use it to move the body. Then to plant it later, when Noah was in the papers as the main suspect.

His number plate: AA.

His white car parked on the bottom section of Rue Chappe.

'Sabine posted a selfie on Instagram the night of Noah's party,' I say, my words coming out fast. 'It had Noah's street sign in the background. If Thomas already had her business card he would have known to watch that account. How to find her.'

Luneau nods. He already knows what I'm telling him. And my mind is filled with images of how it all went down.

Thomas waiting outside for Sabine to leave, him following her and Noah to the bottom of the street. Waiting as they fought. Noah returning to the party. Sabine carrying on to the metro. I imagine her looking down at her phone, watching the footage she'd taken that night. It was a quiet street. Nobody was around, I remember.

He could have waited until she was almost at his parked car.

Thirty seconds. That's all it would have taken to knock her out and bundle her into it like a drunk girlfriend, put his hands around her neck while she was still unconscious and squeeze. Then all he had to do was speed away.

I bite down on my lower lip and tears burn in my eyes.

Moor goes to a desk in the corner and brings me back a couple of tissues.

'Did you find a copy of that video of Matilde and Thomas on the bridge?' I ask.

'No,' Luneau says. 'But there was a second phone in his apartment. The same one we found those photographs on.' He nods to the iPad, 'There were texts from you on it.'

I think back to his iMessage.

This is why my texts weren't there with all the others. With my neighbour's. Mine weren't going to his real phone, they were going to a burner phone.

'And also a text from Matilde's number,' Luneau continues, interrupting my thoughts. He reaches into the pile of papers in front of him and pulls out a photograph. 'One of these belonged to Matilde. Do *you* recognise anything in this photograph?'

It's all forensic lighting and a sterile tray with a selection of jewellery on it.

I glance down at it: a gold necklace with a seashell pendant, an evil-eye bracelet, a silver bangle and a red kabbalah string.

'That's Sabine's,' I say, my voice small as I point to the red string.

And as I say it, the world warps around me. Because I know why Thomas helped me with my story, with finding out information about that bond. It was never about me or the story. It was about the picture I showed him. Sabine's hand was in frame. That red string was right there. No wonder he was so keen to know where I got it.

He knew Sabine had videoed him. He was worried that if that hand was hers and I'd seen *that* video, I'd see the others too; that I'd see the one of him and Matilde on the bridge.

'So nothing of yours?' Luneau asks, bringing me back into the moment.

I shake my head and think of my earrings. How easily they could have ended up in that forensic photograph too.

It's all a blur after that. Luneau says something about Agnès Bisset but I'm not really listening anymore.

And then I stand up and he leads me to the door, walks me back down those corridors, and rides with me in the elevator until it's time to shake hands and go outside.

It's as I stand there, waiting for my Uber, that the notification pops up on my screen: *Killer dead. Abducted woman escapes.*

And that's when I know it's time to go home.

Because, as it turns out, Paris is not always a good fucking idea.

Chapitre quarante-deux

I'm at Gare du Nord at 10.55 am the next morning, my suitcase beside me as I sip coffee and scan the crowd. I tell myself I'm looking for Mr Tall and Creepy, that it's a matter of safety, and in part that's true. But the full truth is never that simple. So here's the other part, the part I'd never admit out loud, not even to myself: I can't help but search for Noah's face in the crowd too.

Of course, it's entirely illogical. Yes, he has been released, but he doesn't know I'm leaving, so why the hell would he be here? And I could call him. Tell him. Make some big rom-com out of the whole thing. But what then? What, we'd run off into the sunset, get the dum-dum-da-dum-dum and the place in the suburbs and live happily ever after? If only it were that simple. If only that would make me happy, make him happy. But even if we started with the best of intentions, a team of two that would defy convention, stay wild and all that, suburbia and low-level resentment is where we'd end up. That's where it always ends up eventually.

So instead I finish my coffee, take my suitcase and head upstairs to the Eurostar, London and Camilla.

~

Forty minutes later I'm boarding the train, putting my luggage in the rack and scanning the seat numbers for thirty-four. I pull out my phone, put in my earbuds and silently pray nobody sits next to me. I scroll through to a podcast and close my eyes until the narrator is running through things I don't want to hear about right now, and so I pull out my earphones and close my eyes until the train is moving.

It's a beep that has my eyes flick open. A text message. From Camilla. A photograph of the spare room she usually Airbnbs out, all made up with throw pillows and a Harrods bear with a green ribbon around its neck we bought together a few years back on a whim.

On your way?

I type back: *Yes, see you soon xxx*

The seat beside me remains empty, so I put my handbag on the chair and scroll through Instagram. But every post reminds me of something I don't want to remember: a jewellery advert reminds me of that gold necklace, evil-eye bracelet, silver bangle and red kabbalah string; of all the corpses still unfound. A shot of a sunset reminds me of the apricot sky behind the Seine in Sabine's video. A positive quote reminds me of Thomas's bookshelf. A shot of a gallery reminds me of that painting on his wall and a shot of a Parisian café reminds me of all the dreams I'm leaving behind.

So instead I go to my emails.

There's one at the top from Hyacinth.

An article is attached. I click on it and glance through the text, the indictments against Agnès Bisset, minus of course anything implicating her in Sabine's death. It's entitled: 'The Paris Affair'.

Her message reads: *It'll be live from 2 pm.*

I got my scoop after all. So why don't I care anymore?

My phone is right there in my hands and I know I shouldn't, but I just can't help myself. I pull up Safari and type in *Thomas Jamison*. I'm met with a long list of articles and his face, his eyes with those long lashes that are pale at the tips, staring back at me. My breath catches in my throat as I click on the first one. It was published yesterday.

> *Thomas Henry Jamison, 38, who died two days ago in a fire after allegedly abducting a woman, Harper Brown, has been implicated in the death of Sabine Roux after her DNA was found in his car and number plate recognition software placed him at le Bois de Boulogne on the night of 15 October. Investigation into the death of Matilde Beaumont continues . . . colleagues and neighbours describe Mr Jamison as a nice, helpful, caring man.*

Maybe one day I'll write about Thomas too. But not now. Because even seeing his face staring back at me from my phone makes my hands shake.

I sit back, listen to nothing but the hum of conversation around me and look at my reflection in the windows as I wait for the darkness of the Chunnel to end.

Chapitre quarante-trois

The next year passes in a blur: soon after my name finds its way into the press, the media figure out which is my Instagram account and so I delete it and every other social media platform too. I follow the story in the papers, and every time I learn a new detail I catalogue it with a forensic detachment that makes no sense to me. Like: Thomas worked in the same large, mirrored building as Matilde Beaumont. The papers speculate that's where he first saw her. He stalked her. He approached her. He spent that evening on the bridge with her. And then, one night, he grabbed her and killed her. Just like I hypothesised. The papers speculate about lots of things, really. But I'm the only person aside from Thomas who'll ever see that photograph of her on the bed in that dark room. Crying. And it haunts me.

Harrison's second album bombs. Melody gets pregnant. They break up. He texts me a long, sad missive, which at first I think is sweet (that he's seen the press) but, then, in true Harrison style, turns out to be selfish (he hasn't written anything since we broke up and needs his muse back). I don't text back. Instead I tell myself I'm strong, independent, don't need anybody, and then mope around the house, scared to go outside, looking out the window for Mr Tall and Creepy. I commit to a daily green juice. That commitment lasts three days. I mope some more. I apply for jobs. I write to Hyacinth to tell her there may be reference calls on the way and find out that *The Paris Observer* has closed its doors. Hyacinth's shitty moods make so much more sense now. This makes me sad on one hand but happy to think that Stan will now have to find a new job and may end up 'freelance' like me. I consider sending him a 'how to write a blog' post but don't. Instead, I apply for more jobs. I get an interview. I have a panic attack on the Tube because someone near me is wearing perfume with a strong note of orange blossom, and as I breathe it in I think of that morning I discovered they'd found Sabine's body. I get a job. I immediately start planning a trip to Japan I won't be able to afford for eighteen months. I have flashbacks all the time. I imagine a world where Thomas wasn't caught, where he moved from amateur to seasoned killer. Would he have developed a calling card? An initial? A flower? Or would he have continued to walk this earth unnoticed, blending in seamlessly with the good and obedient people of the world?

And then I think of his concerned text message that morning after I gave him the flick: *Hi Harper, I'm not sure what happened yesterday but I think you're right, it's best we end things. Just let me know you're okay. T.* And I run through all the reasons he might have sent that. Maybe it was part of some sick ploy to get me to trust him and he got off on duping his victims. Maybe he wanted to feel in control.

Or, the scariest of all, maybe Thomas genuinely saw himself as a good man.

Of course, there's another one too: he thought my mother had a photograph of him. So, if one day she got hold of my phone records, he wanted it logged that not only was our fling over but he was fine with it. Just fine.

But I try not to think about that one. Because when I do, I know what comes next: even though Thomas thought my mother had a photograph of him, even though I posed a mild risk, he didn't just let me go, didn't just pick another victim instead. And I am left asking: why *couldn't* he let me go?

Why did it have to be *me*?

Which then leads to thoughts of Sabine, and how if she hadn't seen him and recognised him, she'd be alive now. And then: guilt. Because Sabine saved me in a way. After her death, I was put on ice until things calmed down.

That is, of course, until one night, I arrived on his doorstep . . .

Those sorts of thoughts will fuck you up at 4 am, it's almost impossible to make them stop, and when I manage it's only to think other equally shit things like, *What would have happened if Camilla hadn't called me that night I went to Thomas's house for help?* The night I showed him that picture from Sabine's video with her hand in frame? What if he hadn't heard me tell Camilla, 'I'm just at Thomas's house'? Would he have killed me then?

Mum and Neville break up for good and she meets a new Neville – this one is called Marc. Camilla realises the guy on the fourteenth floor is not her soulmate but she hasn't had her identity stolen yet either, so maybe both of us were wrong. She gets the job at *Vogue* and is constantly bringing me tops a size too small from sample sales.

Agnès Bisset goes to trial. Her messages are dissected as part of the investigation. It turns out she would have disposed of Sabine herself if Thomas hadn't done it for her.

The Klimt isn't recovered, she claims it was a fake but that doesn't matter because I was right about that not being her first foray into white collar crime. A vast number of artefacts from questionable origins are seized from Geneva Freeport. It turns out she was using emerging art, selling pieces she bought cheap for seriously inflated prices, to move said artefacts. Not once do I read the name Philip Crawford-White in the papers, of course.

DNA extracted from Thomas is added to the UK National DNA Database. There's a positive match with the DNA taken from a 2015 UK murder scene.

I recognise the victim immediately. It's the young blonde girl in that photograph I saw at the cabin. Though she's older in the pictures in the papers, she still has the same eyes, hair and smile. And she's the right type: she looks just like me and Matilde. The newspapers tell us that she was his babysitter years before. That she had a small textiles business hand-painting unique designs onto articles of clothing. They find an email from Thomas in her inbox professing his love. They find her rejection.

And they close the case.

As for me, I'm healing. I'm not healing. I'm healing again. It's a process. I take up jogging. I take up yoga. I take up Pilates. I take up barre. I do none of them. Instead I sit every day and stare at the blinking cursor on my screen and do my best. Because work is the only thing I really have these days.

And I'm okay with that. Work doesn't bundle you into the boot of a car and handcuff you to a bed. Work has a beginning, a middle and an end, and the end doesn't involve tears (mostly). Work is something I can do indoors.

The doorknob rattles and I look up.

'Heya,' Camilla says as she comes inside. 'Please tell me you put on pants today?'

She says this line a lot so I don't take it too seriously.

'Maybe,' I say.

'It's not healthy. Get dressed, it's Saturday night. We're going out.'

She disappears into her bedroom.

'Where to?'

'Surprise,' she yells and then reappears holding up a navy lace top. 'But I'm dressing you.'

I close down my computer and stand up.

'I'm not really feeling like it,' I say.

'Harps, please. How many things have I done for you?'

I roll my eyes, take the top, and go through to my room where I get dressed and run a brush through my hair.

~

Twenty minutes later, in the back of an Uber, it's a blur of traffic lights and headlights and shop windows and beeping and Camilla chatting happily about someone at work.

Then the car slows down and I look outside. Soho. I can see one of my favourite jazz bars up ahead – is that where we're going?

I get out of the car and stand on the pavement.

'Bye, give me five stars!' Camilla instructs the driver. And then he's gone, and Camilla is taking my hand and saying: 'Ready?'

We move up the street a little and then turn sharp left into a doorway. The lights are gentle, romantic. The floors are unpolished floorboards. There are paintings on every wall and the positioning of small lights makes them jump from the walls as though animated. I focus on one of the paintings. Now I understand why Camilla still has a firm grip on my hand. She wants to make sure I don't do a runner.

My face grows warm and everything starts spinning a bit – like I'm one of those miniature ballet dancers in a music box – as I look from painting to painting.

I recognise the gold, the red and the comics. But the girl is different now. She's blonde. And she looks a lot like me.

I look to Camilla. My eyes say, 'Thank you but I'm scared,' and I'm shaking my head as if to say, 'Let's get the hell out of here.'

'You're fine,' she says and squeezes my hand, then skips off to the drinks table.

And so I do the only thing I can think of, I move over to the wall and start inspecting one of the paintings up close. *It's me, it's definitely me.*

I'm a dark-clothed, mysterious figure that seems to almost melt into her surroundings.

I think of that night over a year ago now, the one where I wandered into Le Voltage unannounced to take a picture and he was there.

Is he here?

But all I see are people milling around a small table set up with champagne, Camilla among them, and others talking to each other, saying things like 'his juvenile works' and answering statements with 'Quite'.

'So I have gifts,' comes Camilla's voice as she arrives next to me. I turn to grab my glass of champagne. And that's when I see him.

On the far side of the room.

He looks just like he always did and is wearing a pair of light blue jeans ripped at the leg and a long-sleeved white shirt. I imagine his biceps under it. That tattoo: ka-pow.

And I'm just standing there, staring at him. Camilla frowns and turns to follow my gaze.

And that's when he sees us too.

～

My heart is banging so hard against my rib cage it's reverberating in my ears as he moves towards us in what seems like slow motion.

'I'm going to give you a sec,' Camilla whispers in my ear, and then she's off, to the other side of the room. And I'm left, breathless and not sure what to do with my hands. I clasp my champagne glass.

'Hey,' he says, his eyes still on mine as he approaches.

'Hey,' I reply. It's all I can manage as he moves forward to kiss me on one cheek and then the other. He smells like he always did: like peppermint shampoo and the air after it rains. 'I'm so fucking glad you came. I was worried you wouldn't.'

I feel my forehead move into a frown as realisation hits: Camilla organised this with him. I look over to her and she's watching us, grinning.

'So,' I say, looking at the painting closest to us. 'New model?'

He grins. 'Do you mind?'

'No, it's a shit likeness anyway,' I say.

'Yes, *and* you're wearing your clothes.'

'So a strong fail on all counts,' I say, sipping my champagne.

And I want to say so many things, though I'm not sure what they are. I want to be witty and brilliant and all the things all at once. But for me, when there are things I can't say, or I won't say, it's almost like they clog my throat. And then I can't say anything at all. And so I just stand there, staring at the painting, waiting for him to say something first.

'I should probably go and talk to some people,' he says, watching me.

And I smile and nod and wait for him to go, like I don't care either way, when really my marrow is aching. This is why I never would have come here if I'd known. This exact feeling.

'But I'll be done in twenty minutes,' he says, interrupting my thoughts. 'Can you stick around?'

Chapitre quarante-quatre

Reader, I stuck around. And now I'm waking up slowly, his arms around me, memories from last night flickering through my mind. The gallery. His paintings. I turn to look at him: he's still asleep. I reach for my phone beside the bed. There are two missed calls from Mum. I slowly wriggle out of his grasp and into the cold morning air, pulling my dressing gown around me as I close the door and head through to the kitchen with my phone.

It's still dark outside as I dial.

She picks up on the first ring. She sniffs. She's crying.

Shit.

'He's gone, Harper. Marc's gone.' Her voice so small, just like a child. I've heard this voice so many times.

'I'm sorry, Mum,' I say, my voice flat.

She starts sobbing again. 'I thought it was going to work this time.'

'I know,' I say. 'I can come and see you tomorrow?' I suggest. Tomorrow is Sunday.

'That would be so great,' she replies. And I imagine her there in the same house I grew up in, wearing the same sort of clothes, removing all traces of Marc from her eyeline.

'Okay, see you then.'

We hang up. And I look back to my closed bedroom door and I know what I have to do. Because, ladies and gentlemen, some patterns never change. Not hers, and not mine either. I tiptoe towards the door so I don't wake Camilla, reach for the cool handle and twist. And then I move inside. He's lying on his side. I slip out of my dressing gown, drape it over a chair and get into bed.

He rolls over to hug me. 'Where were you?'

'Mum was calling,' I say, threading my fingers through his and squeezing, then moving towards his face and kissing him on the forehead. 'She can't wait to meet you.'

He pulls back just slightly and looks at me. 'Huh?'

He frowns. His muscles tense up. I make sure I maintain eye contact even though something twists inside me as I see his irises contract.

'She asked us for lunch. It's not until twelve though, so lots of time.' Then I lean across and kiss him on the neck and hold him tight. Too tight. Crazy-girl tight.

'Wait,' he says, blinking as if to get his thoughts right, his forehead a deep frown. 'Why does your mom want to meet me?'

I swallow. This is more painful than I expected. 'Why would she not want to meet you?' I ask.

Fear flashes in his eyes. I might miss it if I didn't know what I was looking for. He pulls away from me just a fraction more and the air beneath the duvet gets cold. His adrenaline is surging now, he's thinking, *How the fuck do I get out of here without upsetting her? A meeting. I'll say I have a meeting.*

I swallow loudly and try to control my breath.

'Harper?' he says.

A sadness flows through me as I wait for the inevitable. 'Yeah?'

He breathes out loudly.

'Are you fucking with me?'

My throat closes up.

'No,' I say. My heart is beating faster now. And his eyes are narrowing. He tilts his head slightly. Then he reaches behind his head for his pillow and hits me with it. 'You are, you fucker.'

He sits up, feet over his side of the bed as he reaches for his phone and starts scrolling through it and my heart is banging so hard against my ribs.

'Oh look, my mom wants to meet you too.' He grins, turning back to me and showing me the screen. 'You're a psycho, you know that?' he says, standing up and pulling on his grey underwear then reaching for my dressing gown.

It's too small for him, but he puts it on anyway and heads for the door.

And my throat is tight. This isn't how it was meant to go.

'Are you leaving?' I ask, my voice cracking.

'No such luck. I'm making coffee.' And then he goes and I'm left staring at the doorway.

And I can hear him in the kitchen, hear cupboards being opened and closed. Hear the kettle flicking on. But it's as I hear the fridge door close that I know exactly how this story ends.

It ends in tragedy.

Love stories always end in tragedy eventually; in death, disillusionment or divorce. There is no fourth choice.

I know that.

But maybe hearts are just made to be broken.

Because as I sit here, on the bed we slept in last night, listening to him opening drawers in the other room, I know with total certainty that, despite it all, I'm going to do it anyway. It doesn't matter that it's illogical and it can only end it tears. It doesn't matter that it goes against everything I know to be true. Maybe biology has finally blinded me, maybe I have PTSD from Thomas so I'm not thinking straight, maybe society has sucked me back into their way of seeing things, or maybe it's just that everything beautiful in life is temporary. I don't know. All I know for sure is when people ask how we met, I'll revel in saying, 'Well, it was Paris in the autumn. I was sleeping with a serial killer and he was married to someone else.' Or maybe I won't. Maybe I'll say none of that. Maybe I'll just smile and say, 'Well, it began like any anti-love story. With *Chapitre Un.*'

Acknowledgements

Thank you to my publisher, Fiona Henderson, for your ongoing belief in me, your invaluable creative input and for always going the extra mile. To Dan Ruffino for your support from day one. To my editors, Deonie Fiford and Michelle Swainson, for your attention to detail and thoroughness – I always know my books are in great hands. To Mark Evans and Katherine Ring for your fantastic proofing skills. And to Anthea Bariamis for checking the French phrases in this book and all your work creating the audiobook.

Thank you too, to Elissa Baillie, Gareth Woods-Jack and the entire team sales team at Simon & Schuster Australia for always championing me and getting my books into the hands of booksellers. To Kirstin Corcoran for your next-level marketing prowess. And to Anabel Pandiella for all you have done to promote my books, for being the most amazing tour buddy, and for making sure I don't overdose on vegetable juice.

To my wonderful agent, Mollie Glick – thank you for being in my corner! You have no idea how much I appreciate you. And to the books to film team at CAA: thank you for taking my stories out into the world of film and TV!

To the international publishers who have delivered my work to a whole new audience – thank you. And to the reviewers who have stood behind me, the booksellers who have pressed my books into the hands of new readers and the bookstagrammers who have supported me online, thank you so much – I couldn't do this without you.

Which brings me to my readers – thank you for all of it. For reading my books, for sending me messages about them and for the on-going love you show my super-flawed characters. Thank you for being on this journey with me.

To Judy Lam, who won the auction for a character name in this book due to her generous donation to Australian fire fighters through Authors For Fireys at the beginning of 2020; I hope you love the character of Judy as much as Harper does!

To my friends in finance, for your patience, humour and the guidance you showed me while I was trying to get my head around various financial systems; sorry for the multitude of questions! Thank you for all of your help and for making it fun.

To the narrators of all the true crime podcasts I have listened to over the years and to the film makers who have put together the many true crime documentaries I have binge watched – I may have lost vast amounts of sleep as a result of your work, but I could never have written this book without you. But especially to

Karen Kilgariff and Georgia Hardstark of the *My Favorite Murder* podcast – as you can probably tell from this book, I'm a huge fan and so is Harper. We both credit you with the fact that we're still alive and kicking.

To my friends and family, of course. Always. In every way.

And finally, to my characters. I learn a lot more from them than they do from me.

About the author

Pip Drysdale is a writer, musician and actor who grew up in Africa and Australia. At 20 she moved to New York to study acting, worked in indie films and off-off Broadway theatre, started writing songs and made four records. After graduating with a BA in English, Pip moved to London and she played shows across Europe. In 2015 she started writing books. Her debut novel, *The Sunday Girl*, was a bestseller and has been published in the United States, Italy, Poland, the Czech Republic and Slovakia. *The Strangers We Know* was also a bestseller and is being developed for television. *The Paris Affair* is her third book.

To find out more about Pip, head to:

pipdrysdale.com

Facebook.com/pipdrysdale

Instagram @pipdrysdale